Peter Michael Rosenberg is a young British author with outstanding talent. His first novel, *Kissing Through a Pane of Glass*, was the runner-up in the 1992 Betty Trask Prize and Awards, and on publication in 1993 it received widespread critical acclaim, as did his second novel, *Touched By A God or Something* (both now available in Touchstone).

Also by Peter Michael Rosenberg

Kissing Through a Pane of Glass
Touched by a God or Something
Daniel's Dream

Because It Makes My Heart Beat Faster

Peter Michael Rosenberg

To Vince + Kathleen,
Hope you enjoy it,
with very best wishes,

Peter Michael Rosenberg
July 97

TOUCHSTONE BOOKS
LONDON . NEW YORK . SYDNEY . TOKYO . TORONTO . SINGAPORE

First published in Great Britain by Simon & Schuster Ltd, 1995
This paperback edition first published by Touchstone, 1996
An imprint of Simon & Schuster Ltd
A Viacom Company

Copyright © Peter Michael Rosenberg, 1995

This book is copyright under the Berne Convention
No reproduction without permission
All rights reserved

The right of Peter Michael Rosenberg to be identified as author of this work has been asserted in accordance with sections 77 and 78 of the Copyright, Designs and Patents Act, 1988.

Simon & Schuster Ltd
West Garden Place
Kendal Street
London
W2 2AQ

Simon & Schuster of Australia Pty Ltd
Sydney

A CIP catalogue record for this book is available from the British Library.

ISBN 0-684-81742-X

Printed and bound in Great Britain by Caledonian International Book Manufacturing, Glasgow

This book is a work of fiction. Names, characters, places and incidents are either the product of the author's imagination or are used fictitiously. Any resemblance to actual events or locales or persons, living or dead, is entirely coincidental.

This book is dedicated to my sister Naomi

Acknowledgements

As ever, special thanks go to my editor Lucy Ferguson, for her assistance and encouragement, and to everyone at the Christopher Little Literary Agency for their continued support.

Part One

1

It was not the first time that Jonathan had been woken in the night by an unfamiliar noise. Although he was not an especially light sleeper, he rarely slipped into the realms of oblivion that had characterised Liz's night-time excursions to the Land of Nod, a comatose collapse that more closely resembled death than sleep.

Awake, at least in part, Jonathan peered over to the alarm clock on his bedside table: two thirty-five. He calculated that he had been asleep for three hours, or just long enough to prevent him from drifting off again.

Whilst Jonathan was unlikely to be woken by a nearby thunderstorm or a noisy car chase in the early hours, neither event being in any way out of the ordinary in his neighbourhood, something strange or unusual was likely to disturb him from his slumbers. Especially if the nature of the disturbance indicated that it had originated from *inside* the house.

Jonathan was not particularly well schooled in the science of acoustics, and would have been hard pushed to explain how one differentiated between a sound generated inside the home and one whose source was further away, but he was aware that a difference existed, and that he could recognise it. It was not, to his mind, purely a matter of volume, timbre or even direction. Clearly these factors played a part, but – as he later mused – how one discerned the directional source of a noise when one was fast asleep, on the first floor of an ageing terraced house and with a thick duvet pulled up over one's head, was something of a mystery. But there was one thing of which Jonathan was sure; the noise that woke him that night, came, as it were, from within.

On first waking, Jonathan had no idea what it was that had disturbed him: none of the more obvious possibilities – a creaking floorboard, a squeaking hinge, a rat scuttling across the kitchen floor – sprang to mind. Indeed, his first inclination was to ignore the noise completely and blame his disturbance on a touch of indigestion; he had eaten sausages that evening – not a part of his regular diet, but now that Liz was not around to scold him for such blasphemies, he had chosen to indulge himself. Perhaps he was paying the price now for such gastronomic heresy?

This particular theory, barely alive and jostling for position amongst a myriad of options, was soon put to rest when, just as he had decided to ignore it, the sound was repeated.

It was clearer this time, and a little louder. The possibilities were endless. A wounded crow beating itself to death in a blocked chimney flue? It was not unknown in houses of that age. Or a larger intruder: a pookah, perhaps? Or a poltergeist?

His mind, recently awakened from dreams and clambering clumsily and sleepily for a foothold on reality, was rarely an ally in these circumstances, happier to conjure up the darkest, most distressing Gothic visions of horror, torture and death than console him with pastoral images of happiness, comfort and joy. Whilst never fully comfortable with such imagery, over the years it had, at least, developed a certain familiarity. Jonathan was still often surprised by the bizarre creativity displayed in his dreams, but he was rarely ever shocked. Had he ever chosen to investigate the reasons why his psyche was thus inclined, he might have discovered a great deal of what his colleagues in the psychology department referred to as 'self-knowledge', an expression that Jonathan particularly disliked, being no fan of contemporary jargon. However, he had never chosen to explore the nature of his nocturnal visions, believing such investigations best suited to those who harboured secret faith in crystal balls, Tarot cards and tea-leaf divinations.

On the few previous occasions when his sleep had been interrupted, whilst startled and still recovering from deeper, darker journeys through the unconscious, he had always been presented with scenarios of splatter-movie dimensions, rather than the more subtle convolutions of animate and inanimate objects that seemed to occupy other people's visions. Rarely would his psyche – or whatever it was that was so keen to frighten the bejasus out of him – oblige with recognisable, corporeal images; whatever the reason, it preferred to provide ghosties and ghoulies rather than something more substantial, or perhaps more obvious. Like an axe-murderer. Which for Jonathan was probably just as well.

Jonathan had never, to the best of his knowledge, undergone any experience that could truly be described as supernatural, but for some reason (fear of the unknown? fear of confrontation? fear of being hacked to pieces by a madman with a hatchet?) he felt that, if push came to shove, he could more easily deal with an apparition, no matter how nasty, no matter how noisily it rattled its chains, than even the most politely mannered cat-burglar.

Although he was not especially weak or feeble, Jonathan was nonetheless of slight build. He had straight, light brown hair that he wore longer than was currently fashionable. Although for a short period during the eighties he had sported 'designer stubble' (more out of laziness than any desire to follow trends) he now kept his lean, rather gaunt face clean shaven, thankful for a well-defined chin that required no camouflage. His eyes, steely blue, could deliver a most penetrating stare; they were not kind eyes, but neither were they shifty or cruel, suggesting instead an ever-alert intelligence.

At five feet ten he hardly towered above his contemporaries, and although not a featherweight, was not the sort of person one would automatically call upon to help shift a piano. He was fit, yes; his weekly bout on the tennis courts with Dougie kept him trim, and he could certainly wield a racket with reasonable force, but he was not otherwise especially strong. Men who are not, in this way, overtly physical, naturally shy away from confrontation with anyone who has, at some time in their life, wielded a sledgehammer, barbell or sack of cement. Jonathan was no exception to this rule: not categorically a coward, he would be amongst the first to move away from any altercation that included flying fists or toe-capped boots.

Which is why, if he had had a choice in the matter, Jonathan would rather a stranger enter his house by dematerialising and then filtering through the plasterboard, oozing slimy globules of fluorescent green ectoplasm, than by jemmying a door lock or kicking in a windowpane with his size fourteens.

But Jonathan did not have a choice, and the noise from below suggested anything but unearthly and ethereal interference with his possessions.

Inevitably, finding himself awake and alone in the middle of the night, his thoughts turned to Liz. Liz could sleep through anything. She could be lying in bed, deeply engrossed in a book or magazine, and a moment later her eyes would close and nothing short of a controlled explosion would rouse her. The bedroom light could be shining in her face, next door's teenage tyrant could be attempting to loosen the cement between the house bricks by placing his loudspeakers up against the wall and playing *Guns'n'Roses* at full volume, and still Liz's breathing would plunge to such a shallow ebb and flow that one could no sooner measure its intensity than quantify the effect of a butterfly's flapping wings on the global weather condition.

And her heartbeat: quite bizarre. Jonathan had once even been moved to take her pulse, shortly after they had started sleeping together. He had woken in the night, and with the last remnants of sleep still clouding his consciousness, found himself momentarily surprised to find the beautiful and enchanting stranger lying beside him. They had not known each other more than a few days at that stage. He had propped himself up on one elbow and stared tenderly at her profile, back-lit by a rising full moon that reflected its wintry, platinum illumination through the open curtains. She was so lovely – the image of those fairy-tale illustrations of Sleeping Beauty over which he had pored as a child, all blonde tresses and finely sculpted cheekbones.

Just as he had begun to lose himself in dreamy, whimsical indulgence (and even though he was still half-asleep) he suddenly became aware that Liz was making no sound at all, that there was no movement in her, not even the faintest twitch. When he put his hand to her cheek, her flesh was frozen, as cold as if she were a slab of meat recently retrieved from the deep-freeze.

He had felt for her pulse, but had found nothing. He was overcome with a momentary panic as the sudden, startling thought struck him that Liz was dead. So shocking and so real was the notion that it was as if he had been stabbed in the chest. He had gasped out loud, and in panic had taken hold of her and shaken her roughly. That she did not respond with an immediate yell or shriek only further confirmed what he had seen with his own eyes. Liz was dead. It was only in the following moments, even as his distress was rising to hysterical levels, that Jonathan saw her eyelids twitch. Slowly, reflexively, one eye had opened blearily, and a touch of moonlight had caught her glistening, sky-blue iris. But it was not until he had forced a noise out of her – a rather somnolent grunt that was anything but attractive – that Jonathan had stopped shaking her and gently, very gently, eased her down onto the mattress. Only then did he accept, with perhaps the greatest relief he had ever known, that he would not have to spend the remainder of the night explaining to the appropriate authorities the presence in his bed of a young, naked, dead woman, whose surname was still an unfamiliar rubric, scribbled down on the back of a bus ticket, but not yet committed to memory.

It was the following morning, after he had told her the details of this mid-night incident (of which she had no recall) that Liz confessed that this was not the first time she had alarmed someone as a result of her nocturnal drift into insensibility, and that she had meant to tell Jonathan all about it, on the off-chance that he might wake in the night *et cetera, et cetera.* Jonathan was a sound sleeper, but he had always envied Liz her deep excursions into dreamless night, journeys that seemed to be of an altogether different cast to his own.

On hearing the noise for a third time, Jonathan identified it as something undeniably from the real, wide-awake world rather than the more nebulous dimensions of his sleeping world. Much to his astonishment, his disturbed psyche flashed a detailed, photo-realistic image of a man in dark clothes creeping around his living-room. This was even more disturbing than the sort of blood-guts-and-gore imagery that he usually woke to, and as such, Jonathan chose to treat it as an aberration and ignore it.

Despite the noise, despite this vision, and even taking into account the fact that it was the middle of the night, Jonathan did not take the opportunity to lock his bedroom door and barricade it with as much bedroom furniture as he could shift. He did not arm himself with a heavy, blunt instrument. He did not telephone the police to inform them that, in all likelihood, there was a prowler in his house. He did not open the windows and scream into the night for assistance. Instead, Jonathan slipped out of bed, put on his bathrobe, opened the bedroom door, stepped out onto the landing, and began to tiptoe downstairs in the pitch black as stealthily as if *he* were the cat-burglar and did not want to wake up the owner of the house.

Although he was vaguely aware that his behaviour was, at the very least, inappropriate in the circumstances, at the back of his mind Jonathan thought that the noise might simply have been caused by Liz, returning to the house, however unlikely that might be. She still had a key, after all, although it would be hard to explain why she should choose to creep around the house at this hour rather than telephone first to say she was coming over. Alternatively, there was still the possibility that the noise had been caused by some oversized rodent attempting to gain access to the contents of his refrigerator, or the afore-mentioned disabled bird.

In the midst of all this confusion only one thing was clear. Jonathan had no idea what he intended to do in the event that, rather than confronting Liz, a ghost, or a half-dead crow flapping pathetically in the chimney flue, he in fact found himself face-to-face with an intruder in the very act of stealing the family silver. That there *was* no family silver, no valuable portraits, no bundles of currency stashed away in a wall-safe was partly the problem. In Jonathan's opinion, he possessed nothing valuable enough to warrant anyone breaking into his house in the first instance, *ergo* whatever was thumping around his living-room with all the grace of a hobbling hippo could not possibly be a burglar. *QED*.

The stairs creaked annoyingly as he descended to the hallway. Even as he approached the bottom of the staircase he knew that the first thing he would have to do was to turn on the light; he was now sufficiently awake to realise that it was, at the very least, perverse to stalk around his own house at night in the dark. Why hadn't he switched the light on at the top of the stairs? Not that there was any real danger; he had never been broken into before, and he seemed to remember reading somewhere that real intruders did not carry out their burglaries at such unseemly times.

These misplaced notions, combined with overexposure to too many television thrillers, had clearly distorted Jonathan's sense of what constituted real danger. The closest he came to any sense of what might really happen if there had been a burglar in the house was to make the rather feeble assumption that, once he had switched on the light, anyone groping his furniture would be off like greased lightning, presumably making escape through whatever opening they had used to enter the house.

This cavalier behaviour was not mere ingenuousness – Jonathan was a relatively sophisticated city dweller and had been for many years. Nor was it solely due to his tiredness, although it was true that he had not had a full night's sleep for several weeks. This was something else altogether. Jonathan's distraction, if that is what this wholly inappropriate case of light-headedness might be called, was, in some complex way, tied up with the fact that he was not used to being on his own in the house. He had never before had to deal with an incident of this nature, alone. Since Liz's departure he had not been sleeping well. Had Liz been there that night, it is likely he would not have woken at all. And even if he had woken, he would in all probability have turned over and fallen asleep again. After all, Liz would have slept through it – herds of wildebeest could have swept through the bedroom and Liz would have remained deeply ensconced in sleep. But, of course, Liz had not been there, and he had woken, and what was more, in her absence he was acting like a complete idiot.

Consequently, it was only as he was creeping, stealthily, down the last few stairs, that Jonathan began to realise just how ridiculous he was being. What was he thinking of? At once he resolved to re-establish some control over the situation and introduce a note of reality into what had become a decidedly unreal scenario. Tentatively, he called out his wife's name.

'Liz?'

No answer. No sound.

He tried again.

'Liz?'

Nothing. Jonathan was just a few steps from the bottom when he suddenly sobered up. It was the silence that did it. No more creaking, squeaking or tapping. No scuttling of paws, beating of wings or rattling of chains. That was when he should have stopped. That was the moment when he should have taken a deep breath and run back up the stairs to the relative safety of his bedroom. But Jonathan's momentum carried him forward, and as he stepped onto the hallway floor, a huge blackened claw tore out of the darkness, its thick fingers splayed like some mutant, five-limbed spider, and with acrobatic ease clutched hold of his throat and hurled him back against the wall with such swiftness and fury that he had neither time nor sense to respond.

The breath was knocked out of him so totally, so completely, that he thought his lungs had given up the ghost. It was as if he had exhaled the very essence of himself, given birth to some phantom, a life-spirit or something that, unbeknown to him, had always resided within, but had now been forced from his body like the air from a burst balloon. The back of his head hit the wall with a deafening crack that reverberated throughout his skull, a sickening report that travelled down into his stomach. It was a sound that conjured visions of bones snapping and organs rupturing, and Jonathan felt immediately faint. The foul taint of sick rose to the back of his throat. The vice-like grasp tightened, constricting his breathing still further, and just as he thought he might pass out, a face appeared before his eyes, like a vision. It seemed to float before him in the darkness, not quite corporeal or solid, but something discrete and singular, and seemingly unconnected to whatever it was that was gripping him about the throat with ever-greater fervour. Jonathan could not speak, breathe or react in any way. He was pinioned to the wall so effectively that he had been rendered immobile, like a chloroformed moth, pinned by a collector to a piece of cardboard, wings outstretched, ready for labelling and cataloguing.

Jonathan had not reached the light-switch in the hall, so everything was still in darkness, the only light a shimmering of yellow from the street lamps that radiated ineffectively through the frosted glass fanlight above the front door. In addition, Jonathan's eyes were watering readily, so he could not clearly make out the details of the floating visage, save to say that it was certainly a man's face, though wholly devoid of expression or animation. Again, before sufficient time had elapsed to assimilate these images, Jonathan experienced another new, strange sensation. His mind had raced ahead at fantastic speed, expecting another blow, to the stomach, the genitals, the soft, vulnerable underbelly, but it had not come. Instead, something dense, cold and metallic was pressed to his left temple, hard against the skin so that he could feel it bruising the flesh beneath. He had not, until that moment, allowed any question to enter his head – no who, what, why: nothing. There had not been time. Less than a second had passed since he had stepped off the bottom stair. Time – the sort of time he was used to – had ceased to function. Now, something else took over, something other than strictly conscious thought. Suddenly Jonathan knew, with an eerie, prescient clarity, what it was that was pressed to his head. It was as if he heard a voice telling him quite clearly: This is a gun.

No one had ever pressed a gun to Jonathan's head, so he had no notion of where this image came from. The vision of a gun being forced against one's skull was not, he was sure, embodied in the collective unconscious, a genetic memory just waiting to be triggered by the real event. He could not see it, and yet there was no doubt in his mind that it *was* a gun – rather than, say, a steel pipe or a jemmy or a wrought-iron poker – that was currently bruising his skin.

And yet, even in this undercranked, slow-motion

universe in which he found himself immersed, there was not sufficient time for Jonathan to express these thoughts clearly. They remained vague and ethereal, like clouds coalescing in a blue sky to form something recognisable, but then shifting to create other, less familiar shapes.

He was just on the threshold of making some sense of what was happening to him when a noise – a loud, metallic click, like the sound of a car door closing – echoed close to his left ear. It was impossible, but he knew that sound. He had never heard it in real, waking life, but still he knew what it was; it was the sound of a revolver being cocked.

A second or two passed without further incident, just enough time for Jonathan to become more consciously aware of what was happening. The hand that gripped him around the throat, the face floating before his eyes, the gun pressed to his head were, of course, all connected, and they all belonged to the intruder that he had not believed existed. It all became suddenly, horribly clear. But still he could not move. Neither could he see. He thought about raising his arms suddenly, knocking the gun away, but fear had paralysed him. At the moment the hammer had been cocked into position Jonathan had closed his eyes, squeezing out frightened, terrified tears from between the clenched lids, and all he could see was a vision of a gun going off, in slow motion, sparks flying and wisps of smoke spiralling out from the muzzle, images from some old Peckinpah movie perhaps, replete with blood and gore, and flesh brutalised by the impact of a bullet.

'This is a gun'.

It was strange, an echo of the words he had heard

so clearly inside his head a moment previously, only this time the words had emanated from in front of him, words enunciated clearly, with a particular accent that he vaguely recognised but could not identify there and then.

Jonathan was starting to feel groggy. He still could not breathe; there was no let-up in the powerful grip. He wanted to say something to this effect, to point to his throat, but he had been stunned into immobility.

'This is a gun, it's loaded, and if you try to scream, shout or move in any way, I shall shoot. Is that clear?'

No words had ever been clearer. Two or three more seconds had passed and Jonathan was still alive. He tried opening his eyes, he tried to nod, he tried to answer ... but he could not do a thing. At some point in the previous few seconds, he felt certain that his heart had stopped beating altogether, but now as he began to assimilate what was happening, it had gone into overdrive, beating faster than he believed possible.

'Do you understand?' The voice was harsh, urgent. Jonathan had to find a way to respond.

The intruder loosened his hold on Jonathan's neck slightly, just enough so that he could exhale an agonised 'yes'.

There was a long silence, during which time Jonathan fought hard to regain his breath. He felt sick, anguished, terrified. He needed someone to tell him that this was not real, was not happening, that it was just a nightmare or a bad trip or a hallucination.

But the only person in a position to tell him what he wanted to hear was, at that very moment, pointing a loaded handgun at his forehead, and was not about to tell him anything of the sort.

2

What's happening here? thought Jonathan. What the fuck is going on? Who is this man, what does he want? Is he going to hurt me? To shoot me? Jesus fucking Christ, is that it? Is he going to do that, to shoot me? Oh God, Oh God, no, no, no . . . I don't want to be hurt, I don't want to die . . . Fuck it fuck it fuck it . . . Why is he doing this? What have I done? I haven't done anything, doesn't he know? I haven't fucking done anything, I'm innocent, I've done nothing . . . nothing . . . nothing . . .

Jonathan was starting to lose consciousness. His breath was constricted, his vision completely blurred. He was beginning to weaken, his knees were giving way. He was totally incapable of acting, of imposing himself on the situation, which was taking its swift, desperate toll. His mind, a kaleidoscope of confusion, half-reasoned questions, half-forged answers, spun like a carousel. He could feel himself losing touch with his surroundings, like in those moments before he fell asleep, when realities became blurred, when priorities become confused. He recalled something vaguely about a tutorial he had to take in the morning, but could not remember why it was important. He had made a promise to someone about something... what was it? He thought he could hear someone talking to him, whispering, a child's voice. What was he saying? Was it important? Liz would know; Liz would be able to tell him. He would have to call her, ask her to help out... but where was she? Where was Liz? And why wasn't she here now? Perhaps she was out shopping. If so, he hoped she would remember to buy some food; he had hardly any food in the house, had not had any food in the house for ages now. Not proper food. Why was that? He could not remember. Something else now. Something else trying to edge its way into his thoughts, his dreams, his visions, something to do with food. Yes, he had to get some more food in, something nice; he hadn't been eating properly, just junk, sausages and burgers, it wasn't good for him, he would buy steak, from a cow, cow's steak, that was it, cow steak, cow shake, how shake, handshake...

He was slipping into a complete stupor now, his thoughts jumbled and baffling. For just a moment he registered the force around his neck once more, the dull image of the man's face, the discomfort of cold steel pressed to his head... and then it was gone.

He could see the surface now, see the sunlight glinting on top, the rays penetrating through the clear blue waters, he could feel himself rising, his hands reaching to the surface. He would break through in a moment, he just had to keep concentrating, keep reaching out, and in a short while he would be out in the open, in the air, in the light. It was coming closer now, the glittering sunlight was brighter, not far now, just another few yards and...

The intruder relaxed his grip on Jonathan's neck but did not let go. Reflexively, Jonathan drew a huge draught of air into his lungs; he felt groggy and deeply confused for several seconds. Where was he? What happened to the water? Then he realised what had happened and felt, with a probably wholly inappropriate gratitude, the relief of being able to breathe again. He took full advantage of it too, not knowing how many more individual breaths there were left to him. Jonathan inhaled the sweet air voraciously; huge, dynamic lungfuls, sucked up greedily like a vacuum cleaner on full power, as if he could store it for later use, like a camel drinking water in readiness for a trip across the desert. It made him feel quite faint.

His eyes were still tearful and his vision still blurred. There had not been sufficient time to assess what was happening to him. Despite the real feelings of distress, there was still something horribly unreal about the experience; everything was disconnected, uncertain ... it had all happened so suddenly. Not like a movie, but like a nightmare. In movies, you saw it coming; you saw the lead-up, the scene being set, the clues being laid. Things did not just happen, out of the blue, with no explanation. It was all too quick, much too quick. Jonathan wanted a moment's space to consider, to weigh up the situation. But there *was* no space, and he just had to suffer, stranded momentarily in a terrifying limbo, knowing neither what it was that had happened to bring this state of affairs into being, nor what was going to happen next.

And what did happen next was as deeply shocking as anything that had gone before.

In the rush of feelings, emotions and bodily reactions that were tearing through him, it was clear that certain of these responses were wholly appropriate to the circumstances: shock, surprise, fear, terror, confusion, bewilderment, pain, anxiety, sweaty palms, aching limbs and dry throat. All these were not only clearly recognisable, but — given the situation — quite natural. However, shadowing these feelings, and every bit as real as the fear and terror that, like a drug injected into the bloodstream, coursed around his system, was an altogether less appropriate reaction.

A complete stranger whom he could barely see, let alone identify, was perhaps about to blow his brains out with a loaded revolver, and Jonathan had a hard-on. He could feel it, fully erect, straining against his bathrobe. Consumed in that same moment by conflicting feelings of shame and pleasure, of being aroused and repulsed, his greatest fear was that the man with the gun would see it, would find out. What then?

Jonathan was relieved of the disagreeable responsibilities of anticipating the consequences, for no sooner had he registered this rather shocking response than he was forced to re-direct his attention to his assailant.

The intruder loosened his grip a touch more, and perhaps sensing that Jonathan was in no state to run and was not about to faint or throw up, released his neck from his grasp.

'Don't even think about running,' he said, pressing the gun barrel even harder against Jonathan's temple, preventing him from nodding assent. Jonathan's eyes, fully adjusted to the dark but still bleary with tears, started to smart. However, he could now see sufficiently well to make out some of his assailant's features. He was a big man, six feet two, perhaps more; sixteen or seventeen stone. His hands were huge, oversized, like a boxer's, and his wrists were thick, giving onto hairy, muscled forearms; little wonder that he had been able to pin Jonathan so effectively with just one hand. He was still standing close, and Jonathan felt nervous looking directly into his face. The man's breath was ripe and tainted with stale tobacco.

'Is there anyone else in the house?' His voice was gruff, coarsened by too much shouting on the terraces, too many cigarettes.

'No,' said Jonathan, his own voice reduced by fear to a pitiable, cracked whisper. He was so relieved at being given permission to speak that he found himself tripping over his own tongue in the rush to get a few words out. 'Please . . .' he said, still breathless, desperate to make his plea heard. 'Please . . .'

'Shut it,' said the gunman.

'Please don't . . .'

'I said shut it. Begging won't do nothing.'

Jonathan stopped abruptly. Did he dare to speak again? What did he mean: 'begging won't do nothing'?

He saw the intruder's hand tighten around the gun. What was going on here? Surely . . .

'Please,' cried Jonathan, terror rising in him rapidly as the gunman started to press the muzzle of the gun still harder against his forehead, forcing his head back against the wall. 'Please don't shoot me.'

It was then that Jonathan started to cry. He could not believe what he had just said. Please don't shoot me. Like: please pass the salt, please wash your hands, please stop nagging me. Please? What was he thinking? That good manners would stop this gorilla from blowing his brains out? Never in his life had he believed he would ever be reduced to uttering words such as these. It was absurd. It was terrifying. What good was pleading? He had to do something; he had to act.

Not surprisingly, the intruder just stared at him. Jonathan was in mental agony. Was the man going to shoot him? What could he say to stop him, what could he do? There must be something. There had to be.

Jonathan still felt immobilised. He tested the muscles in his arms, trying to flex them ever so slightly, just so that he could ascertain that he was still capable of moving, but it was as if nothing would respond. All he could do was stand there, like a puppet, a shop-window dummy, a cripple.

'Take what you like . . .' started Jonathan, but dried as soon as he saw the intruder shake his head. There was something in the air, the hint of something terrible, like a bad smell, just recognisable. Jonathan started to panic.

'Listen, it'd be better for both of us if you just don't say nothing, okay?' said the gunman, then took a deep breath. He closed his eyes for a moment, during which Jonathan saw his assailant's whole body tense up, as if a set of internal strings had suddenly been pulled taut.

'Please . . .' started Jonathan, the word dying before it reached the air.

The intruder's face tightened suddenly. 'It's your time to die,' he said, then pulled the trigger.

3

Jonathan had been a shy, quiet child. The youngest of two sons, he had grown up in the shadow of his older, and altogether tougher brother, Steven. Whether Jonathan's retiring nature sprang from his genetic make-up – both his mother and father had been the gentlest of parents – or if, in fact, he was the product of a deliberately benign nurturing process, would never be known. Jonathan, however, had his suspicions: 'I'm the daughter they never had,' he used to claim, only half-jokingly, in later years. Not that there was any genuine resentment on his part. Despite these occasional comments, in truth his parents had never treated him as anything other than a normal little boy. However, they had noted – as good parents should – that Jonathan was a quieter, more introverted child than their first-born, and they modified their expectations accordingly. As young children are apt to pick up the subtlest cues from their parents, perhaps it was this modified attitude that Jonathan had tuned into, and which had suggested something altogether more insidious than that which had been intended.

Whatever the reasons, Jonathan was aware that he had a very different nature from his brother and, indeed, many of his contemporaries, but he never felt especially disadvantaged by this. After all, what real harm did it do if Steven used to tease him unmercifully in the playground in front of all his friends? It wasn't as if he was ever physically abused. And what if he had a tendency to cry easily? There was nothing actually *wrong* with being a sensitive little boy; his mother had assured him of this on many occasions. It was just a little embarrassing at times.

If, in the end, it made any difference to his overall development, then it was certainly not discernible in the young, pre-teenage Jonathan. Jonathan came from a secure, loving family, who valued him for what he was and provided an environment in which he always felt safe, so his shyness was never seen as an impediment or handicap in real terms.

However, secure and protected habitats can bring their own problems. It was only in later years that Jonathan came to suspect that, if anything, his own home environment had been too safe. In their efforts to shield their youngest son from the less pleasant aspects of the real world, his parents had been guilty of overprotecting the boy, so that when the real world eventually intruded so rudely upon his life, Jonathan was less well prepared for dealing with it than others of his age and background.

And there *was* an event in his youth – a not very happy event – that awakened Jonathan to truths of which he had hitherto been kept sublimely ignorant. It was not anything that could rightly be defined as tragic – nothing earth-shattering or soul-destroying – but none the less it had a profound effect on his adolescence, with repercussions that were to echo down the line and, in time, affect his adult life too.

* * *

It happened shortly after Jonathan started high school. Moving up from his suburban primary school with its small pool of recognisable pupils and friendly, accessible teachers had been more of a trauma for Jonathan than his parents had realised. Finding oneself in a new and complex environment, surrounded by several hundred strangers, most of whom are older, wiser and physically more imposing, can cause considerable anxiety in even the most extrovert of eleven year olds. It was no fun suddenly becoming a small fish in an immense pool when previously one had been a veritable whale: prefect, top of the form, and a good inch taller than most of the other scholars.

But Jonathan had coped. Wanstead County High was no different from dozens of other big grammar schools perched on the edge of the capital. But it *was* big; an ageing, three-storey Victorian red-brick building arranged around a central quadrangle, and several other lesser buildings of more recent vintage scattered over a considerable area. Into this were poured seven or eight hundred pupils and innumerable staff; the sheer presence of so many people in one institution had caused difficulties for Jonathan, who was simply not used to engaging – on any level – with so many other human beings. Then there was the timetable to deal with. It took a few days just to get used to the idea that every lesson did not take place in the same room, that the powers-that-be actually allocated ten minutes between periods to allow the pupils to race from one end of the school to the other ... it was all very strange. And Jonathan, being a nervous type, had spent the whole of the first week fretting over the possibility of getting lost or of being late.

It was while he was still in this slightly troubled, rather apprehensive state that Jonathan's first brush with real life occurred.

It was a Monday morning. The physics lesson, which had taken place in one of the science labs, had concluded, and along with his classmates Jonathan had trooped out, turned left along the corridor and marched into room F2 for their first English lesson of the week. F2 was their form room, so everyone had their own allotted desk in which they could keep their books and satchels or, in Jonathan's case, a shiny new black briefcase.

Jonathan took his place at his own desk. Whilst his new friends chatted all around him, Jonathan opened the desk lid to retrieve his English exercise book. Consequently, he did not witness the arrival of a tall, red-haired and freckle-faced second-year boy who tore into the classroom and strode angrily to where Jonathan was sitting. Indeed, the first he knew of the boy's presence was when the desk lid slammed down in front of him. Jonathan leapt in surprise.

'What are you doing in my desk?' yelled the boy. He had a long, narrow face and small piggy eyes; the freckles were sprinkled liberally across his nose, cheeks and forehead, and he seemed to tower over Jonathan.

'I . . .' began Jonathan, still shocked from the slamming of the desk lid, but he did not have a chance to phrase or even compose a response, for in that same moment the freckle-faced second-year boy pulled back his arm and, with the dynamics of a coiled spring releasing all its energy, ploughed his fist into Jonathan's face.

Jonathan screamed.

'Hey Malcolm,' yelled a lad from the door. 'Wrong room. We're next door. Come on!'

Through a veil of anguished tears Jonathan saw his assailant run out of the classroom. He put his hand to his lip which felt sore and wet, and when he pulled his hand away and saw the blood drip onto his clean white shirt, he started to bawl.

He was not in pain, not physical pain, but he was distressed beyond all measure. A moment before everything had been fine. There had been nothing that day to suggest to him that he was in danger, that something unpleasant would happen: no clues, no omens, no hints of foreboding or intimations of dread. It had been a perfectly ordinary day. He had arrived at school in good time, chatted with a few of his friends, and marched off to his first lesson when the bell rang. The physics lesson had been good fun, involving some practical experiments with springs and weights that nobody had understood. After the lesson he had wandered to his form room along with his friends, and taken his place at his desk. In other words, into an environment as safe as he was likely to find outside the confines of his own home.

And then, out of the blue, for no discernible reason, a complete stranger had wrongly accused him of some misdemeanour and, before Jonathan could assimilate what was happening, had punched him in the face. Jonathan had never been hit before. Afraid of violent or even excessively rowdy behaviour, he carefully avoided potential flashpoints. He had never been in a fight whilst at primary school and his parents, liberal in action and mindful of their own childhoods, had never struck the boy.

And now his lower lip was bleeding. Profusely.

Two of his new friends, acting with the mature responsibility that often comes in times of crisis, helped Jonathan to his feet and led him outside into the corridor. As Jonathan continued to bawl pathetically, one of the boys rushed off to find a member of staff, whilst the other boy did his best to calm the injured victim.

By the time a teacher arrived, Jonathan had brought his hysteria under control, but he was still sobbing bitterly. The boys related, to the best of their ability, the events of the previous five minutes. The teacher in question was a Mister Robinson who, coincidentally, was new to the school himself, having taken up his appointment as head of the history department just a few days earlier. Not at his best with snivelling boys, Robinson did his best to calm Jonathan with suggestions that Jonathan, being an Englishman, should adopt a stiff-upper-lip in this matter, before handing him over gratefully to a passing caretaker who took Jonathan along to first-aid, where his split-lower-lip was bathed and he was given a cup of tea to calm his nerves.

Whilst this event would hardly constitute a trauma for most eleven-year-old boys, and even at the time would have paled into insignificance besides some of the beatings administered by older, tougher pupils, Jonathan was still extremely distressed by the incident. As he would later recall, it was not the fact that he had been hit that had upset him so greatly (although it had been a great shock); it was the fact that he had been hit *for no reason*. He had done nothing, perpetrated no crime, committed no sin, not even by omission. He had been minding his own business when some lout who was in the wrong place assaulted him. How could things like that happen? It was so . . . *unfair*.

Worse still, the freckle-faced bully had got away with it. Jonathan had been hurt, his pride and dignity injured, and there would be no justice. Surely that couldn't be right. And to add insult to injury, as he rushed back home that afternoon, looking over his shoulder at regular intervals lest the bully be following to finish him off, he concluded that he could not even tell his parents about the incident. He had cried. He had bawled and squealed like a stuck pig; it was just too embarrassing.

Thus it was that Jonathan's first year of high school was tainted by the after-effects of this formative incident, the repercussions of which would, in time, affect his whole life: never again would Jonathan feel completely safe and secure. As he learnt that day, unpleasant, even terrifying things happened to people for no reason at all, and there was nothing you could do about it.

For the rest of the year, and for some considerable time afterwards, Jonathan lived in fear of meeting the freckle-faced boy. Thankfully it was a large school, and although Jonathan sometimes spotted the boy, he never had to come into contact with him. It wasn't until several years had passed that it suddenly occurred to Jonathan that the boy probably had no idea of the effect he had had, and would probably not have remembered the event even if someone had delivered an accurate, blow-by-blow account. More to the point, he would not have recognised Jonathan if he had been thrown at his feet. Whilst this knowledge was, on one level, quite comforting, and allowed Jonathan to enjoy the remainder of his time at high school free of the fear that had plagued his first year, he could not help but suffer from the rather damning corollary to all this: that individuals could wreak havoc on other people's lives without having any idea of the damage they were doing.

He never entertained seriously the idea of taking his revenge; the possibility of getting hurt prevented him from taking such risks. He knew he would never initiate any action that could result in his being damaged again. If pushed, however, he might have admitted to a fantasy, a wishful daydream, in which a bigger, stronger – perhaps older – Jonathan, victimised again for no apparent reason, took the opportunity to level the score. Not in some high-minded, superior fashion with clever words or ingenious plans, designed to get even in some intellectually satisfying manner, but in the very manner that had brought him such distress: brute force. Consequently, despite his superior imagination, there was nothing very discriminating about his vengeance daydream, in which fists flew, feet kicked, and blood – not his own, this time – flowed in copious amounts from wounded flesh to mother earth. But just because his fantasy was not especially refined, that did not mean it was not, at some level, deeply satisfying.

It was with a wry smile, many years later, that Jonathan greeted the news that the freckle-faced boy who had punched him in the mouth for no reason at all had become a Conservative Member of Parliament, risen through the ranks of the Party and succeeded to several Cabinet posts, most recently that of Minister of State for Northern Ireland.

*   *   *

This early lesson in injustice undoubtedly went some way to deciding Jonathan on his later career as a sociology teacher. Certainly, when it came time to choose a direction, it was notions of social justice and the desire to understand how human beings behaved when brought together that most fully contributed to his decision.

By the time Jonathan had secured a place at university he was well aware that the world cared not a jot for its people. The frequent and devastating incidence of earthquakes, floods, fire and famine throughout the world paid graphic testament to the fundamental indifference that the planet displayed towards its human inhabitants. However, such indifference did not mean that all was lost. As Jonathan reasoned, in the face of cosmic neglect, there were areas of existence over which human beings still had some control, namely: how to behave properly in company, be it family gatherings, football crowds or on the battlefield.

His university years, whilst not especially distinguished, did at least furnish him with plenty of first-hand experience of how people behaved both in general and in particular. Whilst a university was hardly a microcosm of the 'real' world, there was no doubt that one could learn a great deal just from careful observation. When Jonathan began applying his new-found knowledge of sociology to what he saw, a number of fairly basic but none the less intrinsic truths became evident.

In particular, it soon became clear that there was no such thing as absolute morality, or even a widely held system of ethics that operated, even amongst the students at the university. People behaved well or badly depending upon a number of factors, not the least of which was a sense of what they, as individuals, believed they could get away with. Societies – all societies – were constructs, systems held together by convoluted and often complex rules that had to be adhered to and obeyed if the society was to function. However, they did not have to be obeyed by everybody; incidence of deviant or criminal behaviour could be found in virtually all societies the world over. It was the occasional 'lost tribe knows no violence' article, that might appear once in a while in some sociological or anthropological journal that was the exception. Even within the university one could divine a hierarchy of socially acceptable behaviour, a sliding scale as it were, that spread from the most well-behaved, wholly rule-abiding individuals who would not even question whether the rules were appropriate or fair, to those who avoided banishment or incarceration by the slimmest of margins.

These proto-criminals seemed to thrive on pushing the system as far as possible. They had little or no respect for the laws, rules and regulations laid down by the society in which they operated, and yet knew how to work it so that they could profit personally. Occasionally, of course, as in all societies, one such deviant would get caught, and would inevitably pay the price for his actions by either being placed on probation, suspended, or sent down. Banishment from the society, it seemed to Jonathan, was ironically the greatest ill that could befall these non-conformists: they may not have wanted to abide by society's rules, but they sure as hell did not want to be isolated from it.

This realisation – when it finally came – was a revelation for Jonathan. The true rebels in a society were not the criminal fraternity with all their ducking and diving, flaunting of the law and desire to be seen as 'outside' the system, nor was it the deviants who flirted with pushing society's tolerance to its limits by ignoring social mores, promoting taboos and seeking recognition of their daring. No, the true rebels were those who opted out completely, who did not say 'I don't have any respect for your rules and will defy you' but who refused to integrate or have any interaction with the society at all. It was interesting to note that, in most Western societies, the former outnumbered the latter by several degrees of magnitude.

What interested Jonathan the most was what kept people in line: why did the majority adhere to the rules set down by their peers and ancestors when such adherence, in even the freest of societies, was to put a curb on individual liberties. Clearly most people, if they questioned the matter, must have believed that the benefits of society outweighed the drawbacks. By and large people behaved responsibly and within the limits prescribed by the society, because overall that was how they prospered the most.

And yet, the very existence of individuals who, for other reasons, refused to abide in this way suggested that there was something intrinsically foreign about social systems, that they interfered with that most base of attributes, human nature. Was it human nature to do according to other people's will rather than one's own? Was it human nature to bend one's will to that of others rather than exercise one's own to the full extent? And was it human nature to conform to rules and regulations that were clearly at odds with one's own growth, freedom or prosperity? For Jonathan, the very existence of individuals who refused to toe the line was evidence enough that socialisation was in essence in complete conflict with human nature. Which made the abundance of working, functioning societies throughout the world all the more startling. And, by extension, worthy of investigation.

By the time Jonathan had completed his studies and graduated from the university with an upper second-class degree in sociology, many new lessons had been learnt, and new discoveries made which, in one way or another, sought only to compound the essential truth of his first, brutal experience of real life when he was just eleven years old. His studies, both academic and personal, of how people behaved when they were brought together, convinced him of one thing: you could lay down the law, you could ensure that by adhering to those laws people would benefit, and you could make the exercise both pleasurable and painless (as in the best democracies) and yet there would still be people who believed that living by their own laws was of greater importance.

Consequently, of the myriad discoveries made during these three years, the most profound, and far reaching — learnt, like the others, through personal experience — was perhaps the most devastating of all in its implications: despite social conditioning, despite the rules and regulations that were instilled into individuals throughout their lives, given certain circumstances, ordinary people were capable of committing the most terrible crimes.

The study of people and their interactions was, for Jonathan, the only area of intellectual pursuit worth cultivating. And if, when spoken out loud, such declarations sounded both pretentious and extravagant, then it is only fair to say that Jonathan was aware of this, too.

But no amount of study and tuition prepares someone for an event like the one in which Jonathan found himself ensnared that night. No amount of deliberation, reflection and consideration can be of use when, without prior warning, a total stranger holds a gun to your head, tells you that it's your time to die, and then pulls the trigger.

More to the point, even a deep understanding of human interaction is of little use when, having passed through such an experience, one finds oneself – as Jonathan did – unscarred, unbloodied, but still facing a strange man with a loaded weapon.

The intruder laughed – an ugly, sickening cackle – and pulled the gun away. Jonathan felt sure he was about to faint, indeed, was praying that consciousness would desert him there and then so that he would no longer have to deal with the surreal but still terrifying circumstances in which he found himself. The absurdity was almost too much to bear. It was still dark, he was still being held captive by an armed, probably violent, intruder who was clearly off his rocker, and he still did not have a clue what any of this was about.

In his terrorised state Jonathan could not be completely certain of anything, but he felt sure that the gunman had told him he was about to die, and that he had then heard . . . what? Did his captor pull the trigger? Or, as now seemed more likely, did he merely uncock the hammer, and allow Jonathan to imagine the rest? Maybe the gun wasn't loaded at all? Was it supposed to be a joke? Was that why the gunman had laughed? What sort of joke was that?

Despite the laughter – or maybe because of it, because of its manic, hollow ring – Jonathan did not feel any more safe. The gun was still pointing at him, and other than the bizarre, horrible cackle, the gunman had given no indication that anything about the current situation had altered. Jonathan's mind, still unsettled from this most recent, devastating experience of near-death, slipped into overdrive, and he started to devise strange explanations for what was going on. Perhaps this wasn't a burglary at all. Perhaps this was all some sort of set-up, someone's idea of fun; a 'killergram', or 'terrorgram' or something like that. Someone had mistaken the date of his birthday; it was all just for laughs. Perhaps it was over now, and once Jonathan had tipped the performer, he could go back to bed and forget all about it. Or maybe it was ... what was that terrible programme on television in which people were always being set up and filmed? Jonathan couldn't remember, and as he thought hard to recover the programme's title he realised how absurd he was being, how, far from being over, whatever it was that was happening to him had probably only just begun.

With this last thought an immense weariness suddenly overcame him, sapping him of what little energy he still retained. Jonathan looked at the gun, then at his assailant. He was too shaken up, too upset to speak. And yet as he became aware that neither the assailant nor his own consciousness were about to release him from his ordeal, his mind started to race around in a mad panic, without discipline or direction, desperate to find something solid, something real to hold on to, something that could keep him from cracking up, from falling to pieces, from crumbling into a pile of dust.

Sadly, he could find nothing that was of any use to him. There were no personal experiences from which he might draw succour, no events in his own life that might indicate his next move, nothing in his own history to help him out. The man had threatened his life, for Christsake! What in his own life could he possibly draw upon that offered support? There was nothing. Instead, after floundering around amongst the flotsam and jetsam of his own memories, he found himself returning to the same dim memory, a vague recollection of something he had once read about a famous author – one of the great Russian novelists perhaps – who, Jonathan was sure, had once been subjected to the same torment as this, a mock execution . . . and how it had turned him into a total wreck.

Jonathan could not be certain of the details, but he thought the author in question might have been Dostoevsky. He must have come across the information in connection with his work once. It was all so hazy and indistinct. With nothing else to grasp hold of, he tried to concentrate on this fragile snippet of information, in the hope that it might bring him some comfort, but all he could remember for sure was that, prior to the mock execution, Dostoevsky had been arrested; he had been imprisoned, charges had been brought, events had followed in some sort of logical order, *there had been some sense to it all*.

But not to this; there was no sense to this. This was something entirely different, something not from the biography of the great Russian author, but straight out of the fictional works of another Eastern European altogether. This was like something out of Kafka. Only, if so, it was Kafka on fast forward; Kafka without the introductions, without the scene-setting, without the punctuation; not so much as a comma or colon. There had been no arrest, no trial, no reflections, just a meaningless execution, without foundation, without reason. And even that had failed to reach its expected outcome.

And what *was* going to happen next? Jonathan knew he risked angering his captor by addressing him, but if, as seemed terrifyingly likely, he was destined to die that night, he did not believe he necessarily had anything to lose by such agitation. He had to take the risk.

'Please,' whispered Jonathan, still teetering on the edge of oblivion. 'Please, take whatever you want. You can have everything. You don't need to shoot me.' Jonathan could hardly believe that he had managed to force out a coherent sentence.

He stared blearily into the face of his captor; the light was too poor to be able to distinguish the man's features clearly, although there was the suggestion of something heavy and brutish about the line of the jaw and the thick, bushy eyebrows that dominated his face. And the pits in the skin; were those scars, wondered Jonathan, whose own vivid imagination was now starting to work against him?

Who is this man? thought Jonathan. What is he doing here, in my home? Is he still intending to use the gun?

Jonathan could barely stand the agony of suspense. Not knowing was terrifying, as terrifying as the gun itself. It was like one of those nightmares where the moment of greatest terror is prolonged beyond expectation, beyond its point of resolution, like those dreams of falling for ever through the air and never reaching the ground.

The intruder continued to stare at Jonathan for the

best part of a minute, during which time the gun remained by his side, pointing to the floor.

Jonathan could feel his strength slowly ebbing away. His knees had given out; only the wall against which he leant so precariously was preventing him from collapsing to the floor like a house of cards. His eyes started to close. Perhaps this was it, the beginnings of unconsciousness, the darkness that would spirit him away from all this. He could feel himself sinking, sinking into warmth and comfort. His eyes felt so tired, the lids so heavy. Above him he could see the bright glistening of sunlight on water, and he knew he was descending into the depths. The surface of the water was retreating now, the dappled light becoming dim . . .

'Oi!'

Jonathan opened his eyes abruptly. The intruder had raised the gun to eye level. Oh God no, thought Jonathan, not again; please, not again.

'Over there.' The intruder waved the gun towards the living-room. Jonathan waited a moment, as if needing permission to move. When the gunman stepped back, Jonathan gave a slight nod and then very slowly edged away from the wall.

With the gun still aimed directly at his head, Jonathan staggered to the living-room. He could feel his knees quaking, his thighs and calves quivering as if he had some sort of degenerative muscular condition. He knew that he had to remain upright, that any sudden move, even if it was just stumbling over the carpet or lurching to one side might cause his captor to panic, to tense up, to react reflexively . . . or just shoot for the hell of it. Who could say? After all, *he had a gun*, and what did Jonathan know about people who carried guns? Hadn't he said 'It's your time to die'? Hadn't he?

Just a few faltering steps carried him across the hallway and into the living-room. As he stumbled past he caught a glimpse of the back door at the end of the hallway, and the shards of broken glass on the carpet.

A glimmer of sodium light from the streetlamp outside the house filtered in through the gaps in the curtains, providing just enough illumination to ensure he would not bump into the furniture. He stepped in through the doorway, then stopped.

How had this happened? wondered Jonathan, rather feebly. Why hadn't it been Liz? If only it had been Liz...

'Sit down,' said the assailant, indicating the sofa. Jonathan managed the last few steps to the sofa then all but collapsed on to the cushions; another minute and he would have fallen for sure. His stomach was in spasm, a clenched fist of knots that seemed to be tightening by the second, drawing all his strength from his limbs. He pulled the bathrobe around him tightly, not for warmth, but for protection. Jonathan was wearing nothing beneath the robe; he had never felt more naked, more vulnerable, in his entire life. Much to his astonishment, he was still fully erect; he did not know if the gunman had noticed, did not know what it meant. How could he be excited by this? It was terrifying.

The intruder came around and stood opposite Jonathan, who sat perfectly still, looking up at him, scared and confused beyond reason. The gun was still levelled at his head. Jonathan knew nothing about weapons, but he recognised the small handgun as a revolver of some sort; it looked antiquated, like something from the black and white gangster films of his youth. He had no doubts that it was still an effective tool for maiming and killing, and he was not about to take any chances whilst it remained in the hands of his oppressor.

'I wouldn't go getting your hopes up.'

The man's voice was flat and inexpressive, and save for the accent, which Jonathan had now identified as south of the river, had little to distinguish it from a thousand other voices that one might overhear whilst in a city pub, on the street, or travelling on the underground.

'I mean, you're still going to die . . . I think it's only fair you know that.'

Jonathan's stomach churned once again. From the moment that the man had gripped him by the throat until he had first uttered that dread death sentence, if any clear thoughts had formulated, they suggested that all he was dealing with – or, perhaps more accurately, *not* dealing with – was a burglar, involved in a routine case of breaking and entering. The sort of thing that probably happened in a thousand neighbourhoods every night of the week. Despite attempts to repress them, his initial thoughts on waking had been of an intruder stealing possessions; that, after all, was why they broke into houses. But since hearing the gunman's manic cackle, he was not so sure. True, the gunman had not shot him. However, now that Jonathan was sitting down, having regained some control over his breathing, it became increasingly evident that the man standing opposite with a loaded handgun was probably not merely a burglar, but more likely a psychopath. A nutter. A madman.

And that's when Jonathan got really scared. With sociopaths there was no order, no pattern, no telling what they might do. Burglars robbed, rapists raped, but sociopaths were capable of doing anything, and, worse still, doing it with a clear conscience.

Jonathan's breath started coming in short spasms as the terror seized him. He tried desperately to control it, but he had terrified himself with his own imaginings. He had read enough books, seen enough films, overheard enough stories to be able to picture in graphic detail the sort of acts perpetrated on innocent people by individuals who, for whatever reasons, were so far off the rails that no amount of investigation, understanding or reasoning could make sense of their behaviour. In that same moment Jonathan's mind became filled with a hundred snapshots of gore, torture and horror. Like some malfunctioning machine – a stylus stuck in the groove of an old record, or a computer about to crash – he became caught in an endless, meaningless, repetitive cycle that managed only to heighten his sense of terror: the man had a gun but hadn't used it. He had a gun. But he hadn't used it. He had . . .

Jonathan gagged. He saw sharpened knives lying dormant in kitchen drawers, forks glowing red in the flames from the gas hob, rope lying in twisted piles in the shed outside . . .

His mind raced ahead, beyond his control, presenting him with more and more images of torture and degradation. He gagged, swallowed, gagged again. What was this man capable of? What was he going to do?

And there would be no reasoning with him. Since the start of this ordeal, not for one moment had Jonathan felt anything other than blind panic, but in the brief moment between when he collapsed on to the sofa and when his captor had spoken again, he had entertained, albeit momentarily, the notion that some combination of word, action and reward might just get him out of this fix. With the repetition of the death sentence, however, such thoughts, which had barely lived long enough to have had an independent existence, now vanished into the ether.

'Look,' said Jonathan, barely able to control the fear in his voice. 'What is all this? Why are you doing this?'

The intruder raised his eyebrows but said nothing.

'Please,' said Jonathan. 'Please tell me what's going on. Have I done something wrong? Is that it? Have I done something?'

The gunman eyed Jonathan with disdain, before shifting his weight and leaning forward. Jonathan's automatic reaction was to move away, but there was nowhere for him to move to.

The gunman gave a little sniff, then cleared his throat. 'I don't know,' he said calmly. 'What *have* you done?'

It was quite cool in the house; the central heating had gone off several hours previously, and yet Jonathan could feel the sweat trickling down his back and seeping, oily and clammy, from his palms.

'I've done nothing.'

'Must have done something.'

'No, I swear. There must be some mistake. I mean, I don't even know you.'

The intruder nodded slowly. 'Nobody knows me,' he said, his voice still oddly expressionless, as if he were reciting lines.

Jonathan's stomach gave another convulsion. 'I . . .

I don't understand. If you don't know me then why do you . . .' The words dried in his mouth. He swallowed, somewhat painfully. The gunman did not seem to be objecting to his attempts to engage him in conversation. For some reason this gave Jonathan the merest glimmer of hope. If he could talk with him, converse, find out what was behind all this, then maybe there was a chance, a way out. He tried again. 'Why do you want to kill me?'

There was another pause as the gunman seemed to weigh up this last question. Jonathan watched the man's face carefully, anxious for some hint of humanity to show through, something with which he could connect. But there seemed to be nothing there; the man's face was as expressionless as his voice.

The gunman continued to consider Jonathan's question whilst Jonathan just looked on with mounting tension.

'Because,' he said at last, with just the merest hint of a smile creasing his lips, 'you're the chosen one.'

Riddles. That brief glimmer of hope faded as swiftly as it had arrived. His life was being threatened by a man who spoke in riddles. How could you even start to reason with someone who talked in mystifying epigrams? 'You've been chosen.' What was that about? Jonathan started to feel sick again.

'Please . . . please tell me what's going on. You don't know what this is doing to me.'

'Don't I?' said the gunman, clearly angered. He stepped forward and brought the gun close to Jonathan's head. Jonathan pushed back into the sofa, but could not get away from the muzzle of the revolver that was now pointing straight between his eyes. 'Eh? Eh?' said the gunman, his voice more animated than previously. Jonathan started to panic again. 'How the fuck would you know what's in my head, eh? Jesus ... you people. You're all the fucking same.'

The bile surged up into Jonathan's throat and he fought hard to swallow it; the acid burnt all the way down. His assumptions about the intruder's mental state seemed to be right, and this was no consolation at all. He was going to be murdered by a madman, for no reason, because the intruder had heard voices perhaps, because Jonathan had been 'chosen'. The awful, life-negating lessons of his schooldays reverberated around the inside of his head, an unwelcome echo: terrible things happened to innocent people, and there was nothing you could do about it.

He decided to keep talking; there was nothing else he could do. He was in no position to take on his assailant, who would not even have to shoot him; just one swipe from one of those clenched fists would lay him out for sure.

Jonathan took a deep breath. He desperately needed to sustain a temporary courage, if only to speak to the gunman. 'All the fucking same as what?' he said at last, desperate to shake some sense out of his assailant.

The gunman frowned. 'What?'

'You said we were all the fucking same,' said Jonathan, playing for time.

The gunman looked both puzzled and annoyed. 'Look man, this is a pointless fucking conversation. Now do me a favour and shut it.'

'Do you want to tell me just why you're doing this?'

'I told you; you were chosen.'

'Chosen?' Oh God, thought Jonathan, there it

was again; the religious overtones. That was always dangerous. People could do anything if they believed God was behind it. Men and women had butchered innocent children believing they were carrying out the will of God. Did Jonathan dare ask if God was involved in this? Then again, what did he have to lose? The more he knew, the more likely he was to find out what was behind all this. If time allowed.

'Chosen by whom?' he asked. As long as he kept the gunman talking, maybe something would click; some piece of information might fall into place, give a clue, something. Something that would help him. 'Chosen for what?'

The gunman laughed again, that curious, sickening cackle, like a man who had never produced a genuine laugh in his life, but was merely copying a sound he had once heard. 'You don't give up, do you? Okay. Chosen by fate. For death. Satisfied?'

Jonathan shook his head frantically; he sensed that the intruder was running out of patience.

'Look,' said Jonathan, 'maybe you made a mistake. It's possible, isn't it?'

The gunman snorted in derision. 'No man, it's not possible.' He drew a piece of paper from his jacket pocket and looked at it. 'Is this 17 Hopkirk Way, NW1?'

Jonathan said nothing.

'And is your name J Fairchild?'

Jonathan flinched. The gunman noted the response with satisfaction.

'Then,' he said, with a mixture of both triumph and impatience, 'there's no mistake. Like I said, it's fate.'

He had his name and address. It was written on a piece of paper. Jonathan felt a chill creep over him.

This was no casual breaking and entering, no chance encounter. As the gunman had said, he had been chosen, selected, singled out. The situation suddenly became even more frightening.

'What is this all about?' asked Jonathan, exasperation tensioning each word like a spring so that they shot from his lips like rapid fire.

'Aw, come on man . . .'

'Look, if you're going to shoot me I've got a right to know . . .'

The intruder's eyes narrowed suddenly, and his mouth contorted into a sneer. He placed the muzzle of the gun against Jonathan's throat and brought his face close.

'No rights,' he hissed. 'You got no fucking rights, okay? This,' he said, drawing the revolver away for a moment and waving it in Jonathan's face, 'this is rights; this is fucking rights, understand?'

Jonathan closed his eyes. It was intolerable; the whole situation was intolerable. His stomach had contorted so tightly that it was all he could do to sit upright. How could this have happened? And if, as he was insistent, this man was going to kill him, then why hadn't he done it already? What was the point of this . . . this torture?

But Jonathan didn't dare ask any more questions. Perhaps if he left well alone the gunman would just back away . . .

'Where were *my* rights, eh?'

Jonathan opened his eyes again. The gunman had stepped back and was peering at him angrily. 'No one gave a shit about my rights, did they?'

He was ranting. He's quite mad, thought Jonathan: a complete psycho.

'Someone has to know,' continued the intruder, talking now as if what he had to say was of genuine importance. 'They have to know. Which is why you have to die.'

'But . . .' started Jonathan, in the vain hope that a clue might yet fall into his lap and show him a way to get out of this mess. 'Look, if someone has deprived you of your rights, then maybe I can help? Perhaps I can . . .' Again, he broke off. He could see the intruder shaking his head slowly, disdainfully.

'You don't get it, do you?' he intoned. 'You're all to blame. Every one of you. Someone's got to pay.'

'But . . .'

'And fate chose you.'

There it was again. Fate. What did he mean? 'What are you talking about? What has any of this to do with me?'

The intruder frowned. 'I told you man; you were chosen.'

'You chose me, you mean.'

The gunman shook his head, 'No, man. I just stuck the pin in.'

Jonathan thought he must have misheard. 'What was that?'

'The pin. All I done was stick the pin in.'

Jonathan shook his head in bafflement. 'I don't know what you're talking about.'

The gunman fixed his eyes on Jonathan's. 'I stuck it in the pages. With my eyes closed. You know.'

Jonathan's heart started to race again. There was something awful about what was being said, something devastating, but he did not dare to think about it. He had not fully grasped what the intruder was saying, but he had already guessed what this was all about.

'Telephone book,' said the gunman, as if he had been asked for further clarification.

No, thought Jonathan. Please. Not that.

'North London, residential,' continued the gunman.

Please, no, thought Jonathan. Not this; anything but this.

'Page two hundred and nineteen,' said the gunman, slowly. '"O eight one, eight nine eight, seven nine one six, seventeen Hopkirk Way, Fairchild, J." That's you, innit . . .'

4

Jonathan had a friend, Harry, who spent most of his waking life in the company of computers of one kind or another. Harry was a systems analyst, an occupation that meant very little to Jonathan, whose own experience of computers was limited to the occasional use of the college word-processor. Harry designed computer programs, but as Jonathan did not really understand what programs were, how they worked and certainly had no idea of how they were designed, this meant that, even though Harry was a close friend, Jonathan had little idea of what he actually did for a living. When he pressed Harry for details, Harry would only say that he designed 'business applications', an expression as meaningless to Jonathan as 'liquid assets' or 'quality time' or any other pairing of perfectly good words that had been hijacked to create yet another hideous example of what Jonathan referred to as 'jargonese gobbledegook'.

Jonathan's ignorance of the details of Harry's professional life was more than just casual; it was profound. For most of his life Jonathan had been technologically illiterate. As he had been brought up in an era when computers were the exclusive domain of science-fiction novels and 'rocket scientist', his practical knowledge of matters scientific was limited strictly to a basic understanding of electricity that allowed him to wire up a plug for a domestic appliance without blowing every fuse in the house.

Neither had Jonathan's academic education been enlightened by either an interest in, or understanding of, organic chemistry, applied physics or higher mathematics. (Biology, however, with its strange emphasis on the sexual reproduction of frogs and lesser mammals, did turn his head for a short while.)

Whilst many of his schoolmates spent their days in the science labs, playing with Bunsen burners and pipettes in the wholly spurious belief that they were discovering how the world worked, Jonathan was ensconced in matters which seemed altogether more important, devouring texts with alluring titles like *The Social Animal* and *The Naked Ape*.

Thus it was that he managed to get through school, university and several teaching posts without ever having to answer a question like 'Name the positively charged fundamental particle that is found in the atomic nucleus of every element in the cosmos'. Jonathan would have thought such a conundrum as relevant to his existence as 'why did the chicken cross the road'.

However, in more recent years, that had all changed. Like many of his contemporaries, born, nurtured and released into the world prior to the great computer revolution, once the eighties arrived he found himself more and more baffled by the current state of play in the world of science and technology. New terminology seemed to be erupting into the language at an accelerating pace, with new words like 'on-line' and 'algorithm' entering the vocabulary like the offspring of a pair of profligate rabbits. In an effort to redress this sad and sometimes embarrassing state of affairs, he decided to take action.

This was where Harry came in.

Despite their very different backgrounds and the apparent yawning gulf between them, Harry and Jonathan shared a number of interests. Harry's conversation was not all bits, bytes and algorithms and Jonathan believed that, on a good day, it was even possible to get a reasonably serious conversation about art or politics out of him. However, as happy as Jonathan was to converse with Harry on the state of the nation or the credibility of a bunch of bricks posing as sculpture, it was when Harry talked about the more esoteric aspects of his work that Jonathan found himself genuinely hooked.

It turned out to be a great boon to know someone who, despite the occasional condescending look, could frequently explain, in terms comprehensible to the layman, concepts and notions that would otherwise have passed Jonathan by.

Thus it was that, during the previous year, Jonathan and Harry had met occasionally for the sole purpose of 'discussing science'. These discussions, which consisted primarily of Jonathan asking questions and Harry answering them, took place on average about once a month. On these occasions, suitably armed with enough alcohol to preserve an entire species of small rodent, Harry and Jonathan retired to one or the other's house and, unplugging the telephone, would settle in for an extended session of drink and talk in approximately equal measures.

If Jonathan was hosting the event, they usually

made camp in his study, as it was the sort of room that seemed well suited for chatting about intellectual matters. The study had a certain formal appearance due primarily to the large number of books that lined the shelves. Indeed, they covered the walls so completely as to make the hanging of a certificate (or even a photograph of loved ones) impossible. However, even though Harry claimed that the study shrieked 'academics only!' at anyone crossing its portals, he had the good grace to admit that it was, nonetheless, a congenial environment for discussing important matters.

It was, in all ways, a very different space to that employed whenever Harry's house was the chosen venue. On those occasions, the pair retired to 'the playpen' – a personal laboratory situated in Harry's basement that doubled as workshop and electronic games playroom. The space itself, whilst not exactly poky, was nonetheless quite cramped, due mainly to the fact that it was stacked to the ceiling with circuit boards, relays, video screens, keyboards, several miles of insulated wire of one form or another and other assorted electronic gizmos, most of which tumbled from shelves, desks and drawers in such abundance that the room looked like the badly ruptured interior of some massive electronic beast; an uneasy amalgam of Hieronymus Bosch and Robocop.

The subjects discussed by this pair of mismatched intellects during those well-lubricated, night-time sessions depended very much on what was currently engaging Harry at work. If something was causing him especial angst or, alternatively, excitement, then Jonathan soon learnt that there was no point broaching any subject other than that which obsessed him, as he would have neither patience nor enthusiasm for anything else. Consequently, in the previous few months, at Harry's instigation, they had talked about (or rather, Harry had spoken of and Jonathan had listened to) such intriguing sounding concepts as fractals, cyberspace and ethereal networks.

On other occasions, when Harry was less involved with work projects, Jonathan would get him to explain the ins and outs of a subject which had recently caught his attention, but which made little or no sense to him whatsoever. With a background in physics, Harry had been able to explain, to a reasonable level of satisfaction, such concepts as black holes, virtual reality and the difference between fission and fusion reactors. Such matters were, in truth, all rather old hat to Harry, but he always managed to make his explanations fresh and accessible.

Jonathan was never bored by Harry's attempts to explain these purely scientific matters, as in many of these supposedly logical constructs, there lurked the whiff of the imaginative, the fantastic and – to Jonathan's mind – the insane. This was in itself exciting.

Without a grasp of the most fundamental principles of science, Jonathan, like many of his contemporaries, found himself living in a world more and more dominated by machines whose workings (and sometimes functions) baffled him entirely. A hundred years ago there was not an object in the home that a reasonably competent householder could not mend or restore with his own two hands. These days, as Jonathan used to rant, it was all one could do to operate the damn things. The world, thought Jonathan, was a confusing and distressing enough place without making matters worse through a complete ignorance of science and technology. There were enough real fears and concerns out there without having to add technophobia to the list.

Jonathan's interest was further spurred on by the slowly dawning realisation that the concepts that lay at the root of current scientific understanding of the cosmos bordered on the mystical. For example, he was to learn from Harry that, in an arena where logic, clarity and exactness were upheld as the greatest criteria for establishing fact, one of the greatest formulations of scientific thought in the twentieth century went by the name of 'The Uncertainty Principle'. And that currently the most exciting area of investigation in the world of higher mathematics and physics was called 'Chaos Theory'. With tags as wonderful as these, suggesting perhaps that human beings lived not in an ordered, clockwork universe but in an Alice-in-Wonderland style cosmos, Jonathan wondered that the reasonably well-educated but scientifically illiterate individual was not more interested in the current state of play in the world of science and technology. It certainly fascinated him.

And the one area that fascinated him more than any other was that of time, a subject that he and Harry had discussed at length on more occasions than either could remember. Jonathan had his own reasons for being especially interested in time. As he had once explained to Harry, for most people, toiling away at the butt end of the twentieth century, the machine most likely to dominate their lives was not the computer, nor even the motor car, but that great unrecognised warden of socially responsible behaviour, the clock. The unerring, continuous motion of the second, minute and hour hands, as they transcribed their invisible circles in unceasing progression, not only marked off the various segments of activity that delineated a lifetime (working, eating, playing, sleeping) but, with its regular, unwavering certainty, steadily erased what remained of one's life with each insidious tick and inevitable tock. Jonathan was all too aware of this. It had always struck him as extraordinary that, since the beginning of the industrial era in particular, people had frequently banded together in the name of liberty to free themselves from the overbearing repression of some tin-pot dictator or other, but had never risen as one to defeat the greatest tyrant of all, the one that said 'wake up at six, leave home at seven, start work at eight, eat lunch at one, drive home at five, sleep tight at ten' and so on, not just for one day now and then, but more or less every day, in one form or another, from cradle to grave.

The influence of measured time on the lives of ordinary working people was all-pervading. Time – measured, divided, marked off – ruled the very structure of one's life, controlled one's days with such precision as to render the individual effectively powerless in its wake. Was lunch-time the time when you wanted lunch, or was it twelve thirty to one thirty, Monday to Friday, come what may? Did you do the things you wanted to do when you wanted to, or when time allowed? And how often did you use that expression, deferring once again to time, to that great dictator, time that insisted you woke up, not naturally, not when you chose, not when your mind, body and spirit decided, but when the alarm bell sounded? (The very same signal, Jonathan had long ago noted, that warned the inhabitants of a building that if they did not move fast, they would be engulfed in flames.)

Nothing in life was more insidious than measured time, nothing ruled life as completely, and nothing took away the power of the individual to act, to make decisions, as did the humble clock. The majority of the population even wore one on their wrists, against the flesh, where it set up barely audible but no less real syncopations of rhythm with one's pulse, the beat of one's heart. There it was, your own personal little despot, informing you when you could do this and that, and reminding you, with every glance, that your remaining time on this earth had just decreased, again.

Tick tock.

Curiously, for all the supposed deference to time, it was amazing how little most lay-people understood it. Even in the century that produced Einstein, the man who was to re-define the way the West thought about time for ever, it was still difficult to think of time in ways that divorced it from its measurement and direction. Time passed, in seconds, minutes, hours, days, and it passed in one direction, from the past to the future and so on and so on. And a second was a second was a second, more or less, depending on how expensive one's timepiece was. As a rough rule of thumb, the more expensive one's watch, the more likely one was to know the exact length of a second. As if such things were important.

And yet things were not quite as clear cut as that, a fact that had first alerted Jonathan to the complexities of time. For on occasion time had a peculiar habit of speeding up. Like when one was enjoying oneself, for instance. Like on holiday. Or when having sex. At just the moment when one wanted time to stretch out, to take it easy, even to stand still for a few seconds, that was the very moment when time girded its loins for the big dash to the finish line in a variation of Sod's Law that everyone recognised but about which nobody ever complained: time flies when you're having fun.

Sociologically, time was a phenomenon that deserved greater investigation, and in the back of his mind Jonathan believed he might be the person to bring it into the syllabus. As he once remarked jokingly to Harry, only time would tell.

Unfortunately, whilst Harry was able to explain a great deal to Jonathan, such as the need (with the introduction of computer-generated simulation) to differentiate between the notions of 'real' time and 'virtual' time, he was never able to satisfy Jonathan's need for an easily comprehensible model of time, something he could refer to when, as was frequently the case, he needed to understand one or other of time's peculiarities.

Like why, for example, the most terrifying ten minutes of his life to date had elapsed so slowly that it felt as if several hours had passed.

To Jonathan, sitting stationary on his sofa in the middle of the night, a gun pointed at him, time had become fixed, static, as animated as a corpse or a rock or, of course, the stationary hands of a stopped clock.

He gave a deep sigh, and tried not to focus on the weapon that was still pointing directly at his head. He noted, with some relief, that he no longer had an erection. The intelligence Jonathan had received from his captor had devastated him, and he was still trying to make sense of it whilst trying to deny its very existence.

'Let me get this straight; you selected my name at random . . .'

'Not me; I didn't select nothing. Think of it as fate.'

'You stuck a pin in a telephone directory!'

'Oi! Don't you shout at me, you little shit! Think I'm afraid to use this?' He pressed the gun so hard against Jonathan's forehead that it split the skin; a thin, broken circle of blood seeped from the wound. Jonathan flinched in pain.

'Like I said, you were chosen.'

'But I . . . don't . . . understand,' said Jonathan, still fighting hard to prevent himself from throwing up. 'What good will it do to kill me?'

'You'd do better to shut up.'

Jonathan sighed. Most premature death was probably pointless, but to be singled out by a psychopath who had taken your name by plunging a pin, blindfold, into a telephone directory seemed not just pointless but also farcical, a pathetic way to end a life. If the gunman was serious, then Jonathan knew that it was not just his death that would have been futile, but somehow his whole life too. To die this way: it was not only pathetic, it was undignified. It made a mockery of his whole existence.

'You must have a reason for wanting to go through with this.'

'Must I? Who says?'

'You're going to commit murder for no reason?'

'Perhaps. I wouldn't be the first. Haven't you ever wanted to kill someone?'

Jonathan was shocked by the question. His initial response was to answer immediately, to refute the very idea, but he sensed that to protest too loudly, or to behave too vehemently in any manner, was probably to court further trouble.

'I mean,' said the gunman, eyeing up his captive as if he knew something, a secret perhaps, that Jonathan thought hidden from the world. 'I mean, there must have been a time when you've just wanted to, you know, snuff someone out, like a candle flame. Pfoof! Just like that. Someone who annoyed you, all the time, every day; a bastard boss or something. Haven't you ever felt: I'll do him. I'll do him good, so he never does that again. Eh?' He paused.

Jonathan squirmed uncomfortably beneath his interrogator's gaze. What was it that he thought he knew?

'Oi! You're not answering me. I asked you if you ever wanted to kill someone.'

'I don't believe so,' replied Jonathan, the words catching in his throat. There was something particularly menacing about this new turn of conversation, and he did not like it at all. What was the man trying to do? Seek some sort of justification for his actions? He could imagine it all now, the gunman in the dock, pleading diminished responsibility or some such on the grounds that all he was doing was rubbing out a potential killer: 'But he admitted it to me, your honour; he told me he wanted to kill people . . .'

It was like a sick joke, only there was nothing funny about it, not for Jonathan.

The gunman sneered. 'I don't believe you, man, I don't believe you. We all want to do it to someone, at some time in our lives. I'm sure of it.'

Jonathan gulped noisily; there was a terrible dryness in his throat, tainted with bile. 'Look, even if what you say is true, it doesn't explain why you should want to kill me. I've never done anything to you.'

'Yeah? You seem pretty sure.'

'I swear, I've never seen you before . . .'

'Don't mean nothing. There's all sorts of ways you might have done me damage. You don't know.'

'What do you mean?'

'Forget it.'

Jonathan frowned. There was something here, something he had been missing. 'I mean, have I . . .'

'Leave it,' interrupted the gunman. 'I'm not here to answer your questions.'

But Jonathan would not let go. There was a lead here, and he was determined to follow it through. He had to make some sense of what was going on. 'But you're implying that I'm indirectly responsible in some way for harming or hurting you . . . am I? How can that be? Is this to do with a friend of yours or something? A relative? What did I do?'

'I said, leave it.'

'Just tell me what it is I am supposed to have done!' Jonathan was surprised, and not unhappy, to find his anger rising to the surface.

'You're raising your voice again.'

'For fucksake! This has gone on long enough!' Jonathan started to stand but at that same moment the gunman cocked the revolver, stood up and planting the sole of his right foot firmly on Jonathan's chest, shoved him back on to the sofa.

'Sit down!'

And as if training an animal not to misbehave, having forced Jonathan back into his seat, the gunman slapped him once, heavily, across the face with his open left hand. The blow shocked Jonathan into silence.

Jonathan sat still, not daring to move or say anything that might further enrage his captor. He brought his hand to his cheek, slowly. The gunman watched him closely, suspicion etched into every line of his face. Jonathan sensed then that, in truth, hope as he might, he did not really have a chance with this man; there would be no way of getting through to him.

'You wanna know why I'm gonna kill you, right?'

Jonathan nodded slowly. His face felt raw from the slap; he wanted to cry again.

'It's a sign, innit. Call it a statement. My address to the nation. This is what you done to me, so this is what I done to you. Okay?'

'But I didn't do anything,' complained Jonathan, aware how ineffectual his whining tone would seem.

'You survived. You got lucky. Nice house, good job, some respect.' The gunman snorted derisively 'People like you . . . you got no idea.'

'Tell me then . . .'

'Sure. Like you're really interested, eh?' The gunman shook his head. 'You see, that's my whole point. You think showing some concern now will save your skin. But it won't. It won't make no difference. You don't give a shit about me, not now, not never. And it don't matter how hard you try, it won't change a thing. I've made me mind up. Someone has to be sacrificed.'

'But surely . . .' began Jonathan, hoping vainly that he could use reason to shift the impasse, 'surely if you want to make your point, wouldn't it make more sense to go for someone who has been responsible for your ... your situation?'

'You know nothing about my situation, man.'

'I realise that. All the more reason to confront someone more appropriate.'

The gunman laughed. 'Oh yeah? Like who? The Prime Minister? The Queen? Some big nob official somewhere? Nah, that wouldn't do it. Choose someone like that and they'd all say that it was political, and it ain't. They'd make out I was some kind of lefty nutter, and it ain't like that. I don't give a fuck for all that politics crap. Take a member of the public though ... then they'll start fucking thinking. I mean, we ain't living in a dictatorship. If people had wanted to do something about the likes of me, they could have done it. But they didn't, see? None of you did. You just let us suffer. And you're as much to blame as anyone.'

Oh God, thought Jonathan, sinking further into despair. He had thought his attempt to talk, to reason, might free him from what had become an ever-worsening situation, but it was doing nothing.

His concentration was starting to waver now, but he knew he had to keep going. He would never be able to tackle the man physically; he was too big, too strong. And he was armed. Words were his only chance. He took a deep breath and tried again.

'But how have you suffered?'

'There you go again man. I told you, it's too late. No point showing concern now. Waste of energy.'

'You have to let me try . . .'

'Uh-uh . . . I thought I'd already explained. I don't have to do nothing. Not now. Free agent, see?'

'But this is madness; I'm just an innocent party in all of this.'

Jonathan could see that this last comment did not go down well. The gunman sneered.

'No one's innocent,' he intoned cryptically.

Keeping one eye on Jonathan, the gunman crossed the room to where the dining-table stood, grabbed one of the four straight-backed chairs, and positioned it across from the sofa so that he could sit directly opposite his prey.

Jonathan was now totally bewildered. The man had said he was going to kill him. He had said it twice. He had even made some sort of explanation – incoherent bullshit though it was – and yet he was still here, he was still alive. If this psychopath really was going to kill him, what was he waiting for?

'How long . . .?'

'You in a hurry?'

Jonathan shook his head. 'If someone put you up to this . . .'

'No one put me up to nothing.'

'Then this is some sort of joke, is it? Terrify some innocent member of the public . . .'

'Do I look like a man with a sense of humour?'

Jonathan decided against answering. Instead, he tried a different tack.

'This isn't fair.'

The gunman laughed then, another of his hollow, sour laughs.

'Fair! That's a good one, that is. Didn't no one ever tell you? Life ain't fair. It's all I ever heard. You complain, and they turn round to you and say: "Who told you life was fair?" Like that lets them off the hook or something. Well right you are. You got it taped, brother: life ain't fair.'

'But this . . .'

'It's chance man: hazard.' He gave a small, eerie chuckle, then suddenly became quite animated, waving the gun around for emphasis. 'Wild, eh? I mean, what do you suppose the odds are of something like this happening to you, eh? Let's see . . . what, three, four million names in the London directory? Gotta be, right? So: four million to one.' He nodded slowly, as if in awe at the immensity of the figures. 'Four million.' He paused, working something through in his head. 'Coulda been the pools though, right? Odds like that. Only happen once in a lifetime. It's just a pity it wasn't the pools, right?'

Jonathan did not think the comparison with winning the pools either appropriate or heartening. Still, in the last few moments, his assailant's mood had seemed to lighten, if only infinitesimally. Perhaps now was the time to challenge him somehow – not physically, obviously, but rationally.

'But you can't seriously be thinking of going through with this?' said Jonathan, attempting to sound perfunctory, as if the notion of killing him was just plain silly. Unfortunately, it seemed only to anger his captor. Instantly Jonathan regretted his actions. It seemed that he was to be defeated at every turn.

'Serious? You don't get it, do you? I'm nothing but serious. Like I said, no sense of humour. Had it stamped out of me. Flushed out of me. There ain't nothing funny left inside me.' The gunman thumped his chest for emphasis, as if he were hollow and would resound like a drum or an empty barrel. 'Tell me a joke; go on. Tell me a joke, see if I laugh. I guarantee it, I won't laugh. In fact . . .' and here, ironically, the gunman smiled, 'in fact, if you can make me laugh – a real laugh that is – I'll break my promise to myself.

I'll leave you alone. I will. I'll just walk out that door and pick some other poor bastard's name out of a hat. I will. I'll let you live.'

There it was; the escape clause! He knew there had to be something! Jonathan suddenly realised that all was not lost. It was a chance. The adrenalin surged into his bloodstream, readying him for action. This was it, this was it. He had been offered a way out. Now all he had to do was . . .

'But don't get your hopes up,' continued the gunman, unaware of Jonathan's sudden excitement, 'because like I said, there ain't nothing funny left inside me. Right. You got thirty seconds.'

Jonathan looked at him blankly. 'What? What do you mean?'

'Exactly that. You got thirty seconds to make me laugh.' He stared Jonathan straight in the eyes, then lifted his left wrist and squinted at his watch. 'Twenty-eight, twenty-seven, twenty-six . . . you'd better get a move on.'

With a shock, Jonathan suddenly realised what was happening. It was a game, a horrible sick game. The man had given him a chance, offered it to him like a gift, only to draw the thing away in the next moment. He was being given thirty seconds to make some nutter, some gun-wielding maniac, laugh. Thirty seconds! What could you do in thirty seconds? Jonathan was overcome with a bewildering sense of agony and frustration that welled up inside him like the gases in a bottle of champagne shaken too vigorously. Panic flooded through him. Half a minute – less now – to make a complete stranger fall about in hysterics. Or just giggle, perhaps. Twenty something seconds to make this madman laugh! It was outrageous, impossible.

It was insane.

'Twenty.'

'Wait! Stop!'

'You don't get a second chance. Better make it quick. And no riddles. I hate riddles. I mean, I promise you, a riddle won't even raise a smile. Fifteen.'

And of course, in that same moment, Jonathan's mind went completely blank. Empty. No jokes, stories, tales, riddles, anecdotes, smutty one-liners, funny names, stupid rhymes ... nothing. As the seconds ticked away, all he could think was: this is completely absurd; completely fucking absurd. Suddenly, there was nothing funny in the entire world. He wanted to cry.

'Ten. You ain't doing too good.'

The bastard! How could he do this to him? How dare he! Pick him out at random like a fucking raffle ticket! Threaten his life, submit him to this, this indignity, this ...

'Five seconds ...'

Jonathan screwed up his eyes in one last, desperate attempt to remember a joke. There had to be something he could say! He could not let the moment pass without trying. There had to be something, anything ...

Then he remembered. A schoolboy joke. One of Harry's. It was his only hope.

'Wait, wait! A man ... a m-m-man walks into a bar. Oof! It was an iron bar.'

Silence.

He looked in desperation at the man opposite for the merest hint of a smile, an amused twitch. But there was nothing; not a flicker. Of course not. It was pathetic. Stupid. Not a joke, not even one of his despised riddles. Just a feeble excuse for humour, worthy only of contempt.

What was it they said, the stand-up comics, when they did their routine and no one laughed? When they dried up, when they failed?

'I corpsed.'
'I stiffed.'
'I died on stage last night . . .'
'Nice try,' said the gunman, sniffing. 'Really. But I've heard it before. And it didn't make me laugh then, either.'
Oh God, thought Jonathan. I just died.

5

From where he was sitting Jonathan could see the clock on the mantelpiece. Two fifty. Fifteen minutes ago, thought Jonathan, I was safe. Twenty minutes ago I was still asleep, unaware that some ape was tramping around my house. He sighed. He thought about that all-too-familiar expression, about not being able to turn the clocks back, and sensed, with considerable anguish, just how much of a lie it was. Clocks were turned back every year at the end of every summer. People talked about getting 'an extra hour', as if it had been conjured out of thin air. But of course, it was not an extra hour at all. Time remained sacrosanct, unsullied by the games people played with it. You could tinker with conventions but you could not touch time, and turning the clocks back did not fool anyone. Half a year later and the reverse process was adopted, and that precious hour gained was lost once more. You never got something for nothing, thought Jonathan; never. And it was time itself that Jonathan needed to change. If he could just go back fifteen minutes . . .

'Bet you're not used to this,' said the gunman, interrupting Jonathan's pathetic reveries. 'Not being in charge, I mean. I should imagine this all makes you feel a bit uncomfortable. Powerless.'

Jonathan did not think that answering rhetorical questions would get him anywhere, so he said nothing.

The gunman, however, seemed keen to air his views. 'That's the trouble with this society; it takes the power away from the masses and puts it in the hands of a select few. Like them that got money. And them that can use words. They're the most lethal of all, man. Politicians, lawyers, salesmen . . . they're the real dangerous ones. If you control words, you can control anything, right? Right?'

'I suppose so,' said Jonathan. He was only half-listening to his captor's rant; he had other things on his mind. Like how the hell could he gain the upper hand in this situation. It all looked hopeless.

'Of course, I can understand why people should want to have power; it's a trip. No two ways about it. The great thing about being in charge, of having power, is that you get to make the decisions. Y'see, like just then; I had the power of . . . what's the word, y'know, when they let you off. Fuck, what's the word? Y'know, like all that Roman gladiators shit, when the emperors gave the thumbs up?'

'Clemency?'

He paused, turning the word over in his head a few times. 'Nah, I don't think it was that one. Anyway, don't matter. Whatever, they had the power of life and death, right? Just like me now. That's a fucking amazing feeling, man.'

'I'll bet.'

'I tell ya.'

'What about exercising it then? That power?'

The gunman smiled, and brought the gun up high again, levelling it at Jonathan's head. Jonathan drew back into the sofa, the terror flooding through him all over again.

'What d'you say that word was?'

'Clemency.' The back of his throat had dried suddenly, and it was all he could do to get the word out without choking on it.

'Right. Clemency. Funny word, innit. Wish I could think of the word I meant though.'

'Leniency,' suggested Jonathan swiftly. He felt his stomach seize up again. What was this guy playing at? 'Indulgence?' he tried. 'Reprieve?'

'Nah ... none of them. Nothing fancy like that. Still, you're a regular little dictionary, ain't ya?'

Jonathan racked his brains. Words. Words. Somewhere in all this, words were the clue. The gunman had made it clear that he did not trust people who were good with words, and yet he clearly had some respect for them. Jonathan had failed to make him laugh, but perhaps ... oh God, *something*.

'You a writer then, or what?'

'Teacher.'

'Figures. Teachers; they're all bastards. Told me I was a worthless good-for-nothing. Charming, eh?'

'They weren't good teachers then, if that's what they said to you.'

'Can't disagree with you there. And you're a good teacher, are you?'

Jonathan shrugged. What should he say?

'Y'see, the trouble is, teachers always want you to see the world their way. Little Hitlers, little dictators. Forcing their ideas on you, their words ... like "clemency". I mean, what sort of word is that anyway? It certainly ain't the one I was thinking of. Now, if you were *really* good . . .'

'Mercy!' The word burst out of him, as if he had been holding his breath for an age.

The gunman smiled and nodded, knowingly. 'That's it . . . that's the one. Mercy. See, nice and simple. Aren't you the smart one.'

'Going to let me go then?'

'What, for guessing a word right? Sorry friend; you had your chance.' The gunman looked at his watch, rotating his wrist to catch the light.

What was he waiting for? Was this all a bluff, some sort of game? Would he really shoot him? Did people do that: draw names out of a hat and then murder them for no reason? Even psychopaths? Jonathan looked closely at his captor; he did appear to be waiting for something, in which case, maybe there was still time for him to act, to find a solution to his predicament. The gunman appeared calmer now that they were both sitting down; perhaps there was a way through, a way to shift the situation. Jonathan figured that as long as he 'accepted' his position in this bizarre relationship, made no demands, trod carefully, then there might still be a chance. It was certainly worth a try. If, as still seemed to be the case, the man was intent on shooting him, Jonathan certainly had nothing to lose.

'What good will it do, killing me? Apart from assuaging your anger.'

'Do what?' sneered the gunman.

'*Relieving* your anger . . . I mean,' said Jonathan, covering quickly. He would have to watch his language. 'Is that what this is about?'

'Could be.'

'Would you explain it to me? After all, if I'm

going to die, it would be ... comforting ... to know why.'

The gunman thought about this for a moment, then nodded slowly. 'You won't understand.'

'Try me. Please.'

'It's pointless. You can't understand unless you've been there.'

'I appreciate that. But how do you know I *haven't* been there?' Jonathan now felt like he too was talking in riddles, but he did not care. If he could just make some sort of connection with his captor.

The gunman sneered. 'Come off it, man. What would you know about it?'

'Well, if you don't explain what "it" is, I can't tell you.'

The gunman sighed. 'You ever been homeless? You ever have to sleep rough, beg for money? You ever really been hungry? I mean, *really* hungry? Hungry 'cause you haven't had nothing to eat for three days? You can't know what that's like, man. And being cold; not just ...' The gunman pulled a strange face, then in a curious attempt at a posh accent, said: '"Ooh, bit parky, innit".' He dropped the accent, clearly a touch embarrassed at his performance. 'Nah, I'm talking about ice cold, about deep-freeze cold, about cold so cold it takes up residence in your muscles, in your bones, in your balls, so cold they're just frozen fucking little meatballs trying to climb back up into your body. And the head pains, man; you've never known pain like that. I'm not just talking about a little headache from sleeping too much, or a hangover, I'm talking about pain that splits your head in two, pulverises your brain. That's what it can do, the cold; it's like long, sharp, steel claws, reaching inside your head and gripping at bits of your brain.' He stopped for a moment and looked at Jonathan, as if wanting to ensure that this was all getting through to him.

Jonathan said nothing, even avoided looking at the gunman whilst he was talking. He knew he should be feeling something – sympathy, horror, outrage – but he found himself left curiously cold by his captor's descriptions of suffering. Initially he assumed this must have been due to a lack of empathy; why should he give a shit if this bastard – this bastard who was holding him at gunpoint, who had threatened his life – should have suffered in the past? What was he supposed to do, feel sorry for him? Was that it? Clearly, if that was what was intended, his little ploy was not working.

But then, as the gunman continued with his litany of the hideousness and distress of sleeping rough, Jonathan suddenly realised that his lack of response was not due to a lack of empathy, but to something altogether more straightforward: he did not believe him. He listened to his captor talking about living on the streets, and quite simply did not believe a word. Jonathan felt sure that it was all bullshit, a story meant to impress him, or confuse him or ... or what? What was its purpose? Jonathan could not understand. The more he listened, the more certain he became that this man, this intruder, had never so much as gone camping, let alone roughed it on the streets of the big city.

What did it all mean? Why should he go to such lengths – and he was certainly putting his all into the lengthy descriptions – just to impress upon Jonathan how he had suffered? Did he think that excused him his crimes? Was it some sort of confession? Was he looking for absolution? Jonathan was baffled. He tried to tune in again to the gunman's words, to the content of his rather tawdry tale, but he just could not take it in, he could not believe any of it was true. It was a story, a piece of make-believe, concocted with some effort and performed now for a reason or reasons that Jonathan could hardly guess at.

There was a pause in the proceedings; the gunman had stopped talking for a moment. Jonathan tried to focus in on him, and could see that the man was still in performance mode, still trying to convince Jonathan of something or other. Jonathan waited patiently.

The gunman sighed deeply, perhaps even theatrically. 'So don't tell me you know what it's like: being a victim. Don't start telling me that you know what *that's* about, because I won't believe a fucking word. Y'see, I've got you sussed. Clever with words. Think you can change things just by saying the right thing. I know. I've seen people like you before. You wouldn't last two seconds in a fist fight, but you could probably reduce a bigger bloke to tears by saying the right thing. Am I right?'

Jonathan could see that a response was expected. 'I don't . . .'

'Fuck off. 'Course I'm right. Don't you see? I *know*.'

You're a fine one to talk about the power of words, thought Jonathan, his suspicions alerted by this slight change of direction. What did the man want? What was he after?

'I don't believe I've ever reduced anyone to tears just by talking to them,' said Jonathan, playing for time. He was still trying to figure out what this might be leading up to. He did not feel comfortable. He sensed an increased tension in the air.

'Wanna bet?' replied the gunman swiftly, then looked away, almost as if he regretted what he had said.

Jonathan eyed the gunman quizzically. What did *that* mean? There was no confusing the intention. He was clearly intimating that he knew something, something personal, something that . . .

Jonathan did a quick double-take. Was this a bluff? Was this some confidence game to trick *him* into making some sort of confession? Jonathan was aware that paranoia might start taking over if he continued to think this way, but there was nothing he could do about it.

He looked at the gunman again; he was big, well padded beneath those clothes . . . yes, that was it. He was wired up, waiting to tape Jonathan's admissions, that was it. But what for?

It was becoming clearer now. This was not a hold-up, a robbery, or even a potential murder; this was all some hugely elaborate game, set up by someone – God knows who – in order to trick him into saying something incriminating. Of course, it all made sense: the gun, the threats, the confessions . . . and all under this ingenious cover, this murder-by-chance nonsense. Yes, it was all a set-up; clever, but completely false. The intruder had no more intention of using that gun than . . . well, of course not. Someone had planned all this. It was just a great, elaborate game . . .

'Your sort,' said the gunman, interrupting Jonathan's attempts to make sense of his increasingly senseless situation, 'make me sick. You think that just because you never get in trouble with the law that you're safe. But I know the sort of things you get up to. I know the damage you've caused.'

'What damage?' said Jonathan, a touch cockily. If this was just a game, he could afford to play it up a bit. 'What are you talking about?'

'You're no more innocent than me, man. You've done your stuff. You just got away with it, that's all. Till now, that is.'

What did the gunman know? What could this stranger possibly know about him? They had never met, of that he was sure. Jonathan was a law-abiding citizen; everyone knew that. He had never been in trouble with the law, he paid his taxes, he didn't do drugs . . . what could the gunman be talking about? What was he implying? What had Jonathan ever done that could warrant such a comment. Unless . . .

Jonathan shook his head. No way. It couldn't possibly have anything to do with that.

The gunman snorted angrily. 'That's why I'll have no problem doing away with you. You're guilty, man. Guilty.'

'Look, you've got this wrong . . .'

'There you go again, telling me what to think. I ain't got it wrong. *You* got it wrong.'

Jonathan was waiting now, waiting for an opportunity to show that he was on to him, that he had figured it out, but he needed more information, more clues. He needed to know who had set this man up to do this, and why. He decided to play along for a bit longer; eventually, he felt sure, the necessary clues would slip out.

'But what am I guilty of? What am I supposed to have done?'

'You know.'

'I don't! I don't know! Why play games with me? Why don't you just tell me?'

'What, so you can defend yourself? I ain't falling for that. Like I said, I know all about your sort and your clever words. Well it won't work, not with me.'

'I have nothing to defend. You, however, will have plenty to defend if you kill me. You'll be caught, sentenced, sent to prison for life . . . it can't be worth taking the gamble, can it? Just to make a point?' said Jonathan, no longer caring if he provoked the gunman.

'Don't you worry man. They won't catch me. No one will catch me.'

A sad, knowing smile seemed to creep across the gunman's lips and Jonathan, watching this slow, repulsive transformation, guessed immediately what the gunman meant, or at least, what he was intimating: he would use the gun on Jonathan. And then on himself.

Jonathan felt a chill creep over him. This last intimation upset him; the tone of his voice, that creepy smile. If he was acting then he was doing a damn good job of it; too good for Jonathan's liking.

Perhaps it was all true? Perhaps it was all as he had said. He had had enough, he was going to make an example of someone, and his victim had been chosen with the aid of a pin and a telephone directory. As bizarre, as awful as it sounded, it was suddenly no less plausible than Jonathan's alternative, that this was all a clever set-up, designed for some nefarious purpose that Jonathan could only guess.

He had to know. He had to know the truth. Jonathan steeled himself for another attempt at breaking the deadlock. He decided to take a chance, to bluff it out.

'Don't you think this has gone on long enough? I

know what this is all about. I know someone set you up to all this, and I know why. Now then, why don't we just call a halt to the proceedings right now. If you're expecting me to make some sort of confession, then you're out of luck.'

'You got a big mouth.'

'This is absurd . . .'

'Do me a favour . . .'

'Don't you see? The game's up. Now if you just tell me who is behind all this, we can call it a night. I won't call the police, I won't press charges. You can just walk out the door as if none of this happened, and I can take up the matter in person with whoever's paying you for this little performance. Okay?'

The gunman continued to stare at Jonathan. It was an expression of such coldness, such emptiness that just looking at his face Jonathan could tell that the man was missing something, some sensibility or other that, had he possessed it, would have made him wholly human, but without which he was somehow reduced – not an animal, but something almost mechanical, robotic. Not animal, no; but not human either.

After a moment the cold stare metamorphosed slowly into a smile. 'You know something?' said the gunman. 'You almost made me laugh there. Good try. Still, it would have been too late. I gave you your chance for that, remember?'

Jonathan sighed. He felt sure his approach would get a rise out of him. But the gunman had not responded at all; surely if Jonathan had hit the mark then . . .

He was fast running out of ideas. He did not know what the gunman was waiting for, but one thing was certain; if the gunman was for real, then Jonathan had to come up with a good idea soon, or else he might as well forget all about it. Time was up to its old tricks again. Before long, it would run out, and with it would go Jonathan's last chance of survival.

The gunman rose slowly and stretched. He peered around the room, as if searching for something in particular. Jonathan flinched as the gunman suddenly walked away from the sofa and headed towards the mantelpiece. It was too dark to see clearly what he was up to, but from the sounds Jonathan figured he was picking up the various items on the mantelpiece and examining them. This confused Jonathan. There was nothing of importance on the mantelpiece, not even anything especially interesting, and certainly nothing that could interest this lout; just a few gewgaws from his travels: a wooden carving from Indonesia, a small porcelain sculpture of Priapus from Greece, a bronze figure of the elephant-headed Hindu god Ganesh. Jonathan would rather the stranger did not touch his possessions, but he certainly was not going to make a fuss about it.

Should he make a confession? Some sort of admission of guilt, clearly trumped-up and nonsensical, just to get this oaf out of his house and on his way? Would that do it?

'Who's Liz?'

Jonathan started. He had been so lost in his own thoughts that the question had quite surprised him.

'What?'

'Liz. I heard you call it out as you were coming down the stairs.'

Jonathan said nothing. The gunman was standing over him again now, and Jonathan could see that he held, in his left hand, the small silver-framed photograph of him and Liz, taken shortly after they had started seeing each other. He felt a bit sickened by this, and by the turn in the conversation. The gunman had asked him nothing of a personal nature until then, and he was not sure he wanted to reveal anything about himself. And what difference could it make to him, anyway? He decided to keep quiet, in the hope that it would put off his assailant.

It did not work.

'Well?' The gunman was growing impatient.

'She's my wife,' said Jonathan reluctantly. 'What's this got to do with anything?'

'I thought you said there was no one else in the house.'

'I did. There's no one else here. But when I heard the noise I thought it might be her, coming back. Okay?'

'So you're expecting her?'

'Not really, no.' Jonathan really did not want to get into a discussion about Liz, but he was not sure how he could veer the conversation away and on to a different topic.

The gunman looked at Jonathan suspiciously. He reached across and put the framed photograph on the small coffee table in front of the sofa. Then he started to fiddle nervously with the gun.

'You're not making yourself very clear.'

Jonathan noted the anxious fidgeting. 'I wasn't expecting her. It's just that she has a key, so when I heard a noise I thought it could easily have been her coming home.'

'She's away then.'

'In a manner of speaking.'

Suddenly, and in great anger, the gunman leant forward and shoved the muzzle of the gun up against

Jonathan's face, burying it into his cheek. Jonathan cried out in pain. The gunman ignored him.

'Don't play games with me you little shit, or I'll blow your fucking head off right now! Now where is she?'

'She's left me!' cried Jonathan. 'We're separated! She walked out three weeks ago. I keep expecting ... I keep hoping she'll turn up one night! That's all! She left me ...' He started to cry then, half in fright, half in pain, pathetic little snivels that did not do justice to the horror of his predicament. Any thoughts he had entertained that this was just a piece of theatre disappeared. How could this be happening to him? What had he done to deserve this?

The gunman relaxed, took the gun away from Jonathan's face, and sighed noisily.

'That's better. Now next time I ask you a question, just fucking answer it straight, okay?'

Jonathan nodded. He put a hand up to his cheek and winced. He thought a tooth had loosened in his upper jaw. He spat surreptitiously into his hand and was alarmed to see so much blood. He looked at his assailant with a mixture of terror and disgust. This was not play-acting. This was real. Until that moment he had not even dared to think about fighting back, but now Jonathan began to see that if he was to have any hope of getting out of this situation, he would have to do something. He had no idea what, all he knew was that this last action – bloodying him, hurting him – had triggered some internal reserve of energy and anger, and he was damned if he was going to be shot to death in his own home.

'It's a terrible thing, pain,' said the gunman malevolently. 'Terrible to live your life in fear; fear of being hurt.'

Jonathan looked at him suspiciously. What was this leading to? Was this where it began, the torture that he had suspected would be the logical outcome of this scenario? Was this when the real terror started?

Oh God, he thought to himself. Why couldn't it have been Liz? If only it had been Liz . . .

Part Two

6

It had not been her sparkling personality that had first attracted Jonathan to Liz. Neither was it her keen intelligence nor subtle and clever sense of humour; these were all attributes that he would discover later. The first thing Jonathan noticed about Liz were her ankles. They were sufficiently enticing to make him stop in his tracks, turn and – with an intention that many would consider incorrect for all manner of reasons – follow her. He did so up a set of stairs which led to corridors along which (in two years at the college) he had never walked, and upon which he might never have set eyes, had it not been for that momentary, serendipitous triggering of aesthetic delight and pure, unadulterated lust.

Jonathan was what men of an earlier generation would have labelled a 'legs man', although he would never have defined himself in so narrow a fashion. None the less, when it came to matters of women and sexual inclination, it was to legs, feet and ankles in particular that Jonathan was drawn. A slender, well-proportioned ankle was more likely to raise his blood-pressure than bare shoulders, exposed necks or even naked breasts. Where this fondness derived from Jonathan could not say; nor had he, in honesty, spent much time pondering the origins of his own preferences. It was sufficient for him to know and be aware of it. It was also, however, a source of considerable frustration that he was obliged by current trends to keep such matters, by and large, to himself.

In the period during which Jonathan had progressed from a frustrated, inexperienced teenager to a sexually active adult there had been an equivalent shift in certain aspects of what Jonathan thought of as 'everyday language'. Or rather, there had been a change in the acceptability of certain phrases, metaphors and similes, to such an extent that expressions like 'a legs man' were no longer considered appropriate amongst folk who thought themselves educated. In fact, as innocuous as it seemed to him, many of his contemporaries considered such expressions dangerously offensive, implying, or so it was suggested, that they degraded women. This, to Jonathan's way of thinking, was nonsense, as the only person implicated by such an expression was the man to whom it referred. As the years passed and Jonathan found his speech being corrected by more and more people on more and more occasions, he found himself rebelling, sometimes vociferously. To his mind, this movement (that in more recent years had become termed 'political correctness', but which had its roots in the first flowering of feminism) was in danger of distorting, amongst other things, human sexuality itself.

To Jonathan, for whom language was both a utilitarian tool and a sacred blessing — the one concept that set man apart from the rest of the animal kingdom – one might just as well pretend that men were not sexually aroused by looking at women as deny them a *lingua franca* in which to express such notions. The logical extension, for those who objected to colloquialisms connoting sexual matters, would be to insist women donned the *chador* and veil so that men would be deprived of the opportunity to make the sort of comments that the new language police thought offensive. It was to his mind an especially insidious form of censorship, a sort of linguistic fascism, which in its most extreme manifestation threatened to bring about the death of ideas. After all, if one is denied words to express concepts, the concept soon ceases to exist, and that was something that Jonathan could not tolerate. Sex was such a fundamental part of human thought and activity that to deny it its own expression was to stifle the life-force itself. Which is probably why, these days, whenever he was confronted by these flag-wavers for the PC lobby, he made a point of littering his conversations with dangerously prejudiced words like 'chairman', 'wife', 'black', 'dwarf', 'queer', 'spastic' and 'girlie'. Not, as one might think, in order to offend those groups for whom such expressions might well appear derogatory, but merely to point out the absurdity of censoring something as vibrant and essential as colloquial English. 'It'll be a black day when intellectual dwarfs like you queer our speech to such an extent that it is turned into a spastic, stuttering excuse for language,' he said on one occasion to a PC acolyte, emphasising each forbidden word with relish. It was, of course, a well-rehearsed line, but he felt it made the point.

By the same token, he would say 'fuck' a lot, very loudly, whenever he got the chance.

So even though he did not say it aloud in so many words, Jonathan was, unequivocally, a legs man, and consequently it was his keen appreciation of Liz's shapely ankles that caused him to divert his attention from an afternoon tutorial and follow her up the stairs to the dark, unexplored regions of the second floor.

It was an instinctive response, and whilst he had never previously reacted so strongly to such a stimulus, it was not out of keeping with his usual response to things that attracted him. Jonathan gave in very easily to his own desires. If something took his fancy, be it a new shirt, a steak dinner or a pretty face, he rarely delayed in pursuing it. After all, why procrastinate? You could only lose by putting things off: lose sight, lose interest or lose enthusiasm. Consequently, in Jonathan's opinion, if you didn't strike whilst the iron was hot, you were likely to forget why you were striking at all.

As he ascended the stairs, his musings, such as they were, were of the most basic kind, barely nudging the edges of conscious thought, and if it were possible to put them into words, they might best translate as something like: 'Good legs, good sex!'. That Jonathan had never actually proven a causal link, to his or anyone else's satisfaction, is neither here nor there; logic is just one product of consciousness that is overtaken (or even run down) when hormones get hold of the reins.

Good legs, good sex? Perhaps one does not need to believe in such an unlikely correspondence, merely hope for it. Jonathan's own sexual predilections were such that, in this instance, as Liz's ankles had swept past him at head height (she being already half-way up the open staircase when Jonathan first encountered her), that wondrous, inexplicable bolt of desire shot not to his heart or head, but to his groin, where it was most likely to cause the greatest impact.

Caught, for just those few moments, in a world where ankles and lust were the two preoccupying motifs in his world, there were many things that Jonathan did not notice about Liz. He was, for example, only dimly aware that she was wearing a rather pretty dark blue cotton skirt that came down to mid-calf and swirled about her as she walked along. Nor had he fully appreciated the rather soft white sweater that, had be been a 'breast man', would probably have had him foaming at the mouth, Liz possessing what many women (as well as men) would define as a perfect and generous bust. And he certainly hadn't noticed her startling blue eyes, generous lips and high, sculpted cheekbones that had turned many a head that term, but to be fair this was because he had not yet seen her face. Neither did he glimpse her profile as she turned from the corridor into the classroom, because, poor man, he was still preoccupied with those extraordinary ankles.

Such was his preoccupation that it was not until he was standing in the doorway to the classroom, being addressed by a fellow member of staff, that he realised he was not where he was supposed to be.

'Can I help you? Mister Fairchild? Jonathan?'

'What?'

'Are you looking for somebody?'

Jonathan looked blankly at Susan Hastings, senior lecturer in media studies, and then peered around the room at the dozen or so students who were still taking their places. He had the common sense to shake his head and smile.

'Uh . . . not really, no.' He gave a deep sigh. 'Actually' . . . he started, 'I was . . .' He paused as he caught sight of Liz, descending gracefully into her seat, and felt his mouth dry suddenly and completely, as if someone had just poured a large bucket of sand down his throat. Oh God, thought Jonathan, she's beautiful.

He excused himself swiftly with a mumble about a misplaced textbook, and then headed back down the corridor, his breath catching in the back of his throat, his palms hot and sweaty.

Back at his office he dismissed his tutorial students with a feeble excuse that, when set against the bright blue skies of a hot, sunny day, caused not the slightest alarm or consternation. He spent most of the following hour wondering how he could get to meet the vision in white and blue, date her and bed her by the end of the week, without losing his job. He thought about following her home from college in the hope of setting up a casual meeting outside her front door later that week, but soon realised that such ideas were fraught with problems, not least the possibility that he be deemed a stalker or pervert. Furtive measures were therefore out of the question, too risky. He toyed with the idea of asking Susan Hastings, strictly in confidence, for the girl's name, but could not devise a suitable or plausible pretext on which he could approach her. He thought about asking Dougie Francis to assist in some way. Dougie taught a first-year foundation course in social studies and had, therefore, probably met the young woman – or at least had some contact with her. Dougie was also Jonathan's only close acquaintance at the college – not so much a friend, more a drinking buddy – and was probably the only person in a position to help him. But even this seemed precarious; Dougie could well have his own agenda regarding her; it was not unknown for him to put in a bit of spade work at the beginning of each academic year with the occasional pretty, fresh-faced undergraduate. No, Jonathan would have to rely on his own devices if he wanted to fulfil what he now believed was his – or rather, their – destiny.

Two days later, whilst still bumbling along in a haze of confusion and inaction, fate intervened and saved Jonathan from a great deal of effort and heartache. Hurrying to his afternoon tutorial session, his head in the clouds and his mind on holiday, he bumped into her, quite literally, as she rounded a corner near the library, and sent her and her assorted files and books flying.

'Jesus, I'm so sorry . . .' said Jonathan, realising in an instant who it was he had just propelled across the corridor. He leant over to help her up, but in his anxiety moved too swiftly, slipped on the polished tiles and went crashing into her.

'Ow!' yelled Liz as Jonathan's forearm collided with her shoulder.

'Oh fuck!' said Jonathan, as the enormity of this slapstick farce bore down on him.

He rolled away quickly and struggled to his feet. Thankfully there was no one else around to witness his blundering behaviour. He took a deep breath and, ensuring he was stable, held out a hand. 'God I'm sorry,' he said, trembling both from the ordeal and the sight of Liz's ankles, calves and thighs, all bared thanks to the manner in which her skirt had risen way above her knees. 'Are you okay?'

Liz looked up at the shambling sociology lecturer and started to laugh. Oh God, thought Jonathan; that's just what I need.

'I'm fine,' said Liz. She accepted Jonathan's offer of help and pulled herself to her feet.

'You're not hurt? God, I'm so clumsy . . .'

'No, really, I'm okay,' said Liz, brushing herself down and re-arranging her clothes. Jonathan watched in fascination. Even in his highly distressed state he still found himself getting excited as Liz ran her hands down over her body, tugging at crumpled material, straightening creases.

Jonathan managed to tear his eyes away for a moment to survey the rest of the damage. Her books and files were strewn across the width of the corridor. Putting his own case – a tatty leather document folder – to one side, he set about helping to collect the scattered fragments. Liz followed suit, and in one of those wonderful movie-moments, Jonathan and Liz both reached down for the same book at the same time and found themselves, for just an instant, holding hands. And in that same instant, rather than pulling back in horror or embarrassment, they both prolonged the contact, for just a second longer than expected, enough time for something, for the merest hint of attraction, to pass between them. It was so slight, so tentative, that had Jonathan not already been obsessed by her, he (being a man and by definition less sensitive to such subtleties) would almost certainly have missed it.

But he did not miss it. On the contrary, it registered with the impact of a slap in the face, and as they both straightened and Jonathan handed the book to Liz, he felt the first stirrings of genuine sexual excitement, the warm, tremulous buzz of ardour and lust, as it vibrated through his limbs and torso, converging on his lower stomach and groin. This is it, thought Jonathan as he looked, a touch too longingly perhaps, into Liz's wondrously clear blue eyes; this is my chance.

'I really am so sorry.'

'I'm fine, really . . .'

'You might have sprained something.'

'Honestly, I'm okay . . .'

'Well at least come and sit down for a moment.'

Liz shook her head. 'I'm late as it is . . . if I hadn't been rushing . . .'

'But I feel awful.'

'There's no need . . .'

After a couple more rounds of this perfunctory pussyfooting, with Jonathan making ever more conciliatory and unnecessary apologies and Liz insisting that she was fine, Jonathan struck home.

'Well you must at least let me buy you a drink . . . no, I insist.'

Liz sighed. 'Well . . .'

'In fact, let's make that dinner. Are you busy this evening?'

Liz frowned. 'I don't think . . .'

'Really, it would make me feel better.'

'Are you going to let me finish a sentence?'

Jonathan was quiet for a moment. Nerves always made him garrulous and he had barely allowed her to get a word in edgeways. He smiled, sheepishly, then nodded.

Liz smiled sweetly. 'I was just going to say that I don't think it's wholly appropriate – you know, staff and students?'

Jonathan shrugged. 'There's no law against it. And it's only dinner.'

Liz thought for a moment, then shook her head. 'Thanks all the same.'

For a moment Jonathan seriously considered begging, but realised it could compromise him unnecessarily. But it was a tough call; she was, quite simply, stunning. Dressed in a simple cotton skirt and sweatshirt she looked somehow softer and even more appealing than when he had first set eyes on her. And then there were her ankles. Oh God, thought Jonathan; those ankles.

'Well, if you won't come voluntarily, I'll just have to invoke the ancient college bye-laws concerning speeding in the corridor. If I report you to the appropriate authorities it means three days stable duties or a morning in the stocks. Of course . . .'

Liz tried to keep a straight face, although it was clear by now that she was finding this sort of attention very enjoyable. 'That, sir, is blackmail,' she said rather theatrically.

Jonathan nodded. 'I can see why they let you in. Well, what's it to be? Mucking out the horses or *tagliatelle al funghi* at Alfredo's?'

'Correct me if I'm wrong, but it's been over a hundred years since the college kept horses.'

Jonathan said nothing. He took a pen from his inside pocket and fished around in his other pockets for a piece of paper, eventually finding an old bus ticket, which he handed to Liz. 'Write your name and address for me and I'll say no more about this unfortunate lapse.'

Liz laughed this time, scribbled the details, then looking at her watch, started to panic.

'I have to go . . .' she said, and turned to go.

'Eight o'clock?'

'Fine,' she said, and started heading swiftly down the corridor. As she rounded the corner at the far end, Jonathan fell to his knees and, shaking his fists in triumph, threw his head back and proclaimed a victorious 'yes!' to the ceiling.

'Won the pools, have we?'

Still on his knees, Jonathan looked sideways to see the vice-chancellor staring at him in bemusement. Jonathan rose swiftly and brushed himself down.

'Something like that,' said Jonathan, collecting his document case.

The vice-chancellor nodded. 'Aren't you supposed to be somewhere, Mister Fairchild?'

Yes, thought Jonathan, nestling between that young woman's thighs. 'Just on my way,' he said. Lost in his deeply sexually oriented reveries, he pushed past the vice-chancellor and, despite his efforts to maintain control, skipped down the corridor, laughing.

7

Liz had fallen into taking a degree course more by default than by any positive decision. Stuck in a dead-end job that had barely exercised her intellect or abilities, she knew that she had to do something about it or face a lifetime of frustration.

Unfortunately, she had no idea what else she should do, and when someone suggested she go to college, it seemed like a sensible option. A qualification would broaden her horizons, equip her for more than the mundane and menial tasks that had become her lot. But still she had not known what to do, what subject to study. It all came down to the same question, one which had bugged her for years and to which, for all her efforts, she still did not have a satisfactory answer: what did one do with one's life? Or more particularly, what should she do with *her* life. It was a source of constant amazement to her that other people knew what they wanted; not just what they wanted to eat, or where they wanted to live, but what they actually wanted to do. When did they discover the answer to such a forbidding question? How did they find out? How could they be so certain?

Of course, what Liz did not recognise – and what no

one had told her – was that most people did not know what they wanted; like her, they had fallen into their jobs and relationships in a largely random fashion with little true self-understanding or realisation. People did what they did because, like that terrible cliché that had somehow become common parlance during the eighties, it seemed like a good idea at the time. Or, in fact, was the only idea at the time. In truth, like Liz, most people had no idea what they wanted in life; they had no knowledge of what was truly important to them. And it was not for lack of intelligence or even imagination. It was simply because no one had ever taught them that such questions were important, perhaps the most important questions they would ever have to ask.

Were choices really so limited that smart, clever, witty people chose to become teachers rather than artists? Or was it that, at an age when the decisions had to be taken, one simply was not in possession of sufficient information to make a qualified decision? Nobody had ever told Liz that 'Film Director' was a bona fide profession, that you could even study to become a film director, that there were actually schools that would teach you such things. When Liz left high school, disenchanted with lessons and exams and the general lethargy she encountered amongst teachers and pupils alike, no one told her that you could make a living as a songwriter or an actress or a designer. Admittedly, she had no right to point a finger at anyone in particular and she knew that, in the final analysis, she was responsible for her own life and her own decisions. But how different it might have been if someone – anyone – had just held up a light in the darkness and said: 'Liz, you don't have to take shorthand and dictation for the rest of your life; instead you can be a professional photographer!' Or a philosopher. Or a beach bum. Or something like that.

College may not have been the answer, but at least it might help her to ask the right questions. Certainly it was a case of 'so far, so good'. London was new and exciting, her flatmates were all good fun, and she was coping easily with the course work. And now this. Only three weeks into her first term and already new things – new, *different* things – were happening to her.

Why did I wait so long, she wondered to herself as she applied a touch of colour to her lips. She didn't want to overdo it, but at the same time it was nice to make a bit of an effort. It had been rather a long time since she had had an excuse to dress up.

Jonathan rang the doorbell and waited impatiently for someone to answer. He hated hanging around on doorsteps and often wished he had lived in the days when people left their keys in the latch so that anyone could knock and then enter immediately: it would have been so much more civilised. Instead, in this current, less trustworthy age, he was reduced to the same status as the gas man or a Jehovah's Witness.

The door opened and Liz appeared, wearing a long, navy blue coat which, revealing very little, gave a quite inappropriate impression of chasteness. 'Hi,' she said softly, then smiled nervously. 'You won't mind if I don't invite you in, only . . .' She looked behind her into the darkened hallway. 'It's just, I share with three others, students at the college, and . . .'

'Say no more,' said Jonathan, only too pleased to

get away. He led the way to his car, a beaten-up old Volkswagen that, despite having done yeoman service for the best part of five years, was long overdue for replacement.

'Italian okay?' he said, as he opened the door for her.

'Fine,' said Liz, as she settled into the front passenger seat. 'Only this is German, isn't it?'

'No, I meant . . .' started Jonathan, only to see the smile creep across Liz's face. 'Right,' he said with a sigh. 'I can see I'm going to have to watch what I say.'

'You certainly are,' said Liz. 'And Italian's fine.'

'Buono,' said Jonathan, as he slipped into the driving-seat, taking care with the door. He had slammed it earlier that day and a little shower of rust-coloured snow had shaken loose from the side panel and fallen to the ground. He would have to get it looked at.

'So what do I call you?'

'"Sir" will do fine. Until we get to know each other better.'

'I'm serious; it was only after I dashed off down the corridor that I realised that I didn't know your name.'

'You mean you didn't check up on me?'

Liz looked a little startled. 'Well actually, my spies are all on vacation at the moment.'

'Well, I'm Mister Fairchild to my new first years, Jonno to my family and "that long-haired lout in sociology" to the vice-chancellor. But you can call me Jonathan.'

'Very well, Jonathan.'

'And how about you?'

'Me? I'm just plain Liz.'

'Hardly plain.' Jonathan looked around him furtively. The restaurant – a friendly little trattoria just off Camden High Street – was only half full, as one might expect on a Monday night, but Jonathan was still a little uneasy about bumping into one of his colleagues: Alfredo's fell comfortably within the college's catchment area, and it was not unknown for members of staff to celebrate special occasions – birthdays, anniversaries, meagrely pay rises – with a pizza and a bottle of Chianti.

Liz blushed and, taken off-balance momentarily by Jonathan's flirtatious remark, tried to change the subject. 'Didn't you burst into our media-studies class the other day? I'm sure it was you; you were talking to Professor Hastings.'

'Professor? Susan's not a professor, she's just a lowly tutor like me.'

'But she introduced herself . . .'

'Yes, I'm sure. That's Susan. Delusions of grandeur.'

'Oh . . . but it *was* you.'

'Yes. I was following you.'

'I see.' Liz fingered her wine glass nervously. She could see she was going to have her hands full. She was not used to men being so brazen. It was an interesting new approach; Liz was used to men either fussing nervously around her or just being plain vulgar.

In the momentary silence that followed, Jonathan took the opportunity to re-fill their glasses. He knew he was coming on a little strong, but that was just his way, and he figured that if she did not like it she would let him know. Besides, he did not believe in disguising his usual behaviour with false niceties. Why pretend to be a sheep when wolves were perfectly attractive in their own right?

'I'm serious. I saw you on the stairs and . . . well, actually, I was captivated by your ankles.'

Liz was taken aback by the stark confession, but did not believe him for one moment. She took a mouthful of frascati; it was colder than she had expected, and her tongue went slightly numb for a moment. Her ankles? No one had ever said anything about her ankles before. Was he being sarcastic? What was wrong with her ankles?

'Why are you making fun of me?' she asked, a touch of peevishness evident in her tone. 'You don't even know me.'

Jonathan balked at the accusation. 'I'm serious. The most pleasing set of ankles I've ever seen passed in front of me the other day, and I had no choice but to discover who owned them.'

'But . . . ankles?'

'I have a mild but incurable foot-fetish.'

Liz smiled this time. Was he being serious? Or was this just his idea of a chat-up line? 'How revealing.'

'Is it? What does it reveal?'

There was something rather charming about him, she thought, noticing how his eyes twinkled mischievously like a little boy's. She decided to relax and enjoy the slightly suggestive banter; after all, it seemed pretty harmless.

'Something darkly sexual, I suspect,' she said. 'Did you ever see your father naked, save for his shoes and socks?'

'God, I don't know,' said Jonathan, as the rather

distasteful vision flashed to the forefront of his mind. 'Did you?'

'No, I've never met your father.'

Jonathan laughed. 'I see. And *your* father?'

Liz paused for a moment. 'Ah. No. Not that I recall, but that doesn't mean anything, does it?'

'I wouldn't know; you're the psychology major.'

'Yep. Three weeks in and already I'm an expert.'

Jonathan smirked, rather unattractively. 'I always pick the smart ones,' he said, almost to himself, and regretted it immediately.

Liz looked at him askance, took another sip of frascati, then nodded slowly. 'I'll bet you do.'

'No, I . . .' started Jonathan, realising his error. He was about to refute the notion, implicit in his smart-arsed boast, that he was always picking up bright, inexperienced students and making a play for them, but suspected he would be chastised for protesting too much. He decided to send himself up in the hope this would cover his apparent conceitedness. 'Actually, you're the third this week.'

'It's only Monday.'

'One for breakfast, one for lunch. I'm a quick worker.'

'Indeed. And do you use the same technique with all your conquests?'

'Are you my conquest?'

Liz smiled coquettishly. 'We shall have to see, shan't we. Now then, about this technique of yours.'

Jonathan smiled. Clearly she was not the least put out by his remarks and, in fact, was countering at every opportunity. He was going to enjoy this.

'My technique? It's foolproof.'

'Is it really?'

'Absolutely. Even if nothing else happens between us I can go around telling people that you've fallen for me.'

'And I have the bruises to show for it.'

This time it was Jonathan who was taken aback. There was something in her manner, something in the way she had said it that had given him pause. There was an edge to her voice; something that suggested there was more to the remark than just clever repartee ... Jonathan was not sure this time whether she was joking or not, and consequently found himself uncertain of how to take it, or how, in fact, to respond. This was no naive young student. In fact, now that he looked at her closely, it was clear that she was older than the usual first-year intake. He did not want to risk upsetting the atmosphere, which was light and frivolous and fun. Ever since they had taken their seats at a corner table the conversation had flowed easily, without awkwardness or the sort of gaucherie for which, despite his greatest efforts, Jonathan was renowned, and he did not want to spoil anything now.

'I'll have to make it up to you,' he said, a touch solemnly perhaps, before finishing the contents of his wine glass in one swift and unintentionally noisy gulp.

Alfredo's was a favourite haunt of his, and although he visited infrequently, he always enjoyed it there. The food was first class, the atmosphere friendly and cheerful, and the management had somehow conspired to create a relaxed ambience with a mixture of informality, uncluttered decor and tasteful, intelligent background music which was neither as bland as Muzak nor as distracting as the collections of classical arias that many Italian restaurants mistakenly believed added 'authenticity' to their venues.

The restaurant was quiet that night, and the waiters had left them to chat for a while before bringing across the menus. Jonathan had checked that Liz drank wine before ordering the frascati, and then had made a bit of a show of letting her order before folding his menu swiftly and saying 'same for me'. Unfortunately, he had put so much effort and concentration into perfecting this seemingly casual foreplay that he had not paid attention to what Liz had ordered. It was only now, as they awaited the arrival of their first course, that Jonathan started to feel a little uncomfortable. If she had ordered anything with seafood, he was in big trouble. He was allergic to seafood – in fact, allergic to anything that had spent a major portion of its life underwater – and although he knew he would look foolish or even pernickety leaving his starter untouched, he also realised he would look a lot sillier turning blue and throwing up over the table.

Other than this minor concern, Jonathan was in his element, thoroughly enjoying himself. Despite the joke remarks about 'conquests' he considered it a notable achievement to have enticed Liz out that evening. Liz was quite simply charming, with none of the rather callow, juvenile posturings beloved of first-year students that so irritated him. Perhaps she was a mature student, with a few years 'real life' experience under her belt? She certainly carried herself with great assurance. Her whole approach to the evening had been refreshingly direct, and Jonathan had found that very appealing. When it came to female company, he much preferred wisdom to wistfulness, knowingness to naivety. At least, that is what he would have professed, had anyone bothered to quiz him on the matter.

'Have some more wine.'

'Uh . . . I've already had two glasses and we haven't even finished the garlic bread.'

'It's okay,' said Jonathan. 'I know they have another bottle in the cellar.'

'That wasn't what I meant.'

'You're being far too circumspect. Don't you enjoy drinking?'

'Yes of course . . .'

'In which case you're just being polite, or worse, mistaking moderation for decorum, and I won't stand for it.' He poured the wine.

Liz sighed, a touch theatrically, then lifted her glass. She was, in truth, already feeling a bit light-headed; not drunk or even tipsy, but just entering that pleasant, relaxed, loosened state of drooping one's guard just a little and being prone to say things that might best be left unspoken. But there was nothing for Liz to feel guarded about; she could tell. She leaned forward, her voice dropping to just above a whisper. 'There's no point trying to get me drunk,' she said, hoping the comedic overtones in her voice were crystal clear. 'If you want me to sleep with you, you'd be better off coming straight out and asking.'

Jonathan gulped noisily, ignored all indications of irony or humour, and wasted no time in concocting a suitable response. 'Really? Great. Let's fuck.'

Liz nearly choked on the wine. 'Straightforward and to the point . . .'

'Well you did say . . .'

'It was meant as a point of information, rather than a direct invitation.'

'Oh ... my mistake,' said Jonathan, who, despite the commonly accepted definitions of the words he was about to use, was adamantly, defiantly, not apologising. 'I tend to be a bit prosaic when it comes to talking about sex. Sorry.'

Liz, who felt momentarily out of her depth, stumbled to find a suitable response. Had her attempt at a joke misfired? Had she miscalculated so badly? Surely not. She was better at reading people than that. Surely this was just part of the game.

'No,' she said calmly. 'I think I should be apologising.'

'For leading me on?'

'For underestimating you.' Liz replaced her glass carefully on the table and looked around her. Although she was not a prude, she was rather pleased the restaurant was so empty.

Jonathan nodded sagely. 'Well?'

'Huh?'

'Is that it? Is the offer withdrawn?'

Liz shook her head in astonishment. 'What offer?'

'Well ... the suggestion, then.'

She noted Jonathan's cheeky smile. How was it that this man could say the sort of things that would normally have her reaching for the nearest sharpened instrument, and get away with it? It had to be something about the playfulness, the ease with which such outrageous comments were made. There was no threat, explicit or implicit; it *was* just a game. She chose to continue in the manner that she first intended, and if he really was that prosaic, then at least she knew where she stood, could make suitable excuses and leave at the first possible opportunity.

'Do I get to eat my *antipasto* first or would you rather violate me right here in front of the grated parmesan?'

'I'm game if you are.'

Liz paused a moment, as if mulling over the proposition. 'I don't want to miss out on the *tiramisu*; it's not exactly a regular part of my daily diet.'

'Spoken like a true student.'

'Thank you; I'll take that as a compliment.'

'That's only the start. I also think you're beautiful.'

This time Liz blushed. This was certainly not what she had expected. Just more fun? She chose to treat it as such, although her sixth sense suggested something altogether different. 'Mister Fairchild!' she said mockingly, hoping to hide her embarrassment. 'I think you're being rather forward.'

'It's my nature. I have a tendency to speak my mind.'

'I'd never have guessed.'

'Does it worry you? Some people do find it a bit confrontational.'

'You surprise me.'

Jonathan studied her expression for a moment longer than Liz found comfortable. 'But that's just it,' he said at last, a touch more seriously than one might have expected. 'I don't, do I?'

'Don't?'

'Surprise you.'

Liz shrugged. 'Let's just say that I'm starting to get used to it.' She paused a moment, taking time to size him up. 'I suspect you may have the wrong impression of me.'

'Yes? In what way?'

'All this smart banter. You'll think I'm ... Well, put it this way: I'm not *worldly*. My background is strictly working class. I come from a small country town – not much more than a village, really – and this is my first experience of the big city. I've never been to the opera or a classical concert and I don't know what's fashionable in the art world these days.'

Jonathan nodded. 'So?'

Liz shrugged. 'Let's just say I'm not used to sophisticated, cosmopolitan types. I don't know what the rules are here.'

Jonathan smiled, not knowingly or cruelly, but sympathetically. He was surprised to find himself touched by her confession; he doubted whether he was capable of such honesty. 'Do I frighten you? Is that it?'

'Intimidate, perhaps.'

'I'm sorry. It's not intended.'

'Oh, it's okay. To be honest, it's quite refreshing. Most of the students in my year talk a lot of bullshit most of the time.'

'They just want to make an impression.'

Liz smiled. This was the feed-line she had been waiting for all evening.

'I think if you want to make an impression you're better off knocking people to the ground and then finishing them off with a forearm smash. What do you think?'

Jonathan laughed. 'My view exactly.' He started to pour some more wine but Liz put her hand over the top of her glass.

'You are trying to get me drunk, aren't you?'

'Can't blame a man for trying.'

'Well, if that really is your intention, then you'll succeed.'

'That's what I like to hear.'

'Well, I wouldn't be so sure. When I'm drunk the only thing I can guarantee is that I'll throw up all over your car, then pass out. If, after that, you want to have your way with me, it'll mean carrying me to a suitable bed and then ravishing me without my participation. So, does necrophilia feature up there with the foot fetishism? If so, pour away.'

Jonathan put the bottle down smartly, Liz's graphic descriptions dancing merrily in his mind's eye.

'Best not to overdo things, eh?'

The meal was, as ever, excellent, with not a prawn or mussel in sight, for which Jonathan was profoundly grateful. And, like the true gentleman he was, when they had finished eating, drunk their fill of espresso, had one more *amaretto* for the road, he drove Liz back to her flat, walked her to the door, and made no attempt whatsoever to talk her into bed.

This was something for which Liz, who had begun to take to Jonathan, was also profoundly grateful. Although Jonathan was not to know it, she was especially attracted to men who had sufficient respect, restraint and good taste not to try it on after the first date. Many a potential relationship had gone the way of all things as a result of over-zealous boys on first dates who thought a pizza and a pint entitled them to a paw and a poke in some seedy bedsit at the end of the evening. So, even though he did not know it, in Liz's eyes Jonathan had just passed an important – perhaps even crucial – test.

'There,' said Jonathan as they stood on the doorstep. 'Safe and sound.'

'Thank you. It was a really lovely evening.'

'My pleasure. It was the least I could do after beating you up.'

'That's all forgotten. Besides, it's been a long time since someone swept me off my feet.'

'Bulldozed, you mean.'

'Perhaps.'

Jonathan sighed, then took hold of Liz's hand, a touch formally, before raising it to his lips. He kissed it gently, and Liz was so surprised by the old-fashioned gesture, which had been performed without so much as a hint of irony or mockery, that she found herself speechless. And before she had had a chance to find a suitable response, Jonathan had taken his leave and was heading back to the street.

At the bottom of the path he turned, smiled and waved casually before jumping into the car and heading off into the night, leaving Liz standing in the doorway, smiling with delight.

8

They saw each other on two more occasions that week. On Wednesday they met for a drink after college at a newly opened tapas bar off the Marylebone Road. The eager consumption of a large jug of sangria and several portions of Spanish omelette and spicy sausage lengthened what was supposed to be a brief rendezvous into a marathon eating and drinking session. To the strains of the ubiquitous Gypsy Kings, Jonathan and Liz ate and drank with considerable gusto, interspersing mouthfuls of tortilla with gobbets of spurious information on subjects as diverse as aerobics and astrology. They spoke easily, casually, in a manner that, Jonathan later reflected, would have suggested to onlookers that they were old friends rather than recent acquaintances.

The owners of the bar had gone to some considerable trouble to re-create a sense of authenticity, and the place was festooned with Spanish artefacts and regalia. They had even made a point of employing itinerant Spaniards behind the bar, most of whom looked as if they could not wait to return home. Still, on that unseasonably warm autumn evening, the exotic sounds of flamenco and the distinctive odours of Spanish herbs and spices wafting in from the kitchen created such a strong, Mediterranean feel that by the time they had ordered their second jug of sangria, Jonathan felt as if he were sitting, not on a busy, congested road half a mile from King's Cross, but in some small, family-run *bodega* on the outskirts of Granada.

Unsurprisingly, given the circumstances and atmosphere, conversation soon turned to the subject of holidays in the sun, and trips that they had taken, both as children with their families, and as independent adults. As Liz had travelled abroad very little, her recollections were primarily of family holidays in Devon, simple affairs which, softened by the passing of the years and filled with images of bright blue skies, buckets and spades and vanilla ice-cream cones, she held in great affection. Whilst Jonathan could identify easily with Liz's memories, having gone through much the same experience as a boy, he was more preoccupied with later trips, as a late adolescent and then as a young adult.

It was not difficult for Jonathan to infuse others with his love of travel, and especially his passion for southern Europe. His abiding love of Italy, Spain and, in particular, Greece, was so strong that, had one not known otherwise, one would have assumed he had Greek ancestry. In actual fact Jonathan was at least three-quarters traditional Home Counties stock, and the closest he could get to claiming Greek blood was when he received a transfusion of three pints following a nasty altercation concerning a donkey, a moped and half a bottle of Metaxa in Corfu back in 1981. Nonetheless, he could totally beguile an audience with his travel tales, capturing somehow the very essence of Greece with his deeply evocative descriptions, so that, as one of Jonathan's stories unfolded, one could virtually smell the pine needles and taste the retsina.

That evening Liz found herself on the receiving end of this extraordinary tale-telling ability. She soon found herself caught up in the spirals and convolutions of Jonathan's anecdotes, as he whisked her from one island to the next, through sun-dappled groves of gnarled olive trees, along pine-scented gravel tracks that snaked up the mountainsides, and into the vine-covered tavernas with their red-checked tablecloths and ubiquitous *bouzouki* music.

Liz listened to all this with a sort of awed fascination. Her confession – that she was not worldly – had not been prompted by unnecessary modesty; she had never been on a proper holiday abroad, and save for one school trip to France when she was fifteen and a disastrous weekend in Amsterdam with her first serious boyfriend, she had never ventured beyond England's shores. That Jonathan could conjure up such pictures she thought a rare and wonderful talent.

But despite her pleasure at hearing Jonathan's exotic reminiscences, at some point in the evening, she also became conscious of a deep, nagging, unfulfilled desire which she could not clearly identify. Although she could not name it, whatever it was somehow intimated both risk and excitement. It was only towards the end of the evening that she was able to recognise the feeling as a rather startling urge to accompany Jonathan on a trip abroad. Not next year or next month, but right there and then. So strong was this yearning that, at midnight, as they walked out into the still warm London air, she had already made a decision; although she hardly knew him, somehow – and sooner rather than later – she would travel to Greece with this man who could conjure visions of Elysium out of thin air.

On Friday evening Jonathan took Liz to see the latest Merchant–Ivory film at the Curzon West End. He was not a great fan of the duo's overly tasteful interpretations of English classics, but he knew it would be a safe bet for a date.

Afterwards they had a bite to eat at Kettners. Despite the fact that it was nothing more than a jumped-up pizza joint, Kettners was probably Jonathan's favourite mid-town restaurant. The mock-elegant air – Regency styling, a pianist playing innocuous cocktail jazz – was countered perfectly by the paper tablecloths and choice of food, so that the place was, at one and the same time, quite genteel and enjoyably informal. It was also a great place to chat, as there was always a lively atmosphere without it ever getting noisy or boisterous.

They worked their way easily through two bottles of ripe, luscious Valpolicella as they munched their quattro stagioni and discussed, with fun and fervour, the film they had just seen. They talked at some length about the actors, the locations, the soundtrack, the lighting, the direction, the costumes and the script. As the evening progressed they went on to talk about all-time favourite films, best-loved authors, music to die for and six things they would take to a desert island. They both became garrulous and effusive on the subject of consumerism and how it was destroying value systems and human decency. They avoided any specific talk of politics, as whenever they edged towards it one or other would become mildly petulant. However, they both agreed on the need for greater investment in the health-care system, and disagreed on the need for greater censorship of videos. They also argued quite heatedly about the best way of getting into a hard-boiled egg. To their joint delight they both harboured secret passions for Belgian fresh cream chocolates, and neither had any wish to jump out of an aeroplane with or without a parachute, or to shoot a bow and arrow. Neither had strongly held opinions on the Church of England, the rise in popularity of Perrier water, or the desirability or otherwise of Laura Ashley fabrics. And throughout the evening they both laughed, freely and frequently, out of amusement, appreciation or just sheer pleasure.

Thus it was that they were half-way through their third bottle when Jonathan, just slightly sozzled (but not yet drunk), reached across the table and took hold of Liz's hand.

'You do realise,' he said, his voice warm, fuzzy, wine-drenched, 'that we've spoken about everything except us.'

Liz clasped his hand. 'I know. I was trying to avoid it.'

'Me too. Why do you suppose that is?'

'Scared?'

Jonathan nodded. 'Probably. But why should we be scared? We're both brave, grown-up . . .'

'. . . and categorically Anglo-Saxon. Didn't anyone ever tell you that you're not allowed to talk about personal things?'

Jonathan smiled wildly, gripped Liz's hand with an unanticipated fervour, only to find his own passions being returned with interest. He gazed into her startling, sky-blue eyes and felt his pulse double. He knew that look, knew what it meant: it made his heart beat faster. He was also sure that the same desire was lighting up his own expression with equal animation.

'Let's get out of here,' he said, and dropping two twenty-pound notes on to the table, dragged her out through the door.

She had never known a man undress her with such care, such gentleness. Whilst her experience of men was limited, she had been to bed with enough of them to know that, by and large, what they wanted was to rip off her knickers as quickly as possible in order to bury themselves inside her with equal fervour and fury. Whilst this had its own attractions – the surge of lust and passion in another could be something of a turn-on in itself – it meant that certain other aspects of love-making such as care, consideration and tenderness were lost in the rush of excitement. As her first few partners had all followed a near identical pattern, Liz had naturally assumed that all men were tarred with the same wild brush, so it came as both a surprise and a pleasure to discover that it need not always be the way.

Not that Jonathan was not passionate, excited or – to some extent – desperate to get into Liz's knickers. It was just that he – being perhaps a little older than Liz's previous partners – had learnt that there was more to sex than a quick wham-bam, and that the greatest pleasures came with exercising a certain restraint. For Jonathan, the act of removing clothes was a great source of sexual excitement in itself, and could greatly enhance the pleasures yet to come. Sex could be swift, all-consuming and breathless, but like a good wine, it benefited from decanting, given a chance to breathe so that the more subtle, complex flavours could rise to the top. And on such a warm, sultry night, those exotic perfumes were already percolating through the air with heady abandon.

Jonathan knew how to keep up a head of steam without blowing his top, and how to take his time in the whole arena of foreplay, which for him started with the slow, tender disrobing of his partner, starting, naturally, with the feet.

Despite his previous remarks to her, there was in truth nothing fetishistic about Jonathan's appreciation of Liz's ankles, and on this occasion, whilst caressing them for a not inconsiderable time, he did not linger over them in preference to other parts of her most desirable body. Consequently, having ushered her swiftly but not hurriedly into his bedroom, taken her coat, removed her shoes, lifted her skirt and pulled off her tights, he then eased her back gently on to the bed and proceeded to work his way along her legs, from the toes, in a series of tantalising little kisses and nibbles that, meeting no disapproval from Liz, he continued with until he reached her upper thighs. At this point he diverted his attention temporarily to her torso and the effective and practised removal of blouse and bra, before returning to her loins, where with skilled application of tongue and lips, he soon had Liz squirming with delight. Another couple of deft manipulations and she was free of all her clothes.

Naked and resplendent, Liz was the manifestation of Jonathan's ideal, of everything he fancied in a woman. Without taking his eyes from her he stood briefly and, whilst admiring the curve of leg and breast, removed most of his own clothes swiftly and with ease, and then nestled down beside her.

With long, sweeping caresses he stroked her from the nape of her long, unblemished neck, along the shallow parabola of her slim, taut back to the firm, rounded perfection of her bottom. He loved the strangeness of new flesh, the excitement of coming together for the first time.

Liz's skin was soft, fragrant. With each caress Liz seemed to melt a little, as if whatever inhibition remained in her was slowly ebbing away, vaporising into the ether.

Jonathan was thankful for the weather, an Indian summer. The air was heavy with a velvety humidity that was already coalescing into small, silvery droplets on Liz's soft, silken skin. With each movement, a little more energy was expended, a little more heat generated. The droplets of perspiration channelled themselves into gleaming quicksilver rivulets that streamed across her torso and limbs, before dividing into a multiplicity of tiny deltas that trickled into the secret creases and pits of her body. When he buried his head between her thighs he was astonished to discover that Liz's odour was light, delicate, quite unlike the frequently overpowering smells of the other women he had known. It made his head spin.

With the heat rising steamily from their bodies, the neophyte lovers, goaded on by the promises of greater satisfaction, flexed and contorted their agile bodies, writhing around each other like cobras, seeking purchase on sweat-soaked skin. Liz shifted and stretched in ways she had never thought possible, allowing greater access, exposure, vulnerability, and Jonathan shuffled and strained, pushing his wracked body to its limits, raising the heat, quickening the pulse. Hands touched, lips kissed, teeth bit, tongues twisted and nerve ends tingled where fingers found flesh.

Liz was already riding high when she was startled by a completely new sensation. Aroused to previously unknown levels, her breathing had became irregular and jagged, bursting from her in short spasms as she fought to maintain control, each breath catching deep in the back of her throat. She was wide open to him now, and Jonathan responded with amazing sensitivity. As each stroke brought her closer to climax, powerful waves of pure pleasure started to rise in her, sweeping along her body, until they combined with her shortened breaths to issue from her as deep, throaty laughter, laughter that was both completely uncontrollable and profoundly pleasurable, as if no other response were possible. There was nothing hysterical or comical about it, although Jonathan, delighted that his love-making should reduce Liz to such a state, could not help but find space for a smile amidst his considerable exertions. In fact, as the laughter started to resound around him, he found himself ever more excited as he realised that she was no longer consciously controlling her responses, that he had broken through all the barriers, that she was reacting in a wholly reflexive way, that she was flying.

When, more fully aroused than he had ever been in his entire life, Jonathan climbed on top of her, Liz grabbed hold of his buttocks, her fingernails chiselling into taut muscle, and pulled him inside her. She was already cresting the peak as he entered her, so that as he thrust forward she felt all resistance dissolve, and gave herself up in entirety to the feelings and sensations that now overwhelmed her. Her laughter metamorphosed into a joyful, resonant cry, triggering Jonathan's own intense climax, and in a single, sublime moment the boundaries that divided them disappeared, and bodies, souls, emotions, lusts, desires and passions all merged for just the briefest moment in a breathtaking fusion of flesh and sweat and heat.

They did not talk afterwards. There were no words. Liz fell asleep in Jonathan's arms in a way she had never done with other men, and spent a deeply contented and quite dreamless night, completely oblivious to Jonathan's unrestrained snoring.

She woke feeling as good as she had ever done in her entire life. She looked over at Jonathan and smiled warmly, fully convinced that he alone was responsible for her wonderful sense of well-being, and determined to encapsulate the moment, the feeling, the memory, sealed his lips with hers and made a wish.

9

The problem with ecstasy is that it is both deeply desirable and extremely rare. The sexual euphoria that Liz and Jonathan both experienced that night was exceptional, the result of an almost countless number of factors all coming together at the same time in the same place. The number of variants involved on such an occasion is so vast, and each factor so finely tuned, that it is unlikely the combination could ever be repeated. Like all great moments in a lifetime, it was unique, with its own character and flavour. It was also, in this particular instance, of an uncommon intensity, an intensity raised perhaps by the red wine, the outside temperature, the particular hormonal balance of their respective bodies, the amount of garlic coursing through the bloodstream, and a thousand other possibilities. It is also true that ecstasy, by its nature, is serendipitous and cannot be created wilfully.

So, what is one to do when one has experienced something great and other-worldly, and would welcome a repeat visit? What, in particular, does one do if that experience is something as readily available as sex? Trying to repeat the experience even once would be a disaster. Like many drugs, one can get accustomed to sex, to its particular highs, its specific buzz. Both the body and mind inevitably become de-sensitised. This rules out any hope of repeating the experience on a regular basis. One could say that Jonathan and Liz were both extremely lucky to have had the opportunity of experiencing something as genuinely mind-blowing as they did. On the other hand, how does one live up to the expectations?

At some level, both Jonathan and Liz were mindful of the potential difficulties raised by what had happened. Neither of them had ever previously experienced anything approaching that sort of pleasure in the sexual arena, and they were both aware that whatever it was that had happened between them was exceptional. Which is probably why, when they went to bed together for the second time, they spent most of the night cuddling and kissing and touching and toying but not actually making love. It was not that they were scared (although Liz *had* been shocked by the intensity of her own reactions), but they were, quite understandably, wary of any attempt to repeat an experience that by its very nature was unrepeatable. However desirable it might have been.

When they did next make love again, it was more selfconsciously and with an altogether cooler approach, almost as if the first time had never happened. Not that there was anything wrong with this, and indeed, whilst the mercury did not burst through the top of the thermometer, it still registered high enough on the scale to cause a good deal of whimpering, moaning and general pleasure.

But it was not like that first time. It would never be like that first time.

And whilst that was not then – and would never be – a problem for Liz, in time it would start to play on Jonathan's mind.

'You lucky bastard,' said Dougie as Jonathan approached the bar.

'I'm sorry?'

'That blonde bit... don't think we haven't noticed.'

Jonathan attempted a look of incomprehension, but it did not fool Dougie for one moment. 'Noticed what?'

'Oh come off it Jonathan; it's all over the college. Do you think we're all stupid or something?'

Jonathan avoided saying the obvious. He rather wished Dougie would drop the subject altogether. 'Actually, I'd have thought you had more interesting things to concern you.' He looked around the bar, hoping there were no other staff members around. He could manage a bit of ribbing from Dougie if it was absolutely necessary, but he did not feel up to a public inquisition.

Dougie was not easily discouraged. 'What could be more interesting than discovering that our most deviant sociology lecturer is poking a pretty first-year student?'

'She's mature.'

'I should say...'

'I meant, she's a mature student. This is hardly cradle-snatching.'

Dougie chortled unpleasantly. He beckoned one of the bar staff over. 'Did I suggest any such thing?'

'It was written all over your face.'

'I must remember to wash more thoroughly in the mornings. Pint?'

Jonathan nodded.

'Two pints of best,' said Dougie to the barman, then turned his rather piercing gaze on Jonathan. 'So, spill the beans.'

'What beans?'

'Come on Jonathan. We're all dying to know what it is you've got that the rest of us are clearly lacking. As I've had the opportunity of seeing you in the showers, I was able to report to the rest of the faculty that you are not especially well endowed in the sausage department . . .'

'That's fine talk coming from a vegetarian . . .'

'. . . and so clearly it must have something to do with money and the exchange thereof. Now, what I want to know is, what's the weekly stipend for someone of the stature and appeal of Blondie? I mean, students are always hard up, so I should imagine they'd be grateful for any old crust, eh?'

'You should be well in, then.'

Dougie ignored the intended slight. 'I mean, how much can it be? Fiver a week? Tenner? Whatever, I'd say it was well worth it. Do you suppose she has any good-looking mates in an equally financially strapped position, looking for a saviour to bail them out? You'll of course excuse me using words like "strapped", in the circumstances.'

'You're a skunk, Dougie, you know that?'

'Well, if it's not your plonker and it's not money, then it must be blackmail. What have you got on her? And if its photographic in nature, how can I get my hands on it?'

'Will you calm down?'

'Only if you come clean.'

The beer arrived and Jonathan drank thirstily from

the glass, taking the momentary reprieve to get his story straight. He knew Dougie well, knew that anything he said would eventually filter through to the rest of the department, and consequently it paid to be on guard. Of course, he could always tell Dougie to go to hell, but he didn't like to upset the guy. Dougie was really the only member of staff that Jonathan had any time for, and even if he could be a bit prying at times, he knew the banter was all in good fun, if not in especially good taste.

'Okay. She's a lovely girl. I took her out a couple of times. We get on well.'

'I'll bet you do. So, is it true what they say about students and blow-jobs?'

'I don't know; I don't give students blow-jobs.'

'Touché.'

'I haven't even started yet,' said Jonathan. The beer had revived him, and he was getting into his stride now. 'You can talk anyway. What about that skinny brunette with the cheeky smile that I saw you chatting up in here last week?'

'Brunette?'

'Yes, you know; it means brown hair. As opposed to no hair.'

'Very funny,' said Dougie, reflexively running a cupped hand over his balding pate. 'Anyway, it's a sign of virility.'

'It's a sign of balding, actually. Now what about Twiggy?'

'Jenny, actually. Ah, well, I'm giving her some extra tuition; she just felt a little behind.'

'I bet she's not the only one.'

'She's a slow reader.'

'As opposed to a fast worker.'

'Not as fast as some.'

'I learnt everything from the master,' said Jonathan, doffing an invisible cap to his colleague.

'I'm beginning to think I could learn a thing or two myself.'

Jonathan sighed. 'Like how to be more discreet?'

Dougie laughed. 'Actually, you've been playing it pretty close to your chest. It's only because I'd had my eye on her that I found out.'

Jonathan took another gulp of beer. 'How *did* you find out?'

'I have my spies.'

'Come on Dougie, I'm serious. I really *had* made a point of keeping a low profile.'

'Yeah, well, you should know that nothing stays secret for long in this place. It just so happens that I overhead a conversation.'

'I don't believe you. Liz is as keen to keep this quiet as I am.'

'Oh no, it wasn't her. One of her flatmates.'

'Shit.'

'I don't think she meant to blab. It's just that Jenny heard one of them say "you know, the pretty blonde one" and "out to dinner with the sociology tutor" in the same breath. She mentioned it to me and I sort of put two and two together.'

'Won't be long before everyone else does the same thing then.'

'Like I said, you can't keep secrets in this place. Still, it's not serious, is it.'

Jonathan frowned, but said nothing.

Dougie eyed him closely. 'Is it? I mean, she's . . .'

'We get on really well, Dougie. It's . . . it's good.'

'But she's a student for Godsake . . .'

'She's twenty-five...'

'It's poison.'

'Not at all. She's not in any of my classes...'

'Oh come on Jonathan. This isn't the first time that a student has had a crush on a tutor...'

'I'm not her tutor!'

'You're splitting hairs.'

'Bollocks,' said Jonathan, rather more loudly than intended. He sensed he was overreacting, but wasn't sure he could do anything about it.

Dougie frowned. 'Look, if I've trod on someone's toes here...'

'All I was trying to say is that there may be more to this than ... well, that it may just be different, that's all.'

'Right. I see. Still, there's nothing to worry about in the long term, eh?'

'What's that supposed to mean?'

'Well, by your own admission, you're incapable of making a commitment. I mean, you've always said that.'

'Yeah, well maybe that's changed...'

'And maybe pigs will fly.'

Jonathan flared up. 'What are you saying? You don't know anything about this. Just because all your liaisons are casual little flings...'

Dougie blanched. 'Hey! Take it easy. I'm just trying to set you right.'

'You're trying to piss me off...'

'Not at all. If you tell me it's serious, I'll believe you. Jesus, I've never seen you so touchy before. Come on, Jonathan. Besides, you shouldn't be getting upset about my reactions; you should be worrying about what everyone else is going to have to say on the matter. You know how people look at these things.'

Jonathan took a deep breath. He knew Dougie was right, that student/staff liaisons were open to unusual scrutiny, that he was laying himself wide open to criticism. But that did not explain his agitation. Why had he got so upset when Dougie had suggested his relationship with Liz could not be serious? It wasn't serious, was it? After all, he had known her only a couple of weeks. The relationship, as far as it went, extended to a handful of dates and a couple of nights spent together in the same bed. That hardly constituted a serious relationship, did it.

Unless, of course, there was more to this than even Jonathan had admitted to himself. Could it be that, in such a short time, he had actually fallen in love with Liz? Until that moment he had not even begun to think in those terms, but then until that moment the question had not been raised. It was only Dougie's rather artless attempt to help him avoid future difficulties that alerted him to the true nature of his feelings.

It was not just the case that he and Liz 'got on well'; who was he trying to kid? The other night, when he had woken to find her cold and motionless, he had been overcome with distress. Although at the time he had put it down to mere panic (and quite forgivable in the circumstances) he realised now that what had really upset him was the thought that, if she were really dead, then that would be the end; no more Jonathan and Liz. And they had only just begun. And the more he stopped to think about it, the more he began to realise just how much Liz meant to him, just how exciting it was to be with her. It was only now starting to dawn on him that this was the first time he had ever truly cared about another person. There had been no one in his life before who had affected him this way. It could only mean one thing: he loved her. No wonder he was upset at Dougie's implication that this was just a casual fling, that she merely had a crush on him, that it was not a real relationship. Of *course* it was real. And important. And as this simple, rather obvious realisation became clear, a small still voice told him that he ought to let Liz know about it too. Right away.

He drained the contents of the glass and placed it with great deliberation on the counter.

'You'll excuse me, Dougie. I've got something important to do.'

'Wait . . . where are you going?'

Jonathan smiled. 'To raise Blondie's stipend. I've only just realised how much she's worth to me.' And before Dougie could challenge him, he was half way to the door.

'Liz!'

They all looked round. Liz was standing outside the library talking with three other students – all women – when Jonathan came striding down the corridor. Liz was so surprised to hear him call her name out loud that she found herself temporarily numbed, unsure how to respond. There he was, bearing down on them excitedly, like a man in need of imparting some very good news, and she did not know where to look. One of the three other students, Angie, lived in the same shared house as Liz, so she knew about Jonathan, but the other two were ignorant of their burgeoning relationship. Liz did not know what Jonathan was up to, but felt it was probably safer to pre-empt any difficulties by meeting him half-way.

'Excuse me,' she said quickly, then headed down the corridor towards him.

If she had been surprised by Jonathan's call, she was even more surprised by his greeting. Making no concessions to onlookers he took hold of her hand and pulled her into the nearest available room which, thankfully, was empty.

'What are you doing?'

Jonathan slammed the door shut with his foot, took Liz's face between his hands and kissed her full on the lips.

When he had finished, Liz pulled back slightly and looked nervously around her. 'What are you playing at?'

Jonathan smiled. 'I had to see you. I have to tell you something.'

'But in front of everyone? What happened to "we must be discreet"?'

'Sod discretion,' said Jonathan. 'This is more important than that.'

Liz eyed him closely. There was definitely something different about him; something strange, clear-eyed. Like one of those re-born Jesus freaks, she thought unkindly. 'What can be so important that you accost me in broad daylight in full view of my fellow students? Oh God... you're not pregnant, are you?'

Jonathan grinned, barely able to control his excitement. 'I'm in love.'

'Congratulations. Anyone I know?'

'You,' he said with great delight. 'I'm in love with you.'

Liz laughed. Not because his declaration was funny,

but because of the almost child-like joy with which he made it. Any annoyance she felt at being temporarily compromised disappeared. 'Well . . . that's lovely.'

'I thought you ought to be the first to know.'

'That's very decent of you. Although after the rather flamboyant way you chose to break the news, I suspect most of the rest of the college now know too.'

'Good. I want them to.'

Liz looked at him quizzically. For a moment she wondered if, rather than having seen the light, he was just drunk. 'Why the change of heart? I thought this all had to be kept away from prying eyes.'

Jonathan shook his head. 'It won't work. People will just snigger and talk behind our backs. Every day there'll be a new rumour. Before you know it we'll become public property, the details of our love-life speculated on the open market like a commodity. Some of them will deliberately want to stir things, to cause trouble. If we try to hide it, it looks like we've something to be ashamed of. Why should we put up with that? There are no laws stating that what we're doing is wrong, and I refuse to be a target for other people's malice.'

'And you don't think it will jeopardise your post?'

'Nope. Nor your studies. At the first hint of discrimination I'll . . .'

'Okay okay, calm down. I get the picture.'

'I mean it. I think we should bring it right out into the open.'

'Fine. But I draw the line at having sex in public, no matter how strongly you feel that we have nothing to hide.'

'Spoilsport.'

Liz put her cupped hand to Jonathan's cheek and

stroked it tenderly. He could be so appealing at times. Adorable. 'Want to know a secret?' she said softly.

'Sure.'

Liz hesitated. Should she? Oh, what the hell. 'I love you too. At least, I think I do.'

He took her hand and kissed it. 'Don't think too much; I'd hate it if you changed your mind.'

Liz shook her head. 'I shan't.' She leant close to him and kissed him. He hugged her close and returned her kisses with considerable, barely restrained passion. Liz felt her pulse quicken and her throat dry.

'Let's go somewhere and make love,' she whispered.

'Now? Impossible; I have a tutorial in five minutes.'

'But if you really love me . . .' Liz's expression of mock hurt made him smile.

'What about my tutorial group?'

'No, I'd rather have you.'

'Liz . . .'

'I thought you just said . . .'

'But I . . .'

Liz's right hand had slipped down between them and was now resting comfortably on Jonathan's groin. She gave a gentle squeeze. Jonathan sighed deeply, then brought his hand to her face and caressed her cheek gently. He looked into her eyes, more aware than ever that something very special was happening, something unique.

Liz smiled then took hold of his hand and, bringing his fingertips to her lips, kissed each one in turn.

Jonathan watched this action with strange delight. 'Want to know why I want to be with you so much?' he said, keenly aware of a desire to encapsulate the moment, *this* moment, like a fly in amber, so that it might be preserved for ever more.

'Tell me.'

Should he? How he wanted to tell her, to pour his heart out to her. Was this the right time, the right place? He shuffled about for a moment, nervously. 'Only if you promise not to laugh.'

'Why should I laugh?'

'What I want to say ... it'll probably sound funny.'

'Try me.'

'Promise not to laugh?'

'I promise.'

Jonathan nodded seriously. 'I love being with you because, above and beyond everything else, it's ... so ... *exciting*. Because being with you, just being in your company, instils in me the same quality of feeling that all the truly great things in life bring. Oh God, that sounds so pretentious.'

Liz found herself softening to Jonathan's clumsy attempt to put his feelings into words. She knew how difficult it could be to communicate the subtle nuances of emotion, especially for men, who, in her experience, would rather suffer in silence than actually share their feelings with another. So she encouraged him with a gentle squeeze of the hand and a small, understanding nod. Duly encouraged, he tried again.

'The great things in life are all distinguished by a certain quality – listening to Grieg, reading Shakespeare, walking in the mountains, eating fresh papaya – they all have that certain quality to them.'

Liz laughed; she couldn't help herself. 'Being with me is like eating fruit?'

Jonathan frowned. He knew he was making a poor

fist of it, but he wanted so much to let her know how he felt. 'I told you you'd think it was funny.'

'No, please; carry on. I'm sorry, I didn't mean to laugh.'

Jonathan pushed on; for a man usually so skilled with words, it was amazing how he was now incapable of putting together a coherent sentence. He took another deep breath and tried again. 'All I'm trying to say is that being with you is so wonderful because it lifts my spirits, arouses my desires, makes me hungry for all the good things in life. Because it thrills me, excites me, inspires me. Because it makes my heart beat faster. That's all.'

Liz smiled, but said nothing. Jonathan, who felt sure his little speech demanded some sort of response, waited anxiously. It was not every day that he poured out his deepest, innermost feelings to another human being. Surely she must realise that?

After waiting impatiently for the best part of a minute as Liz, still reeling from the confession, merely stared into his eyes, he had no choice but to prompt her.

'Well?' he said.

Liz stared at him, nonplussed. 'Well what?'

'Oh . . . I just . . . I just thought you might have something to say. In reply, as it were.'

Liz nodded slowly. She sighed deeply, leant forward, and kissed him gently on the cheek. 'I liked the bit about the fruit, best,' she said, then took Jonathan by the hand and led him from the room.

10

A month later, Jonathan invited Liz to move in with him. He thought it a logical and practical arrangement. They were seeing each other two or three nights a week anyway, and they always spent the weekend together. Liz declined, citing probable loss of independence; besides, she wasn't ready. 'Ready for what?' asked Jonathan. 'Commitment?' Liz made out that she wasn't sure.

'It's not that simple,' she said.

'It's nothing but simple,' countered Jonathan. 'We love each other, we love spending the night together . . .'

'I don't know . . .'

'There's plenty of space. You can even have your own study.'

'That's very generous . . .'

'Generosity has nothing to do with it. I want you to live with me. It'll be fun.'

Liz shifted uncomfortably. 'I'm not sure I like what it implies.'

Jonathan frowned and explained that moving in didn't imply anything. What was it, he wanted to know, that she was scared of?

Liz insisted that she wasn't so much scared as apprehensive. She was very touched by the offer, but . . .

It was Jonathan who came up with a suggestion to break the impasse. Liz would keep her room at the shared house, move in with Jonathan on a trial basis, and if after a month it hadn't worked, she still had somewhere to go back to.

The following day, Liz packed a suitcase full of clothes, a box full of books and, with a heart full of hope, moved in.

11

Jonathan's house, a small terraced affair on the borders of Camden and Kentish Town, had been bought with the aid of a legacy, bequeathed by a maternal aunt who had passed away the previous year. He had been living there for only a matter of weeks when he invited Liz to move in with him. Prior to buying the house he had lived in a succession of bedsits and flats, the last of which, a rather dingy affair in Islington with rusty water pipes and peeling wallpaper, had been his home for the best part of two years.

Whilst, on a rather superficial level, he enjoyed having a place of his own, the pleasures he took in it were largely intellectual. To Jonathan, who had never been particularly acquisitive by nature, owning a house meant, first and foremost, that he would no longer have to pay exorbitant rent to a man whom he disliked intensely for a flat that only just qualified as habitable. Why he had put up with living in such dire conditions for so long was something of a mystery. Jonathan was not particularly slovenly by nature, but for some reason he had never pushed himself to complain about the state of the place. Instead, he had just put up with it, as if the whole situation was a *fait accompli*.

The windfall changed all that. Dear old Aunt Harriet. Ironically, he had never been terribly fond of her whilst she was alive, and had believed the feelings mutual. His mother's eldest sister had always been a rather prim, bossy sort of woman with a seemingly puritanical streak a mile wide. She was a statuesque woman with an overbearing manner who managed to terrify most of the family with her stentorian declarations on issues moral and political, none of which accorded with Jonathan's altogether more liberal worldview. She was ever eager to disapprove or raise a censorious eyebrow over family matters, even though her counsel was never actively sought. She was always particularly vocal in the matter of Jonathan's education, rarely sanctioning his decisions. Not that Jonathan cared; he certainly did not allow her to influence his decisions one way or the other, and was not above telling her where to get off when, on occasion, she became unduly vociferous. As a result he was frequently scolded for his disrespect, although interestingly, never by Harriet herself. For much of his life, he saw her only as an interfering old bag, albeit one who probably had his best interests at heart.

In fact, Jonathan had simply failed to recognise that this manner of hers – for manner it was – was applied universally, to everyone and everything, and that in truth, she had been terribly fond of him and rather tickled by the way in which, rather than kow-towing to her like the rest of the family, he had usually spoken his mind, even if that meant disagreeing with her.

Naturally, Jonathan did not realise this until after her death when he inherited most of her accumulated wealth. She had never married, and had had no children of her own. In a brief letter written to him just prior to her death, she confessed that she had always looked upon him as the son she had never had.

The legacy, generous and wholly without conditions, came as something of a surprise to Jonathan. But not as great a surprise as the contents of that final letter. Not for the first time in his life, Jonathan had rather misread someone else's character. It would not be the last time, either.

The only curious aspect of the whole affair was the inclusion in the legacy of a small, gold-plated carriage clock that had once stood on the mantelpiece in Aunt Harriet's old house in Clapham. It was the sort of item that Jonathan found particularly irritating, with its fussy decoration and overly ornate mechanism on display. However, as it was the only personal item that she had left him, he thought he ought to hang on to it. Consequently, whilst his own personal gewgaws had yet to find a place in his new home, Aunt Harriet's ghastly carriage clock took pride of place on his own mantelpiece. Or rather, it was positioned precariously at one end in the hope, perhaps, that some clumsy visitor might knock it off and consign it to oblivion.

Aunt Harriet's money allowed Jonathan to pay in full for his characterful little house. Although this meant that he had no mortgage repayments and was therefore better off financially, he did not think of the house in terms of security, either emotional or fiscal. Bricks and mortar did not, in his opinion, bring peace of mind or stop one from worrying about everyday problems and difficulties. It certainly did not allay serious fears concerning illness, sickness, mortality, disease, social injustice, global pollution, genocide or war. It did not answer any of the Big Questions or stop one from fretting about them in the cold, small hours: is there a God? is there life after death? what is the measure of a successful life? A house, in the final analysis, was just a house; 'a machine for living in'. Jonathan was not a great fan of Le Corbusier, but he could identify with the rugged, down-to-earth, practical implications of the controversial architect's most famous quote. And being, by nature, a social realist, Jonathan had not, at that time, explored the emotional or imaginative possibilities that owning a house could offer him. In other words, although he had been living there for a couple of months, Jonathan's house was not yet a home.

Jonathan had yet to stamp his personality upon any part of the building, inside or out. He had not decorated at all; not so much as a coat of paint. Nor had he hung treasured pictures, posters, plaster ducks or other ornaments on any of the walls. He had not splashed out on new furniture, save for a new double mattress that he had snapped up in a sale just after moving in, and was surviving by utilising a selection of wooden crates, some old planks, a clapped out sofa, and a Formica-topped table that had been left in the house by the previous owners. In fact, although technically he was the proud possessor of his own home, he was living in it as if it were an old squat.

The only room to which he had given any attention was the study, and this was more out of necessity than sentimentality; he simply needed access to the hundreds of books that made up his personal library. Consequently, for this one room he employed the services of a carpenter to build floor-to-ceiling shelving and a sturdy, solid desk on which to work.

Consequently, apart from the study, in which he entertained his friend Harry on their 'science evenings', Jonathan's house was not a place that exuded homeliness. One would not walk into the living-room and think: How lovely, how comfortable, how warm. It was not, as the Germans would say in one of those perfect yet untranslatable expressions, *gemütlich*. It was just an old house that, if it was ever to be anything else, needed a great deal of attention.

On the first few occasions that Liz stayed the night at Jonathan's place, it did not occur to her to say anything to this effect. In truth, such were her preoccupations that she did not really notice the chaos; one darkened bedroom is much the same as another when you're lying on your back with your eyes closed. Besides, it had nothing to do with her. She was just happy that they had somewhere to go to; it would have been impossible to invite Jonathan back to her flat. Even though the other girls knew about the relationship, she thought it inappropriate to have Jonathan stay the night. Perhaps if the others had not been students at the same college, it would have been acceptable. Despite Jonathan's plea to bring everything into the open, she still did not think there was any point in deliberately making either of them vulnerable. What went on in public was one thing; the ins and outs of their private life was something else altogether, and need not be open to the sort of speculation that could start: 'Well, he stayed over last night and you should have heard the noise . . .'

Not that she thought any of the girls would succumb

to such gossip, but they all had friends who often stayed, and you never knew who might overhear something, or catch a surreptitious yet untimely glimpse of something that would better not have been seen at all. Liz was not paranoid, nor did she think herself prudish, but she had the common sense to realise that, honesty and openness aside, some matters were best kept between themselves.

Consequently, whilst Jonathan had visited her place a number of times, had seen the inside of the hall, had had a late-night mug of coffee in the kitchen, and had even spent five minutes waiting patiently in the girls' communal lounge whilst Liz fixed her make-up, he was in no way familiar with the inside of her bedroom. And as Liz saw it, if Jonathan was not to be allowed to stay at her place, then she had no right to criticise, or even comment upon, the state of his.

Even if it was a tip.

Not that Jonathan thought of his home in such terms. Unfortunately, he seemed to have a blind spot when it came to such matters, and it was only when he finally got around to inviting Liz to stay for the weekend, that he thought to do anything about it. In the end, he made only a token effort to adorn the place by draping sheets over the wooden crates and running a vacuum cleaner over the sofa. He was not used to having visitors, and consequently had not even provided the barest necessities for a house guest. It was only when he arrived home one Friday night that he realised there was no spare towel, insufficient crockery, and only one pillow.

Liz managed to entice Jonathan into purchasing an extra coffee mug, two dinner plates and an assortment of utensils that weekend. But as she was an irregular guest, she did not go out of her way to tell Jonathan what was needed to make his place suitable for human habitation. If he wanted to live like a caveman, that was clearly a matter for him. Despite the thoughts that she harboured, she was reluctant to suggest that, whilst Jonathan's home exuded a sort of makeshift informality and casualness, what it really needed was a good clean, a few tins of paint and something comfortable to sit on.

However, once she had moved in – and after a respectable period of transition – she knew she could safely approach Jonathan on the matter of interior decorating.

Despite their physical intimacy, they were still strangers in many ways, so Liz trod carefully when it came to suggesting a few changes. She began by seeking Jonathan's opinions on a number of fairly basic matters, like whether he was happy with the red-flocked wallpaper in the living-room, or, as it was curling away from the walls in a number of places and slowly turning green in others, whether it might not be time to replace it with something less oppressive. At first she found it difficult to elicit any sort of positive or definite response from Jonathan, who clearly did not care one way or the other. Liz, who was nothing if not determined, persevered. Wouldn't it be nicer if the living-room were a bit more airy, a bit lighter? And the bedroom? Wouldn't it be a more pleasurable experience to make love in a cosy bedroom as opposed to a room that looked like a cross between a Victorian hospital ward and a building site?

Eventually Jonathan twigged. One evening, following a particularly enjoyable bout of love-making, he explained to Liz that he had been meaning to do something about the house since he had bought it but what with one thing and another *et cetera*. Yes, he confessed. The living-room was dark, dank and airless and if Liz had any ideas as to how to alleviate the sense of gloom, then she was more than welcome to give it a go. The bedroom too; yes, of course, it should be comfortable, cosy and inviting. Not just a shagging parlour.

Seeing Liz's eyes light up with considerable enthusiasm, he further explained that he would be only too delighted if Liz would take a hand in transforming his happy hovel into something from Ideal Home. And, Jonathan being Jonathan, and never one to do things by halves, he gave Liz his blessing, *carte blanche* and the equivalent of a blank cheque so that she could realise her plans.

Liz possessed all the necessary talents for the job in hand: good taste, good visual sense, a first-class imagination and no delusions of grandeur. She also loved a challenge. She had never owned a house, and had often fantasised about how she would decorate her first home. She had always believed that she possessed a natural flair for interior decorating, but had never really had an opportunity to prove it in practice. So the chance to take Jonathan's place apart and start from scratch was one that she could not resist. Apart from anything else, it would provide a marvellous outlet for her otherwise stifled creativity.

Although Jonathan insisted that she spend whatever was necessary to do the job properly, Liz had no particular desire to squander huge wads of his money. She was not an extravagant person by nature, and nurtured a belief that tasteful, aesthetically pleasing interiors could be achieved simply, cheaply and effectively. She did not have any special caprices to indulge, no penchant for sunken marble bathtubs or Corinthian columns. And yet, where Jonathan saw his house as a machine, Liz thought of it in terms altogether less prosaic. Her concept of home was both extensive and detailed; it was something she had spent a great deal of time thinking about. For her, the perfect home was an environment for experiencing calm, relaxation and pleasure, a place which enhanced and supported good feelings, a playground for adults who could still be child-like. It had to provide comfort and security, and nurture a sense of well-being. A house should reflect the personalities of its inhabitants without being intimidating, so that visitors were not overwhelmed or excluded, but felt welcome. Liz was determined to bring as many of these ideas to bear as possible when decorating Jonathan's house; after all, she was going to be living there too.

They started small, clearing one room at a time. Walls were stripped, curtains torn down, decomposing carpets ripped up and disposed of. Each room was freshly painted in one or other of the then fashionable 'tinted' whites, curtains of bleached muslin were hung and gathered in great swathes, and a wonderful assortment of rugs and dhurries, purchased in a timely Habitat sale, were scattered on the newly sanded and sealed floorboards. The kitchen was dismantled, a new sink *sans* a hundred and fifty years of tea stains put in and a solid wooden table installed. Simple sky-blue tiles were placed on the walls around the work surfaces and the green, corrugated lino that had undoubtedly provided many, many years of good service replaced with something less bilious.

She also convinced Jonathan that money spent on high-quality kitchenware was not, as he protested, extravagant, but economically sound, as such implements would last years. Jonathan, who had no interest in cutlery, crockery or any of the other equipment that Liz was so insistent upon, finally conceded to her demands for Sabatier knives, hardwood chopping-boards and a set of cast-iron saucepans and frying-pans that would have provided sufficient ballast for an ocean-going liner.

Little by little that winter, with Jonathan providing most of the muscle, Liz transformed a cluttered, tatty, terraced house into an airy, spacious new home, which radiated calm, comfort and warmth. Where Jonathan invested his money, Liz invested her self, so that whilst Jonathan could not help but appreciate and enjoy his new home, in truth it reflected not his tastes and preferences, but hers. Which was probably just as well, because as Jonathan would have been the first to admit, when it came to matters of fashion, design and style, he didn't really have a clue.

They spent most of the winter vacation together, although Liz insisted on seeing her parents at Christmas. Jonathan was invited, but he sensed that, as it was still early days, perhaps it was a bit premature to be meeting the family. Not that he had any doubts about Liz or the relationship. In fact, he had never been happier, never felt more secure with another person. It was something of a revelation.

And it was not just sex – although both of them would have agreed that on a list of shared activities, physical contact of one kind or another was undeniably top of the chart. But they seemed well matched in this respect, and there was sufficient openness between them that if, at any time, Liz was not in the mood or preferred to do something else, she always made that clear and Jonathan never put pressure on her. And no doubt the reverse would have been true, too, had such an occasion ever arisen.

At college, everything worked out ideally. As Jonathan had predicted, with their status out in the open, no one bothered them. After the initial frisson of excitement and curiosity, things settled down. By and large, Jonathan and Liz avoided each other at college. Or rather, they made no deliberate efforts to seek each other out. If they did happen to meet, be it alone or in company, then they made no pretence of ignoring each other, neither did they make overt shows of affection. This seemed to go down well with Jonathan's colleagues. Once they had met Liz they were instantly charmed by her, and as most of his male acquaintances would quite happily have stepped into Jonathan's shoes, they were — if anything — rather impressed at the restraint he showed whilst in her company. As for Liz's friends and fellow students, they treated her no differently than before, other than to make occasional saucy or pointed remarks about her tiredness in the mornings.

Altogether, things could not have been better. Jonathan knew this to be true. It *was* true. Liz was wonderful, they were happy, everything was great. And when things were that good, you did not question them. You did not question the whys and wherefores. You just accepted the situation for what it was. Because if you started analysing it too deeply, then like the best dreams and visions, it would probably fall apart. The beautiful things in life were all too often the most fragile, and relationships in particular were unlikely to stand too close a scrutiny. So for Jonathan, the most sensible course was to just enjoy his great gifts and leave intrusive investigations well alone. This was something else he knew to be true. To do otherwise was to invite disaster. To question, provoke, investigate, probe, explore, examine or scrutinise could only lead to difficulty. And if he started to indulge such passions, there would be a good chance that — like the overly curious in a famous, and indubitably true story — he would probably end up with nothing but a dead goose on his hands.

12

That spring they went away together for the first time. Ever since their first few dates, Liz had been planning to get Jonathan to take her to Greece for a fortnight. The visions and pictures that he had painted for her with his colourful, vibrant story-telling had lodged firmly in the forefront of her imagination, and she was determined to experience some of the magic for herself. And who better than Jonathan to act as guide?

The opportunity arose just before Easter. Liz's second term was coming to an end. She had shown herself to be a bright, above-average student, able to grapple with complex concepts with considerable ease. Her essays had garnered top marks and one in particular, entitled 'The Use of Non-verbal Communications as Negotiating Instruments on First Dates' – a clever piece of pop psychology on sex and body language, backed up by some excellent background research – had received particular notice for its originality, integrity and liveliness. Consequently, she was somewhat ahead of the rest of her year, and would not have to tackle any major projects or revision during the Easter break. As for Jonathan, he was merely repeating a previous year's selection of lectures for the summer term, the preparation for which had been done ages ago. So, knowing that neither of them had any time-consuming commitments, Liz had checked out the 'last-minute bargains' at local travel agents and in the 'Getaway' pages of the *Evening Standard*, and had found a couple of exceptionally cheap return charter flights to Rhodes.

Although Liz was on a measly student grant, since moving in with Jonathan, her expenses had been considerably reduced and consequently she had more money to play with. When she gave up her room at the shared house, she made several attempts to persuade Jonathan that they should share the bills fifty-fifty. Jonathan, of course, would not hear of it. As he explained, there was no rent to pay, electricity and heating bills were virtually the same as if he were living alone, and besides, he had more money than she did.

Eventually Liz relented, but made a point of paying her share for food, drink and other basics around the house. That way she did not have to feel beholden to Jonathan, or feel guilty when he treated them both to a meal or a film.

Still, she wanted to find some way to even the balance a little, which was why, by dipping into her meagre savings, she was able to buy the air tickets.

Liz surprised Jonathan with the news just a few days before they were due to fly. She had already made certain that he had no prior commitments. Jonathan, needless to say, was thrilled. He had never been to the Dodecanese before, so it would be something of an adventure for him too, and after the rather damp winter, a couple of weeks of unadulterated sunshine – pretty much guaranteed in that part of the world – would be most welcome.

However, it was not all plain sailing, as Jonathan discovered the night before they left. What with one thing and another, they had not had much chance to prepare for the trip, and it was only at this, the eleventh hour, that either one of them had got around to sorting out what to take. For Jonathan this was par for the course. As an experienced traveller, he knew that the only things to worry about in advance were visas and inoculations. As Greece required neither, he had barely given a moment's thought to the business of packing, which came as second nature to him anyway. For Liz, however, it was a different matter: despite her attempts to treat the business lightly, she found it fraught with anxieties that she had not known existed and which were only now beginning to surface.

'I don't know where to start,' she said that evening as she searched through her wardrobe, trying to divine what would be suitable to take with her. She really had no idea.

'Take as little as possible,' said Jonathan, rummaging through an assortment of rucksacks, holdalls and shoulderbags and dismissing each one with an etiolated grunt. 'Ah, this is it,' he said at last, holding aloft a zipped canvas bag that Liz thought might just hold her make-up and toiletries at a pinch. Jonathan threw it across the room to where Liz was standing.

'Catch!'

Liz grabbed the bag as it sailed past her and held it up for inspection. 'You are joking, aren't you?'

'Travelling light – the secret to a successful trip.'

'Really? What about decent weather, good food and not losing your passport? Don't they count?'

'All superficial matters, my dear,' said Jonathan, returning attention to his pile of bags. 'Believe me, if your worldly possessions become a burden to you whilst you're walking down a deserted road, all it will bring is misery.'

'But Jonathan . . . this is tiny.'

'I promise you that with a bit of thought, some circumspect selections and a touch of imagination, you'll be able to get everything you need in there.'

Liz shook her head in disbelief. 'I think this is a bit excessive.'

'Well, it's up to you. Just remember, you're the one who's carrying it. And just think of the advantages; whilst everyone else is hanging around impatiently at Rhodes Airport waiting for their overweight suitcases to make a long overdue appearance – or any appearance, if Greek baggage-handling authorities have not lost their touch – we'll be out and away with our carry-on bags, heading for the nearest taverna for a couple of ouzos and a *meze*. Trust me.'

Liz appraised the bag once again. Sure enough, it looked the right sort of size for carry-on luggage. How was she expected to cram two week's worth of clothes and necessities into something not much bigger than a school satchel? Didn't Jonathan realise that it was different for girls?

'Err, Jonathan?'

'Uh-huh.' Jonathan had just fished out a similar-sized holdall from the bottom of the wardrobe and was checking the handles for strength.

'Have you ever travelled with a woman before?'

Jonathan held the bag in one hand and gave it a

heavy slap with the other. Several ounces of debris – mostly sand – fell to the floor. 'What? Yes, of course ... oh I know what you're going to say. "Women need more things than men."'

'Well they do.'

'Bollocks. Look, I'll make a list for you.'

'Don't be patronising. I'm just not used to this sort of trip. For me, packing a huge suitcase is all part of the ... the essence of going on holiday. Like the trigger. I'm used to the idea that you take your home away with you for two weeks, just in case.'

'In case what? In case you're marooned there for the rest of your days?'

'Don't laugh at me! This is all new.'

'Correct me if I'm wrong, but this is not the first time you have been abroad.'

'A school trip to France and a wet weekend in Amsterdam four years ago do not constitute world travel and you bloody well know it.'

Jonathan put the bag down and walked over to where Liz was standing, a picture of repressed anger and frustration. 'Okay okay, I'm sorry.' He put his arms around her and gave her a kiss. 'I wasn't being patronising. I really did mean I'd help out.'

'I'm not an idiot you know,' said Liz, not as easily appeased as Jonathan had hoped.

'I never suggested any such thing. But it's only for two weeks. What do you think you'll miss so much in two weeks that you'd suffer for want of having it?'

'Tampax,' said Liz huffily.

'You can borrow mine.'

'I'm serious.'

'Who's denying you Tampax?'

'I'll bet it's not on your smart-arse little list.'

'Well it is now. Number one. Now what else?'

'Well what about clothes? Or do you expect me to wander around starkers?'

Jonathan smiled lasciviously. 'Suits me.'

'Yeah, and about five million sweaty, testosterone-heavy Greek men. Do stop leering Jonathan, it's not pleasant.'

'Why are you so angry? What have I done?'

'I just don't think you understand.'

Jonathan had to agree there. What he had thought was merely petulance at not being allowed to take the kitchen sink, entire contents of her wardrobe and Uncle Tom Cobbley and all abroad for two weeks seemed to have developed into something considerably more virulent. Liz was undeniably upset, and although Jonathan could see this perfectly well, he was at a bit of a loss as to why this was the case. Clearly, something that evening had triggered off this reaction, and although he knew he was probably partially responsible, he suspected his sins were of omission rather than commission. He had failed to take into account something or other, but then, perhaps this something or other was buried in Liz's past, or to do with some peculiar twist in her psyche? After all, one did not normally get so excited or distressed about packing bags.

Jonathan would have been the first to admit that 'the individual' was not his forte, and that such matters were best left to the psychology wallahs. His field was undeniably all about what happened when lots of individuals got together. He saw sociology as a sort of macroscopic version of Liz's own subject, and had always thought that, when it came to explaining actions, motivations, patterns and the like, he had the easier option. You could not always forecast or prophesy how groups of people would behave, but Jonathan believed that by applying a degree of common sense and some well-founded principles, it was possible to explain patterns of behaviour without having to resort to the sort of mumbo-jumbo that passed for rigorous analysis in the world of the Freudians, Jungians, Reichians and the rest. Didn't the word 'psychobabble' sum it all up? Too woolly, too indistinct, too open to individual interpretation. And too much hidden. How could one hope to explain behaviour if such behaviour was dependent upon so many unknowns? Take Liz, for example. Maybe she had once been berated for neglecting to take an important item with her? Going on holiday with her parents and forgetting her bathing-costume, perhaps? Or maybe even physically beaten for leaving behind her Sunday best, her money, house key, medication? Or worse scenarios still. Perhaps it had nothing to do with packing bags. Perhaps it was all tied up with the notion of going abroad. Did it have unpleasant connotations? What, exactly, had happened that weekend when she went to Amsterdam with a boyfriend? Had he done something to her? She certainly didn't like talking about it. Perhaps he had . . .

Exactly, thought Jonathan, drawing in a deep breath as Liz continued to stare at him with steely gaze and little affection. It's all 'perhaps'. And what was worse, even if he were to ask Liz, he doubted that his queries would be answered. After all, wasn't that the whole point of psychoanalysis – drawing out events, emotions, experiences of which even the subject was not consciously aware?

And ironically (or perhaps poetically) the Greeks had an expression that summed this whole situation up. It translated literally to 'You never know what someone is carrying.' At one level – the more prosaic, practical definition – it meant that you should beware of getting into arguments with people, especially strangers, because they could be carrying a knife. Knives are easily concealed, but then so are the accumulation of a lifetime's injustices: the slaps, smacks, verbal, physical and emotional abuses that every human being gathers at some – or even every – phase of his or her life. And who knows what you might accidentally trigger with a word, a phrase, an expression? What dreadful experiences might be dragged up from previously hidden depths by an unconscious motion of the hand, an innocuous shake of the head, a certain smile? Life, thought Jonathan, was a tricky business, littered with concealed traps that lay around like land-mines, waiting for the innocent to stumble across and detonate.

'Look . . . why don't we leave all this for now and go have a drink somewhere?'

'But we're leaving tomorrow and I haven't even started!'

'There's no panic, Liz, I promise. We've all night if we need it. And besides, Greece is pretty civilised these days; there's not much you can't buy out there if you forget to take it along.'

Liz sighed, but made no attempt to clarify what it was that bothered her. For all Jonathan knew, she could be wondering the same thing about him. Why was he so particular and dogmatic about packing some stupid bag? What was his problem? Jonathan did not want to think about it any more. He picked up his wallet from the coffee table, and fished about in his coat pockets to find the house keys.

'Shall we?' he said, indicating the front door. Liz nodded slowly. She looked somehow forlorn, like a little girl who has just thought of something important, but now cannot remember what it was. She picked up a jacket and, with her mind clearly on other things, followed Jonathan out on to the street.

13

As Jonathan had predicted, when they arrived at Rhodes Airport on what could only be described as a gloriously sunny afternoon, the 'travelling light' philosophy that he had espoused paid immediate dividends. Whilst the teeming multitudes of package tourists gathered, with mounting frustration, in the rather close confines of the baggage hall, Jonathan and Liz breezed past with ease and, in Jonathan's case, a certain smugness. They headed out on to the main road and, having waited just ten minutes in the shade of a huge bougainvillaea, they boarded a local bus that took them to the centre of Rhodes town and deposited them, half an hour later, at the central bus station.

The flight from Gatwick had been something of a non-event. Jonathan's experience had taught him that charters were invariably cramped, frequently late and the planes often dirty. Not actually squalid, just grubby from the previous flight. In the interests of economy, planes were rarely on the ground for longer than was necessary to get one set of people off, re-fuel, and cram another load back on. If there was enough time in between for a quick wipe round with a damp cloth, one had to consider oneself lucky. As if all this was not enough to put one on edge, the service was usually perfunctory, any drinks consumed had to be paid for and, perhaps worst of all, if a meal was served it generally erred on the side of familiarity – the sort of familiarity that breeds contempt.

It puzzled Jonathan that the airlines, or perhaps the holiday companies that chartered them, did not take the opportunity of a captive clientele to serve something relevant to the approaching destination. Holidays started as soon as one left home; what a shame it was that one had to wait so many hours, until arrival, before experiencing the promised pleasures of the holiday destination. It did not have to be anything exotic; a *moussaka* perhaps, or even a slice of feta cheese in place of the triangle of processed plastic that accompanied the stale bread roll. Anything rather than a piece of dried chicken, some soggy peas and a couple of sad-looking carrots. And how about a little Greek *bouzouki* music to welcome you on to the plane, instead of that ghastly elevator music? Why not hand out a small booklet of hints, tips and useful phrases to wile away the three hours that would otherwise be spent staring at the seat-back in front? Or, on those charters that had succumbed to the technological advances of the late twentieth century and actually showed videos, why not a film about the destination? It did not have to be specific – a general one on Greece would do fine. Just something to spice it up, induce a sense of excitement or pleasure.

Jonathan realised that all these things cost money, and that in the cut-throat, cut-price world of the package charter, every penny counted, but he expected that what stopped the charter companies from implementing such improvements was not money but a lack of imagination. It would cost next to nothing to implement the menu changes, and even less to buy a few tapes of Greek music. As for the other ideas, a couple of pounds per head would take care of it easily, and Jonathan could not imagine that there was anyone on board who would not willingly pay that tiny fraction extra to enjoy their flight more and arrive at their destination in true holiday mood.

When he put these suggestions to Liz, however, hoping for confirmation and maybe even a few suggestions of her own, he was amazed to find her of contrary opinion.

'No, it wouldn't work,' said Liz bluntly. 'We're talking package tourists here, remember? And British package tourists at that. Most of them will be in Greece a week before they go near a *imoussaka* or Greek salad. For them it's English fry-ups and steak and chips at grotty three-star hotels with karaoke in the lounge bar and English beer on tap, and if you start introducing all those ethnic touches on to the plane you'll have a riot. I can see it now: "Stewardess! My little Jimmy can't eat this foreign muck. Can't you bring him a plate of chips and a pork pie?"'

'You're underestimating people.'

'I'm being realistic. The same would go for the music and the films. They'd be clamouring for Richard Clayderman and *Three Men and a Baby* before you've even left the ground.'

Jonathan saw no point in arguing the case. He did not think he was being particularly idealistic, yet there were times when being anything other than wholly pragmatic in this, the late part of the twentieth century, was both futile and horribly naive, especially when a little imagination was put up against the bulldozing common sense of the hardened cynic. Still, it did no harm to dream.

They arrived at the central bus station with the early evening sun streaming through the trees. Jonathan – who to Liz's surprise had spent much of the flight perusing a guide book – proceeded to lead the way to the old town, as if he had been there just a few days previously.

'How do you know we're going in the right direction?'

'I checked on the map.'

'But you haven't looked at the map – at least, not since the plane landed.'

'Ah ... well, good memory I suppose,' said Jonathan dismissively.

As Liz soon discovered, it was not as simple as that. Jonathan possessed a rare combination of talents – a good memory, a faultless sense of direction, and a nose for rooting out the truth between the lines of almost any guide book – that made him the ideal traveller. And, indeed, travelling companion. He seemed to possess a rare sixth sense that informed him on matters as varied as the right time of the day/month/year to visit a certain attraction and which of a long row of seemingly identical tavernas would serve the best *stifado*.

Although he was looking forward to this trip, Jonathan had not held out much hope for Rhodes. As a major tourist destination for dozens of years, and notably the most 'International' of Greece's resorts, he fully expected the place to sing out with the sort of degraded tourist tack that had desecrated formerly enchanted enclaves such as the Costa del Sol and San Tropez. Many was the time when he had arrived — he felt — two years too late at some noteworthy incarnation of paradise, only to discover that it had lost any pretensions to being an idyll and was now flashing its attributes and advertising its wares with all the subtlety of a hard-up hooker.

The old town of Rhodes was thus a pleasant surprise. Admittedly, there were the expected compromises towards mass tourism, especially along the main drag, Socratous Street. Jonathan was both amazed and slightly offended to see so many glass-fronted shops set into the medieval buildings, brimming with fur coats and heavy gold jewellery. Also, from the rather garish advertising boards placed in front of the tavernas, he quickly established that it would be easier to order a pizza than a *pastitzio*, and in the cafés, the patrons drinking Heineken readily outnumbered those drinking Greek coffee. This certainly had nothing in common with the sort of Greece he was used to. However, the whole of the Old Quarter was a traffic-free zone, which at least made it quiet and pollution-free. Away from the main drag, things changed dramatically.

They soon found suitable accommodation, a charming little whitewashed room, situated above a peaceful taverna which seemed to be the genuine article. The room could not have been simpler: a couple of beds with plain blue bedspreads, a small wardrobe, a mirror, a small table. The door led out on to a narrow balcony which overlooked the exotic Turkish Quarter. Liz was perfectly happy about the shared bathroom facilities, especially as this early in the season, the place seemed virtually empty. This was another surprise to Jonathan who had read that Rhodes had a 'year-round tourist base'. If so, they were thankfully thin on the ground just then, which perhaps added to the pleasing atmosphere.

Once they had settled they went for a stroll, wandering aimlessly through the Turkish Quarter, with its mosques and minarets, wonderful narrow stone alleyways which, in turn, gave on to wide, open squares, empty save for the occasional taverna, café, fountain or – in one instance – bath house. To meander in this part of the town was to walk into a recently refurbished – yet thoroughly authentic – past. The walls were not crumbling, and nothing was in ruins. Although Jonathan usually preferred his medieval cities to smell of sewage and look dilapidated, he was rather pleased for Liz's sake that Rhodes was able to give such an aesthetically pleasing first impression.

Rhodes town, despite its pandering to mass tourism, was still a delight to Liz, who had never seen anywhere like it. It may have been dressed up, but that did not detract from it in the least. Rhodes, or at least its Old Quarter, felt like a place that had evolved slowly. If anything, the fact that it was relatively pristine made it feel more authentic; five centuries ago, much of the city would have been new, not in ruins at all. Liz had fully appreciated that to get to Rhodes she would be travelling through space, but she had not anticipated travelling through time as well.

That first night they ate at the taverna downstairs. Jonathan, whose rudimentary knowledge of the language allowed him to chatter away impressively in fluent-sounding Greek, struck up conversation with

Mister Kyriaki, the taverna owner, much to Liz's amazement. They rattled away for several minutes before Kyriaki, clearly delighted that one of his English guests could converse with him in his own language, scuttled off into the kitchen, returning moments later with three glasses of ouzo.

'Yamas!' said Kyriaki, raising his glass and downing the contents before urging the others to do the same. He smiled broadly, addressed Liz in what seemed a very formal manner – the mellifluous Greek words meaningless to her but a pleasure on the ear nonetheless – and then left them to prepare their meal.

'What a charming man,' said Liz, sipping at her ouzo. She was not quite sure if two weeks would be anything like enough time to acquire a taste for the stuff; aniseed had never been a favourite of hers. 'What was he saying?'

'He said you looked like a horse.'

Liz spluttered into her ouzo, nearly choking.

'What!'

'Don't panic; it's a compliment.'

'Indeed. Off the back of which hand?'

'No, really; he admires your great beauty. It's colloquial.'

'It sounds insulting,' she said, clearly not insulted in the least.

'Not at all. I've heard it before, in the Ionian islands; I don't think it's a universal expression. I suspect Mister Kyriaki may have come from Corfu originally.'

'But a horse!'

'Symbol of great beauty and fine deportment. I should be flattered.'

Liz shook her head and laughed lightly. 'And

what about the rest of it? What were you going on about?'

'We were discussing the current political situation *vis-à-vis* Cyprus and the forthcoming elections.'

Liz frowned. 'Really?'

'Uh, no. I was just ordering, actually.'

'It seemed to go on forever.'

'It appears that Mister Kyriaki is very proud of his kitchen. He says he is one of the last taverna owners in Rhodes town still serving traditional Greek food. He was just explaining the specialities of the house. I think we may have struck lucky.'

If ouzo had caused Liz minor consternation, then the retsina that came with the meal floored her.

'This is, uh . . . this is different.'

'This is the real thing,' said Jonathan, savouring the resinated wine with great delight. 'Produced locally. No chemicals. You can drink as much of this as you like and not get a hangover.'

'Yes, but who would want to?'

'You don't like it?'

'It tastes off.'

'Nonsense. That's just the resin. It's a great complement to the food. Even the best Greek dishes tend to be a touch on the oily side; this acts as a great astringent. You'll get used to it. You see; after the third glass it tastes like nectar.'

Jonathan smiled broadly. In fact, as Liz had already commented once, he had not stopped smiling since they had arrived in the Old Quarter. He was so clearly at his ease here. Even though he had never been to Rhodes before, within a day he seemed able to navigate its labyrinthine streets like a local. Nothing appeared strange or confusing to him, and Liz liked the way he fitted in so comfortably. It made her feel less of a stranger in what was a completely strange land. With Jonathan to chaperone her through the more arcane aspects of the culture ('horse!') she felt sure she would experience the real Greece — if the real Greece was still there to be explored.

They ate heartily that evening, and drank with unrestrained pleasure. After the meal, Kyriaki joined them for coffee and Metaxa, the Greek brandy that Jonathan enjoyed so much. Even in its most refined form it had none of the finesse of Cognac or Armagnac, substituting volatility with body, so that, rather than seducing the senses ethereally, like a light anaesthetic, one could feel it hit the nervous system with a corporeal vigour which was more like a smack in the head than a kiss on the lips.

Jonathan's vocabulary — or rather, its limitations — soon failed him. By this time he had consumed three large glasses of brandy on top of the ouzo aperitifs and the bottles of retsina. Liz, none too sober herself, informed him affectionately that he was now slurring incomprehensibly and in a language that neither she nor Mister Kyriaki could understand. Jonathan, who was just sufficiently *compos mentis* to make a decision, decided in favour of bed. He bade Mister Kyriaki a rather loud goodnight in several languages, on the off-chance that one of them was Greek, then allowed Liz to shepherd him upstairs where, for once, he slept as soundly and completely as his partner.

14

They spent the next day sightseeing. Jonathan was happy to follow the suggested walking tour outlined in the book and investigate some of Rhodes' history. Unlike many travellers, he was not a snob about guide books. He had met purists – self-styled 'real travellers' – who believed that the only way to see a place was to explore it unhindered by other people's ideas and opinions, but Jonathan knew that a good guide could show you things that no amount of independent hunting and scrabbling around could reveal. Besides, when one had a limited amount of time, a guide book was invaluable. It would be foolish to miss the finest, the most unusual or the most amusing sights for the sake of adhering to a rather elitist philosophy. In Jonathan's experience, the only other people who left home without a guide book were the package tourists, and that probably said more about 'real travellers' than anything.

During the morning they explored the Knights' Quarter, starting at the Street of the Knights. This quiet, stately, cobbled lane lined with ancient Inns and Chapels was, for Jonathan, the most evocative part of the old city. There were no shops, cafés, tavernas or traders here, just beautifully restored medieval buildings, mostly from the fourteenth and fifteenth centuries. The Inns — originally halls of residence for the Knights — lined the street in a continuous stretch from the imposing Palace of the Grand Masters downhill to the Hospital of the Knights, now the archaeological museum. If walking in the Turkish Quarter was to recapture a sense of how ordinary people lived five hundred years ago, to wander along the Street of the Knights was to walk in the footsteps of the fearless military who conquered and ruled Rhodes for two centuries prior to being defeated by the Turkish Sultan, Suleiman the Magnificent. It was easy to catch the whiff of history in such a noble and refined street.

After lunch at an almost abandoned taverna near the Turkish Baths, Liz and Jonathan walked out to Mandraki Harbour, with its astounding collection of private yachts and excursion boats. It was here that Rhodes was at its most 'International'. The harbour was the focus for the world's jet set, and the place oozed money and riches. At the narrow entrance to the harbour stood the famous pillars supporting, respectively, a statue of a stag and a doe. According to popular belief, these two pillars — probably the most photographed items in all the Dodecanese — stood in place of the Colossus of Rhodes, one of the ancient wonders of the world. Hearing this, Liz tried to picture a giant bronze statue of Apollo standing astride the harbour entrance, but her imagination failed her.

Placed strategically on the outer mole of the harbour was a fine fifteenth-century castellated fortress, Saint Nicholas Fort, and alongside it a set of three renovated grain windmills. In direct contrast, the landward side of the harbour was dominated by a group of nineteen-thirties municipal buildings built by the Italians. Whilst constituting a rather strange mélange of styles, there was no denying the impressive appearance of the harbour.

Less imposing but, to both Liz and Jonathan, more enchanting, was the quaint, tree-shaded cemetery belonging to the elegant Turkish mosque of Murad Reis which stood in the same area. They wandered here for quite a while, trying to establish the profession of each of those buried, as indicated by the whimsically carved headstones.

In the late afternoon they sat at one of the lush cafés situated beneath the impressive arcade opposite the Mandraki Harbour, and indulged in endless cups of coffee and little silver plates of tooth-decaying *baklava*, dripping with honey and sugar. Once again Jonathan was in his element. He was past the stage where the only acceptable mode of travel was to 'slum it' with the rest of the penniless backpackers. There was nothing wrong with travelling on a shoestring – he had done it himself year after year as a student – but now that he could afford a few of travel's more costly delights, he was not afraid to treat himself. Besides, even luxuries came cheap in Greece.

That night, pleasured by their experiences of the day, relaxed by the effects of the sun, and heavily intoxicated on retsina, they made love with an easy, languid delight that bordered at times on the soporific. Jonathan in particular was much taken by what he divined as traces of Greekness in Liz's odour. Convinced that her perspiration had taken on the taint of oregano, resin and olive oil, he spent the best part of an hour sniffing her arms, legs, neck

... in fact, any part of her that had been exposed to the sunshine that day. Jonathan loved the smell of sun-baked flesh at the best of times, and nowhere was this more arousing, more satisfying than in Greece. He was a firm believer in the importance of pheromone attractors and had already persuaded Liz to go easy with perfumes and deodorants. At first Liz had found this vaguely perverse, and felt uncomfortable about doing without the battery of smelly unguents that, like every other female victim of late twentieth-century consumerism, she applied with religious regularity. But, after a while (and especially after having been told every day for six months that she smelt like a goddess) she finally relented. Although at first she had discarded her perfumes and incense to please Jonathan, in time she had rather grown to like what she saw as a more natural way of being. And as no one had made disparaging comments or wrinkled up their noses when in her company, she felt pretty comfortable about the idea. Of course, now that they were on holiday alone in Greece, she had no inhibitions about her own smell, and had allowed herself the luxury of spending the whole day denuded of all artificial scents. This clearly had a most powerful effect on Jonathan that night, who found himself unable to withdraw his nose from her armpits, initially, and from between her legs, latterly. Had Liz been a little less drunk or a little less relaxed she might well have objected to such close personal scrutiny, but that night she was not bothered in the least and in an odd way, which she was never to understand fully, was even somehow flattered.

'Your snatch,' said Jonathan no fewer than five times that night, 'smells of apple blossom.' Liz, whose own sense of smell was rather less refined, took Jonathan's word for it.

On the third day, without much discussion, they boarded a ferry for Tilos. Jonathan had read the relevant chapters in his guide book several times, checked the ferry timetables and cross-referenced them with the information gathered at the tourist office, and devised a rough plan that would allow them to see three neighbouring islands and still have a couple of nights in Rhodes before flying back to London. Liz was quite happy to go along with this, although she felt slightly miffed that she had not been consulted. She had to remind herself that, with his greater experience and evident love of organisation and research, these matters were probably best left to Jonathan. It was clear that he derived great pleasure from planning each stage of the trip. And, as she had expected, he was extremely capable in this regard. At no time in their two weeks did Liz have to worry about finding accommodation, buying a ticket or checking a bus timetable; Jonathan did everything.

The ferry journey took a leisurely four hours from Rhodes to Tilos. At that time of the year the boat was virtually empty, and Liz found it difficult to imagine the decks swarming with Scandinavian backpackers, which, according to a personable young Greek whom they met on board, was certainly the case during the height of the season. It was all so peaceful, chugging along through the azure waters at a steady, almost stately pace. As a way of getting around it certainly beat speeding up the M1 in the pouring rain or trundling along the commuter lines with a British Rail sandwich in one hand and a cup of lukewarm coffee in the other. Here you could stand out on deck in the fresh, scented air and feast your eyes upon vast stretches of calm blue sea, disturbed only by the occasional fishing caique or the sight of a bare outcrop of rock in the distance. For Liz there was something almost minimalist about all this serenity, as if here, in these wine-dark seas, nature reverted to a sort of Zen landscape, an active emptiness which, when gazed upon, induced a similar, stilled state of mind, like that achieved during meditation or trance. It was supremely satisfying, and as she stood in the brilliant sunshine and looked out on to the clear, empty waters, she had her first direct experience of the magic that Jonathan had conjured up in his stories.

However, such magic was short lived, for as they approached the jetty at Tilos, Liz's heart sank. When they had left Rhodes it had been quite a dramatic event in its own right. As the ferry steamed out to sea, one took in splendid views of the Old Quarter with its mammoth medieval walls rising resplendently above the Commercial Harbour. They had chugged on past Mandraki Harbour with its myriad cruise ships and cargo boats, rounded the top of the island with its multi-storey hotels and crisp white sand beaches and headed out to open sea. It was little wonder that Rhodes was the most popular tourist destination in Greece. It had all been very impressive, and Liz had been looking forward to seeing something equally picturesque, if less grand perhaps, as they approached Tilos. She had, at the very least, expected a tree-lined wharf with dozens of gaily painted fishing-boats, and a plethora of white-washed villas cascading down the mountains ... the sort of thing she had seen in all the brochures, the sort of vision that Jonathan magicked out of thin air with ease.

But the approach to Tilos offered no such visions. Instead, a rather scrappy concrete pier extended into the water from a virtually empty wharf. The only building visible was a rather ugly glass and steel prefabricated restaurant, which bore no resemblance to the sort of island tavernas that Liz had already started dreaming of. A few small houses littered the rise above the wharf, and the land in the immediate area looked very barren, bereft of olive trees or pine. A stone and pebble beach swept around a shallow bay to the left, and in the distance one could make out the bright blue dome and white cross of a church, but otherwise there was nothing to suggest that this place was worth visiting at all, let alone the 'unspoilt gem' that the guide book had promised. She looked to Jonathan for confirmation of her feelings, but found him absorbed in the docking procedures and eyeing the surrounding landscape eagerly.

'Is this the right place?' ventured Liz cautiously. She did not want to sound as if she was whinging, but at the same time, it often paid to come clean at times like this.

'Looks terrible, doesn't it,' said Jonathan, but without any apparent concern.

'Thank God for that . . . I thought . . .'

'Don't panic. It'll probably work in our favour.'

Liz looked at him quizzically. 'Run that by me again.'

'I am assured by the author of our bible here that Tilos is an undiscovered, largely untouched paragon, reminiscent of the sort of place one found all over Greece twenty years ago, before the great tourist invasion. I suspect one of the reasons is that potential island-hoppers are put off by the lack of charm and promise offered up by this harbour. With luck, most of them say something like "Is this the right place?"' – he paused for a moment to allow Liz the pleasure of poking out her tongue at him – then continued – 'and decide to stay on board until the next island. Let's not judge it until we've seen it.'

'Fair enough. But what if you – and your friend in the book there – are both deluded?'

'Then we're stuck here for three days.'

Liz smiled. 'Hardly rates as traumatic, then.'

Jonathan laughed. 'Actually, I think it's going to be fabulous.'

This was something she loved about him; his tireless enthusiasm and optimism. She sensed that even if Tilos was a hole, just being there with Jonathan would somehow turn the experience into something memorable.

She did not have to wait long to have her first impressions of Tilos dashed. Once off the ferry, she followed Jonathan as he made his way confidently around the harbour then into the back streets. As he had suggested, once away from the harbour, the place reverted to type, albeit on a miniature scale. There was just one main street, barely wide enough for a vehicle, which led past a charming old-fashioned local taverna to a village square on which sat one other taverna and a café. There was no traffic and, as they had arrived during the afternoon siesta, not a soul to be seen. Whilst this phenomenon in a northern European country would suggest immediately that a place was dead – or a ghost town, perhaps – in Greece and other Mediterranean countries it was completely natural, indicating instead that a town or village was merely in a state of temporary suspended animation, ready to burst into life just as soon as the ambient temperature had dropped by a few degrees.

Past the square the road became a track. Jonathan followed the instructions in the guide book and they were soon walking down beside the water's edge along a gravel path. The path led to a delightful whitewashed house, fronted by a patio which sat three or four feet above the pebble beach and overlooked the water. A flimsy plywood sign attached to the gate by a piece of frayed string and painted in a rather slapdash style, read 'Rooms/Zimmers'. Jonathan pushed the gate open and was just about to call out when a wonderfully rotund Greek woman, grey-haired and dressed all in black, waddled out from the house.

'Yassu!' she called out in greeting. She smiled broadly. Jonathan returned the greeting, making sure to use the polite form, and asked about the rooms. The woman nodded vigorously and beckoned them into the house. A simple, double-bedded room at the back of the house faced directly on to the back yard. A shared bathroom was for their exclusive use until such time as other rooms were let, and breakfast was 'no problem', although not, it would seem, included in the tariff. A price was swiftly negotiated and, although Liz had no idea what was being said, clearly the landlady was happy with the outcome.

They dumped their bags and the landlady, who now introduced herself as Roda, did her best to make them feel welcome. She was evidently delighted by their arrival so early in the season. She took hold of Liz's hand and dragged her back to the patio. She sat them at a small wooden table beneath a shady tree and then brought them glasses of lemonade. She spoke no English, but explained again in Greek that her name was Roda – they must call her Roda – and that they could stay as long as they liked. It was still quiet on the island, there were no problems. Jonathan thanked her, told her their names, and after she had practised them a couple of times, she patted him on the forearm and left them in peace.

'She's wonderful,' said Liz. 'And this place . . . it's beautiful.' From where they sat they had an unobscured view of the sea. Off to the left the bay curved in a shallow arc. The harbour, at the end of the bay, looked more pleasing from this angle, with the prefab restaurant out of sight, and the hills behind providing an interesting backdrop.

'So, what was all that about?'

'Huh?'

'The two of you jabbering away like long-lost friends. What was she saying to you?'

'Just polite conversation; where are we from, how long are we staying . . . how long have we been married.'

'Married!'

'Well, this is a deeply conservative country remember, and little islands like this . . .'

'What did you tell her?'

'I told her we were on our honeymoon.'

'Jonathan!'

'What?'

'Well apart from anything else, it's a terrible lie.'

Jonathan pulled a face. 'Hardly. And you saw how happy it made her. She was delighted; anyone would think her own daughter had just got married.'

'That's not the point.'

'Lighten up, Liz; it was just to make things easier.'

'It's deceitful.'

Jonathan frowned. 'Oh come off it.'

'No, Jonathan,' said Liz, clearly disturbed. 'I mean it. It's deceitful and dishonest.'

Jonathan, somewhat taken aback by the vehemence of Liz's reaction, searched swiftly for a response that would mollify her. He was not prepared for this at all.

'Well . . . technically, yes; it's dishonest. And I can see you feel uncomfortable about that, so why not think of it as play-acting?'

'Don't patronise me; you know I hate being patronised.'

Jonathan held up his hands in surrender. 'Sorry, sorry. I didn't realise you'd take it so seriously. But it's done now, and no real harm's been done, eh?'

Liz was not to be placated so easily. 'You could have consulted me; now I have no choice but to play along with your deceitful little story. And I hate living a lie.'

Jonathan thought 'living a lie' a bit strong in the circumstances. He knew Liz well enough to know that she was not above a bit of hysteria when she wanted to make a point, and if there was one thing he could not abide it was hysterical women.

'I think you're making a melodramatic mountain out of a barely visible molehill.'

If Liz had thought him patronising before, she now thought him just plain ignorant. 'I'm entitled to have my own response to this situation, Jonathan,' she said, barely containing her anger. How dare he tell her how to behave!

Jonathan was just about to leap in and tell her to stop overreacting when he suddenly thought better of it. Something about his harmless prank had upset her considerably, and while he could make light of what he had done, he had no right to make light of her emotional response to it, even if it did seem hugely exaggerated. He vaguely recalled some homily about discretion and valour; although he had never understood it fully, it seemed appropriate in the circumstances. Even though he was still seething with repressed anger, he decided that a brave retreat and capitulation on his part would be preferable to an all-out war.

'Sorry,' he said after a while, hoping that they could turn to other matters. Unfortunately, his apologies had come too late to appease Liz, who beneath her still calm exterior was steaming.

'It's not good enough. You can't go around making assumptions about how other people are going to respond to your unilateral decisions on matters that . . .'

Jonathan's fist landed on the table with a report like a gun going off. Liz jumped from her seat as if a jolt of high-voltage electricity had been passed through it; the shock made her gasp out loud.

'For Godsake,' hissed Jonathan, unconcerned at the effect he had had on her and angered that his white flag had been shot to pieces. 'Don't you think you're getting a bit carried away? How come you get to commandeer the moral high ground all of a sudden? I mean, since when have you been such a goody two-shoes?'

Liz, visibly shaken, gave a noisy, nervous gulp. 'Since I was born,' she replied bluntly. Still shaking, she got up from the table and went quietly to her room, leaving Jonathan nonplussed and any further discussion on the matter in limbo.

Just after dark they strolled down to one of the village's three tavernas. Roda recommended they try Taverna Irina, which was situated just a few minutes' walk along the shoreline.

This was the sort of place that Liz had been hoping for; a tiny, traditional taverna right beside the shore. The small brick building, containing the kitchen and a handful of bare tables lit by bright fluorescent tubes, was separated from the narrow shingle beach by a beautiful open-air patio; it seemed unlikely that anyone would dine indoors unless it was actually raining or blowing a gale. A dozen or so small, rickety wooden tables were set out along the patio, each covered in a bright red and white checked tablecloth. The vines which grew either side of the main door spread their verdant tentacles along the trellis which overhung the patio. Two larger than average olive trees, their branches decorated with lights, stood like gnarled sentinels at either end, enclosing the patio like a secret garden.

Although all the tables had been set, only three or four were occupied. Liz and Jonathan chose the table nearest to the water. They gazed out on to the placid waters and the darkening sky, drinking in the warm and deeply scented air as if it were an intoxicating draught. The unmistakable sounds of the *bouzouki* emanated from a crackly old record player just inside the doorway, and as the plaintive melodies floated out and up into the vines, they became juxtaposed with the ever-present sound of the cicadas, the rhythms cross-cutting and merging to produce a sound that was, for Jonathan, the essence of Greece.

They ordered a bottle of restina, some *tzatziki* and a plate of *melatzanasalata*, an aubergine dip which Liz had never tasted before. She was soon ordering another plate and another bottle of restina with which to wash it down. It was simply exquisite.

Liz had calmed down considerably since their little spat earlier that afternoon, and now, with a full moon low in the sky and reflecting off the sea, she had started to fall under the peculiar spell of the islands, the spell that Jonathan had conjured up every time he spoke of Greece. There was something especially enchanting about Tilos. It had none of the glamour or glory of Rhodes, no great medieval walls or churches, no glistening white sand beaches. Architecturally, the place could not have been simpler. And as for tourist provisions, other than the fact that the menus at the taverna were written in English as well as Greek, there seemed no concessions to foreigners at all. And yet, the place was captivating; even that simple taverna where they sat and watched the moon on the water and ate their Greek delicacies, was infused with a slow magic that seeped in through one's skin, beguiling the senses, seducing mind and body alike.

By the time the main courses arrived, the taverna had filled up, and all around them couples were chatting and laughing, eating and drinking and generally having a good time. Liz was floating. In part, it must be said, this was due to the second bottle of restina, the contents of which had disappeared swiftly along with the starters. And yet Liz was not drunk. If anything, she felt enlivened and invigorated.

They both ate heartily and with relish, Liz getting

stuck into a grilled fish of some description whilst Jonathan savoured the delights of the best *kleftiko* he had ever tasted. The still night air was filled with the fragrances of the food, laced with oregano and rosemary and hints of lemon, like a giant bouquet. They did not talk much whilst eating, too preoccupied with the task in hand, but when they had finished, when the last morsel of flesh had been consumed, when their appetites had been fully satiated, they found themselves unable to talk about anything else.

The superlatives tumbled out of their mouths for a further five minutes until suddenly they both realised what they were doing, and in the same instant, burst out laughing.

'Anyone would think we hadn't eaten for a week.'

'I know,' said Liz. 'It's crazy. What could account for that? Have we run out of things to say to each other?'

'I think it's just what happens in a place like this. It re-ignites your passions for things, especially flesh-related things. Bacchus and all that. I think we get a bit blasé, in England.'

'No,' said Liz. 'It's more than that. I've *never* enjoyed a meal so much in my life.'

'The weather helps. This warmth . . . it penetrates you, stirs you up, releases the passions. Like warming brandy to release the vapours and aromas. I'm sure of it.'

'Whatever it is,' said Liz, holding her brandy glass in the air to catch the waiter's attention, 'I love it.'

Back at the house, their passions fired by the evening's events, they could hardly wait to get into bed together. Although mildly intoxicated, they remembered that they shared the house with a nice elderly Greek lady and her family, and even though she had been (wrongly) informed that the couple was on honeymoon, when they made love, they did so as quietly as possible. Alas the attempt was doomed to failure, for not only did Liz's attempts to stifle Jonathan's moans also stifle his passions, it also reduced them both, in time, to a serious and sustained fit of the giggles.

Jonathan rose early the next morning. Wine of any kind — but particularly retsina — interfered with his sleep patterns, and instead of being the 'break-of-noon' night-owl that he felt sure was determined by his biochemistry, he reverted to a sort of primordial early bird. In England this usually caused him nothing but distress, but in Greece, especially in the islands, to rise with the dawn was nothing less than magical. As Liz was still sound asleep, he took the opportunity for a little solitude, dressed swiftly and headed outside.

From the back yard he could see over the shadowed hillsides which were bereft of motion and life. All was still. As the sun rose slowly from behind the hills, the sky above them, half-shaded by the spreading penumbra, became gently saturated with colour, like ink spilt on to blotting paper. The previous evening the air had been filled with warmth and scent, which hung heavily within it, as if laced through in deliberately intoxicating concentrations. The richness of the atmosphere had been further enhanced by the profusion of sounds: the music of *bouzouki*, the click-clack chirping of the cicadas and the multilingual buzz of conversation, rising up from the tables like steam from a cauldron. But in the morning all that was replaced by a strange purity.

The air was light and breezy, perfumed with only the merest hint of mimosa and pine, barely discernible. And despite the breeze, which was gentle and steady, there was a remarkable stillness, interrupted only by the occasional movement on the hillsides of a farmer or a lone sheep scrabbling away across the rocks and scrub. Even the lapping of the sea on the pebbles had become attenuated overnight, so that only the occasional trilling of birdsong disturbed the silence.

Jonathan walked down to the beach and wandered along slowly, gazing down now and then to find a brightly coloured stone or piece of broken glass, smoothed by the action of the waves. There was no pollution to speak of, no plastic bags or polystyrene cartons. As the sun crested the hills and began to illuminate the surroundings, he could almost see the landscape waking up. He breathed the cool, fresh air deep into his lungs and positioned himself in the rays of sunshine as they cascaded now over the hillside and down to the water. He closed his eyes and felt the strong, rejuvenating warmth on his face. He smiled. He could not recall ever being happier or more content. He was alive and well on a beautiful Greek island at the very edge of a new day. He was in love with a beautiful, funny, sexy, adorable woman who loved him in return. They were young, clever, playful, and life was easy, easy, easy. And the only grey spot in this otherwise brilliantly colourful canvas was a small nagging voice, somewhere at the edge of the picture, that kept wondering out loud: Why can't it always be this way?

Up in the hills, about an hour's walk from the harbour, was the deserted village of Mikro Chorio.

Jonathan's trusty guide book had suggested it was worth a look.

The island was only seventeen kilometres in length and less than half that in width. There were only two settlements: Livadia, the tiny town by the harbour where they were staying; and Megalo Chorio on the other side of the island. A minibus connected the two towns on an irregular basis, shuttling back and forth along the island's only sealed road to a timetable set very much by the driver's whims. Whilst the only road passed near to Mikro Chorio, the village looked close enough on the map to walk to it.

Although it was not yet ten o'clock when they set out, they were both surprised by how hot it was. They were walking up a long, twisting valley which seemed to channel the heat. The bare, rocky hills acted as highly efficient reflectors and focused the heat to the valley floor. Consequently, by the time they had reached the final approach to the village, they were both hot, tired and sweaty.

The village, or what was left of it, was virtually all in ruins. The buildings had once all perched on this rather lonely hillside, and had long ago fallen into disrepair. Narrow tracks, some of them negotiable but most of them blocked by rubble, connected up the various buildings. As with other deserted ruins, there was something rather eerie about Mikro Chorio. Especially strange was the existence of just one building which was in almost pristine condition, a small pink, red and white painted church, which looked as if it had been dropped into position from above. Whilst architecturally it fitted in perfectly well, aesthetically – even emotionally – it was completely out of place; a well-tended, perfect little church, surrounded by nothing but rubble.

Having trekked across the stones and bricks, they sat down on a low wall in the lee of the church, and sheltered from the sun for a while.

'It's quite creepy,' said Liz, reaching for the water bottle. She unscrewed the cap, raised the bottle to her lips and drank slowly.

'But what is it that makes it like that?' Jonathan held his hand out for the water.

'Well . . . it's a ghost town, isn't it.'

'I see no ghosts.'

'Well, you wouldn't; not in the daylight.'

Jonathan shook his head. 'But I don't even sense ghosts. I mean, the place is a little eerie, but it's not haunted. Just look at this place?' He pointed to the brightly painted church. 'There's still real life here; someone must be responsible for this.'

Liz nodded. 'I think that's what I find so disturbing. Why would anyone bother? Nobody lives here.'

'Ah yes, the powers of the Orthodox Church. It's easy to forget just how deeply religious the Greeks are. Most visitors see only the good beaches, cheap food and glorious weather; the culture passes them by.'

'Maybe, but I don't think *this* has anything to do with religion; this smacks more of superstition to me.'

'Same thing,' said Jonathan, dismissively. He had become distracted by the way Liz's sweat-soaked shirt clung adhesively to her breasts. She was not wearing a bra, and the silken material clung so smoothly to her that it was almost as if she were naked and someone had painted her skin. As Liz spoke he found himself drawn hypnotically to the perfect curves, to the slight, almost imperceptible undulations of flesh as she breathed in and out. He could feel his pulse starting to race, could sense his blood beginning to pump, and the first, pleasurable stirrings of an erection, like a dull but comforting ache, which drew his attention momentarily from Liz's breasts to his own groin. His mind raced ahead to lewd, delicious visions of Liz tearing off her blouse, her breasts, glistening invitingly with her scented perspiration and, released from the constrictions and support of the material, bouncing playfully in the sunlight. The vision moved along quickly. Now she was standing, slipping off her sandals, then her shorts, and Jonathan was upon her now, his own shorts and pants pulled down, his hands reaching inside her skimpy knickers, his cock fully erect . . .

Jonathan's vision ended abruptly as his focus returned to Liz's sweat-soaked shirt. He was suddenly overcome with the strongest desire to reach out and touch her, to let his fingers caress the taut, damp cloth, to mould his hand around those full, firm breasts. And as Jonathan did not believe in stifling his desires, that is exactly what he did.

'Jonathan!'

'Hmmm?'

'Cut that out.' She slapped his hand away.

'What's wrong?'

'There's a time and place for everything.'

'What . . . too early in the day?' He started to resume his fondling. Liz backed away.

'You're deviant.'

'Just showing a little affection.'

'This has nothing to do with affection and you know it. Will you stop that?'

'There's nobody for miles . . .'
'This is a church . . .'
'Liz, it's an abandoned village . . .'
'It's still a church.'
'What, you think God can see us here but not when we're in our room down there?'
'You're missing the point. This is somebody else's sacred spot; what you have in mind would probably be considered defilement by whoever it was who took the trouble to come all this way with a couple of large tins of paint and make this place look the way it does.'
'Well if he's a Greek shepherd you're making an unnecessary fuss because he'll probably have fucked a couple of goats and a handful of younger male relatives on the way up here.'
'Jonathan!'
'Okay okay . . . you win. Besides, for reasons I can't quite put my finger on, this mad lust seems to have forsaken me.'

What was wrong with her? Why the sudden coyness? Couldn't she appreciate the wonderful location, taste the slight danger that accompanied making love in the open and which added that delicious edge? Jonathan shook his head and sighed. 'You know, you can be more effective than a cold shower sometimes.'

'That's not fair.'
'Not fair but quite true.'

Liz stood up, threw a withering look at Jonathan and then stormed off.

'Hey,' said Jonathan rising swiftly, 'where are you going?'

Liz stopped and turned, 'I've had enough,' she said peremptorily, 'and if you don't understand why then you're a lot less clued in than I thought.' She continued walking, and did not look back.

Jonathan chased after her and, after several attempts at berating, ridiculing and embarrassing her – none of which worked – he eventually apologised. Then he apologised again.

He gave up after the third attempt.

15

'Why don't we just stay here?'
'Huh?'
'It's so lovely here. Why don't we just forget about the other islands and spend our time here?'

Jonathan speared an olive on to the end of his fork and popped it into his mouth.

It was early evening and they were sitting outside the local village taverna near the square. Although technically they were sitting on the main road, as there was no traffic it was as quiet a spot as any. Their table, like the half-dozen others, stood beneath a couple of large, leafy trees and caught the last remnants of the sea breeze as it scurried off the water, just visible from where they sat.

They had spent the rest of the morning and early afternoon just wandering around the village, Jonathan taking photographs, Liz scribbling impressions into a spiral-bound notebook that she had brought just for the occasion. Neither of them referred again to the incident up in the hills; no post-mortem was held, no further explanations sought. Jonathan was to remain as mystified by Liz's behaviour as she was by his inability to understand her feelings. That this gap had opened up between them did not seem to preoccupy either of them, and by lunchtime the whole incident had been forgotten.

During siesta they had made love, quietly, and then fallen into a wonderful, dreamy sleep, waking at five in good time for a gentle revitalising walk along the water's edge followed by a few pre-dinner ouzos.

It was never anything less than perfectly serene on Tilos, and this inherent peacefulness had already worked its way into Liz's system. It felt so refreshing, so rejuvenating, that she now wanted to stay and let the island's feel-good vibes seep into her slowly for a few days at least, rather than move on to strange and possibly more stressful places. She could not imagine anywhere else being as relaxing or as pleasing to her; it was nigh impossible to shake off the notion that the island was somehow good for her soul. True, she had been angered by Jonathan's boorish behaviour, but it hadn't lasted long, and besides, it was good to let off a little steam now and then.

They had been in Tilos for only a little over twenty-four hours and already she felt like a different person. The island's simplicity had suffused into her and somehow corrected an imbalance that she could now see had been in danger of tripping her up, of tipping her into some sort of obsessive cul-de-sac. That was the problem with college and study; it was so insular. One committed oneself to academia and suddenly that's all there was: books, words, knowledge, learning, concepts, ideas, all to be assimilated and understood, only to be regurgitated at a later date. And for what? Her health? The edification of others? As Liz sipped her ouzo beneath the verdant branches of the overhanging trees and listened to the *bouzouki* music spilling out of the taverna window, the effort required to find good, convincing reasons for staying at college seemed greater than ever. It all seemed so vague, so futile.

Studying, researching, reading; they could *all* become obsessions, to the point where nothing else seemed important. Particularly when exams were involved. Even the knowledge that her efforts were constantly being assessed, graded, approved made her feel tense and uncomfortable. That did not seem a good way to live, under such pressures, especially when she was having difficulty justifying it all.

Only now, for perhaps the first time, could she see her studies in perspective. They were not the be all and end all of existence. They were not even anything important in their own right. At first it had been a way to pull herself out of the mundane and tedious routines that had come to circumscribe her life. But now that that had been accomplished, college would become just a means to an end, a way to get a piece of paper, a certificate, a seal of approval that would allow her, inevitably, to assist other people to do exactly the same thing. Not only was it all beginning to look rather unimportant, when placed beside the simple, real pleasures she had experienced since arriving in Greece, it was beginning to look downright pointless.

If they could just stay a while, then maybe Tilos and its natural yet potent delights could redress the balance. There was space here, and emptiness; the sort of uncluttered landscape that allowed one to stretch out, both metaphorically and literally. And the way time unfolded was so different; there was no sense of urgency or panic. Liz could not know what life was really like for the people who lived and worked on Tilos, but she sensed that, compared with her own life in London, it was virtually stress free. Here people had time to enjoy and appreciate the most basic, the most fundamental of life's pleasures: a sunset, a stroll beside the water, a glass of wine (yes, she was developing a taste for the local retsina); it was all so easy. She felt as if a clamp that had previously been tightened around her head had now been released. It was just wonderful.

'But what about Nisiros? And Symi? We have to see Symi if we've come this far,' said Jonathan. 'It's supposed to be one of the jewels of the Dodecanese.'

'"Jewels of the Dodecanese?" You're starting to sound like a holiday brochure.'

Jonathan frowned. 'I thought the idea was to travel around a bit; see a few places, get an overall feel of the region. That is what you wanted, isn't it?'

Liz shrugged. 'I just can't imagine anywhere being lovelier than here.'

Jonathan nodded, albeit reluctantly. He was not sure what was going on in Liz's head, but he sensed that she was not merely being perverse. Clearly something was going on, and he decided it would be better to tread lightly than come the heavy and start insisting they stick to their original plans. Still, he was not about to give up the chance to see Symi or Nisiros because of one of Liz's whims.

'Well yes, I agree, it's lovely here. Really, just like the old Greece. But it has none of the . . . the spectacle of some of the other islands I've seen. I really think we should explore the others.'

But I don't, thought Liz; And, what's more, I paid for the tickets. So why don't we do what I want to do?

She sipped her drink. It was not that she was ungrateful – she knew that Jonathan had already made their trip a hundred times easier and a hundred times better than if she had come alone. It was just that she could already see – even though they had barely discussed the matter – that Jonathan was going to have his way, that regardless of what she said, Jonathan would find a way to counter her opinions, find reasons why it was better, cheaper, smarter, healthier or whatever that they should move on. And he would not do it maliciously. Nor would he make fun of her or humiliate her in any way. All the same, at the end of the day, they would be moving on to the next island simply by virtue of Jonathan's will. They had known each other only a matter of months and yet of this she was certain. And the worst bit about it was, he was probably right. It probably was better or cheaper or whatever to see the other islands. Variety is the spice and all that. It was just that Liz felt so comfortable, so relaxed in Tilos. It was not that she did not want to see other places, just that she did not want to leave Tilos. The problem, as she saw it, was philosophical and age-old: how could one be in two places at the same time? Liz was smart, but unfortunately she had not quite got around to finding a solution for that particular dilemma.

That night they ate once again at Taverna Irina. They were a little earlier than the previous night, in time to watch a procession of ducks – about six in all – swim past them along the shore. A couple at the next table pointed to the ducks and started laughing; clearly this was a nightly ritual. Again, in that moment, Liz was enchanted by the simplicity of it all, of a place where the highlight of the evening was to see a family of green and yellow ducks glide past on their way to the harbour.

They ordered some retsina and Jonathan went off to poke his nose in the kitchen to see what was cooking. He came back smiling and laughing. Liz smiled too. She had no idea why Jonathan was laughing; it was as if everything about Greece amused or entertained him. She had never seen anyone so in love with a country before.

'Oh God, you should see what they've got in the kitchen . . .' began Jonathan, and Liz listened attentively to a new story about a not-quite-dead squid and a slightly tipsy cook, a story so recent it was still wet on the page, rough around the edges, yet to find its finished form. Even as he was telling it she could see him refining it, changing certain words, repeating lines for emphasis, practising the measures and beat, building to the punch-line, the pay-off. It was remarkable. She drained her glass and held it out for a refill. Why couldn't life always be this easy? she wondered, aware of how naive she would have sounded had the words burst upon the air as readily as they came to mind. If only the answers came as easily as the questions: what a different world it would be then.

The following morning they breakfasted in the square and waited for the orange minibus to make an appearance. Not surprisingly, they had time not just for breakfast but for two more cups of coffee as well. No great hardship; even though it was early in the day and Liz was still feeling a little fuzzy-headed, she could not help but make the contrast between the activity — waiting for a bus — as it would have been played out at home, and the impossibly casual and delightful air that it took on that morning in the village square.

There was not a great deal of activity in the square at nine in the morning; a young boy helped his father put out the tables and chairs at the other taverna, an elderly woman shepherded her dozen goats across the far corner of the square on her way up into the hills, and two grey-haired, bearded grandfathers with faces the colour and texture of walnut shells sat down at the next table, ordered a couple of ouzos and started playing backgammon.

The minibus arrived eventually, and Jonathan and Liz climbed in for the twenty-minute journey to the other end of the island. It was a pleasant journey along a good, sealed road that wound its way up from the square before snaking a course through the hills on its way to the only other settlement on Tilos, the town of Megalo Chorio.

They disembarked outside a small roadside taverna that looked as if it had not been open since the time of the Colonels. Jonathan checked to see if and when the driver would be coming back, and having established that yes, he'd be back sometime, they started to walk up the hill that led into the town.

Unlike its deserted counterpart, Megalo Chorio was very much alive. Not that there was any great activity to be seen, but then as they had both realised, Tilos was not an island where active pursuits figured very highly. Still, the town was awake, just, and a few locals were meandering through the town's many narrow alleys.

Megalo Chorio was built in a series of steps up the side of a hill. Virtually every house had recently had a fresh coat of whitewash so that the entire town gleamed brilliantly in the morning sun. Splashes of faded blues and greens decorated gates, doors and steps to contrast dramatically with the great explosions of bougainvillaea that burst from every nook and cranny. The hillside was quite steep, the paths narrow, the houses built up in a profusion of styles, all of which were somehow characteristically Greek. Jonathan could barely take his eye from the viewfinder of the camera; around every turn there was yet another fusion of shape and colour that cried out to be captured on film.

In the heart of the town, reached by a series of paths and steps, was a stunningly beautiful church. Like a giant iced cake, it sat on its own plinth, the surface of which was covered in a giant herringbone pattern of black and white stones, like a whimsical chessboard. The church tower stretched up high above the dome, a bell suspended in its highest reaches. It was a magnificent sight, gleaming brilliant white against the intense blue sky. Jonathan went through half a film on the church alone, snatching shots from unusual angles, clambering on to walls to grab the perfect composition. Liz sat and watched his rather frenetic activity with considerable pleasure, noting again that, whatever activity Jonathan was engaged in, he always gave his full attention to it. She realised there was something vaguely obsessive about such behaviour, but she could not help but believe it held the key to Jonathan's contentedness. To do things to the best of one's ability, to throw one's attention at it fully, to engage with it completely: there was something of the nature of Buddhist philosophy in such behaviour.

When he had finished they wandered back down the hill and eventually found themselves on the main road which, just outside the village, forked into two narrow lanes. They followed the right-hand lane which was signposted 'Plaka', and sure enough after about twenty minutes the track fizzled out in a grove of pine trees, beyond which lay a long, sweeping and totally deserted beach. Off to one side, nestling amongst the pines was a small taverna, but save for a middle-aged couple whom they assumed to be the owners, the place too was deserted.

'My God,' said Jonathan. 'I think we've found it.'
'Found what?'
'The ends of the earth.'
Liz smiled indulgently. 'It's beautiful. Do you suppose they're serving food?'
Jonathan shrugged. 'Only one way to find out.'
The couple were clearly very pleased to see Jonathan and Liz and were able to offer them lunch in the form of Greek salad or stuffed tomatoes. With such an extensive menu to choose from, Jonathan plumped for both, whilst Liz was happy with the selection of fresh raw vegetables and pungent goat cheese that had become part of a daily ritual for her.
It transpired that the taverna was a new venture for the couple who were hoping that, with the steady increase in tourism, they would soon be a busy and thriving operation. Jonathan did not want to dampen their enthusiasm, but he did not think there would ever be enough tourists passing through such a remote part of Tilos for the couple to make anything other than a rather meagre living. The couple laughed: they said the same thing about Rhodes once, said the husband, and look now.
After lunch Liz and Jonathan took a stroll along the open, stony beach. They strolled for about half an

hour, stopping now and then to collect unusual stones or shells. They saw no one else. It made the other side of the island seem like a bustling metropolis.

At one end of the bay were a series of large, bronze-coloured rocks sticking out of the water. They clambered up on to the rocks and found a suitable place to sit and rest, overlooking the waves as they lapped gently at the shore. The water was a brilliant aquamarine, highlighted by wisps of white water thrown up by the undulating waves. The sky was an unblemished canvas of graduated blues, spreading from behind them, over their heads and out to the distant horizon where it merged imperceptibly with the sea.

'This is paradise,' said Liz, breathing in the fresh, slightly salty air deeply, so that it seemed to fill her whole body. 'I could live here for ever.'

'You'd get bored,' said Jonathan, injecting what he thought was a necessary note of realism into what threatened to become a rather slushy appraisal of what was a perfectly nice but hardly exceptional scene.

'I would *not* get bored. What you mean is, you'd get bored. How can you do that?'

'Do what?'

'Speak for me. You have no idea how I feel about this place.'

'Oh come on Liz ... what would you do all day? Believe me, a week and a half of staring at the rocks, collecting pebbles and gazing at sunsets and you'd be raring to get back to civilisation — by which I mean the thriving little hamlet on the other side of the island where we are currently ensconced.'

'That's just not true. I really think I could be happy

here. I've never experienced such space before. You don't know what that's like for me.'

'Well, I . . .'

'No!' said Liz sharply. 'You don't know. You can't see inside my head, so how can you presume to know? I wish to God you'd stop doing that Jonathan.'

'Doing what?'

'Imposing your worldview on me, your emotions, your feelings. Just because you feel a certain way about something it does not automatically follow that I do. We may be in agreement on a lot of things but it doesn't mean I don't have my own opinions and feelings. So stop being such a bully.'

'Bully?'

'And don't start getting aggressive about it.'

'Aggressive?'

'Yes. It frightens me.'

'What are you talking about? There isn't an aggressive bone in my whole . . . oh God, I'm reverting to clichés. I am *not* aggressive.'

'You have a violent side to your nature that, like most civilised men, you keep in check most of the time, but let's not pretend that you're docile.'

'Fuck off Liz. What is this, character assassination time?'

'I'm just pointing out that you have a particularly nasty habit of bullying me into agreeing with your point of view . . .'

'There you go again! Accusing me of being a bully!'

'Well you are. You make unilateral decisions without consulting me, you tell me I'm being stupid or ridiculous when I express an opinion that differs from yours, and if I don't concede instantaneously to your desire for sex, regardless of the context, you get irritated.'

'This is nonsense. All I said was . . .'

'There! You're doing it again. I *know* what you said. But do you know what *I* said?'

'Huh?'

'Exactly. You take no notice of what I have to say on these matters – matters, incidentally, that are concerned specifically with me.'

'What bollocks. Where did all this spring from?'

'It didn't spring from anywhere,' said Liz testily. It was clear that she was more than a little annoyed. 'It's been building up for some time now, and I'm not going to carry on letting you get away with it.'

'For Godsake Liz, you're overreacting . . .'

'I am not overreacting! You don't understand, do you? Let me spell it out for you. I have my own feelings, opinions and thoughts and they do not always correspond with yours. I would have thought our little contretemps up in Mikro Chorio would have made that crystal-clear to you?'

'I was horny . . .'

'That's no excuse! Jesus, rapists have been known to say the same thing.'

'What, so I'm a rapist as well as a bully now, is that it?'

'You're not listening. I didn't say that.'

'What's got into you? Why are you so upset?'

'Oh Christ!' said Liz. She stood up and was about to start clambering back over the rocks to the beach when Jonathan grabbed hold of her wrist.

'What are you doing?'

'Let go of me.'

'Don't just storm off . . . that doesn't solve anything.'

'Will you let go.'

Perversely, Jonathan increased his grip on her.

'Ow!' cried Liz. 'What are you doing . . . get off! You're hurting me.' She tried prising his fingers off but he was far stronger than her. 'You'd better let go . . .'

'Or what?'

'Jonathan!' It was then that she looked straight into his eyes and saw something she had never seen before: a look of real anger, so clearly directed at her that, for the first time in his company, she felt really frightened.

She did not respond at first, choosing to stare him out; she was damned if she was going to let him get away with this. She set her jaw firmly and peered straight back into his eyes, returning his anger with interest, saying nothing until, eventually, Jonathan released her from his grasp. She snatched her arm away and rubbed her wrist.

'If you ever do that again . . .'

'Liz, all I . . .'

'No! Listen to me. If you ever . . . *ever* frighten me like that again, then that's it. Finished.'

'But . . .'

'No. No excuses. Hurt me, just once, and you'll never see me again. That better be clear.' She threw a look at him of such scorn and disdain that, for a moment, Jonathan was completely dumbfounded.

'Liz, wait a moment! Look, all I was trying to say was . . .'

But Liz was not listening and as she headed back towards the grove of pine trees that marked the end of the track that had brought them down from the village, Jonathan found himself decidedly disturbed by her increasingly confusing behaviour. When had he bullied her? And how could she say he was aggressive? Because he banged his hand on the table? So he had a temper. Didn't everyone?

Jonathan shook his head in bewilderment. As he started after her it dawned on him that there were things about women that, for all his efforts, he would probably never understand.

16

Whilst the attractions of Tilos revolved, for the most part, around its lack of drama and activity, before they left there was one event that, at least in Jonathan's mind, constituted excitement of a kind.

It was late afternoon. Liz was in the room, dozing happily, whilst Jonathan was sitting alone on the patio, reading a rather lightweight novel and intermittently looking up from the pages to stare across the water. It was, as ever, supremely peaceful. However, on this occasion the peace was shattered rather suddenly when a short, swarthy man dressed in a rather grubby T-shirt and cut-down jeans, burst in through the gate and sat down brusquely opposite Jonathan. Ignoring the fact that Jonathan was engaged in reading a book, the young man addressed him loudly.

'Can you do favour for me?' he barked, his guttural Greek accent stressing and straining the English syllables – like a wrestler forcing a half-nelson on an opponent – until they capitulated.

'What favour?' asked Jonathan, automatically suspicious of his new, unshaven and scruffy acquaintance who, much to Jonathan's irritation, was already beating out nervous rhythms on the table top with the edges of his short, blunt fingers. It was not that Jonathan was feeling particularly unsociable, it was simply that personal experience had taught him that in Greece it was not wise to agree to anything until all the cards were on the table.

The man was clearly incapable of keeping still. As well as beating out the polyrhythms with his fingers, he tapped his feet on the stone patio repeatedly, whilst his head, with its mane of black, shaggy hair, darted continuously to left and right, as if he expected someone to spring out from behind a tree and assault him. His face wore a perpetual frown: a troubled man.

He pointed to Jonathan's camera. 'I need photographs to send to Finland,' he said, as if this were all the explanation necessary. Jonathan, who was not about to agree to anything without clarification, looked at the man blankly. The man managed to frown more deeply, clearly impatient at having to elaborate further.

'My wife – the whore! – live in Finland. I want photos of me, my taverna, to send to the children. You want coffee?'

Jonathan was always impressed by the way the Greek mind could leap from one subject to the next without a pause; no full stops, no semicolons, not even a comma. He had long ago learnt that there was no such thing as a *non sequitur* when talking to Greeks.

'Roda!' yelled the man. 'Thio café, metriou!' There was no sign of Roda but this did not seem to matter. The man pointed again at the camera. 'You can help? I am Spiro.' He held out his hand. Jonathan gripped it forcefully; on his first visit to Greece, many years earlier, he had been misinformed that there was nothing the Greeks disliked more than men with puny handshakes, and consequently he had committed himself to forcing an almost brutal grip on any Greek strangers who chose to greet him in the traditional English way.

'Jonathan,' said Jonathan, not wishing to commit himself any further until more facts had emerged. Finland? Whore? He suspected there was a bigger story behind this simple request, and although he had rather been enjoying his solitude, now that it had been disturbed, he was intent on getting the most out of it.

'I can buy film – no problem,' explained Spiro, picking up Jonathan's camera and eyeing it acquisitively. 'And tomorrow I go to Rodos, so I can develop it there.' Jonathan took back the camera and placed it back on the table. There was no faulting Spiro's English; his vocabulary was extensive, and even if he sometimes tripped up over grammar, it was easy to understand him.

'My wife,' continued Spiro without prompting, 'is a whore, a *putana*!' There was no doubting his anguish. Jonathan waited for Spiro to continue, but it was as if Spiro were waiting for confirmation from Jonathan before carrying on, as if Jonathan had first-hand knowledge of Spiro's wife and her sexual activities. Although Spiro was seemingly looking for support in this matter, Jonathan was unsure how wise it would be to agree with him. What was the correct response when a Greek man tells you his wife is a whore?

'I want to bring the children to Tilos for the summer, but she will not let them come. I tell her, "Anna-Lisa, you must send the children or I will kill you!' but she says no. *Finska! Skata!*' Then without a pause: 'You have whiskey? Vodka? No? Maybe Roda has some wine. Roda!' He banged the table in genuine anger. 'She has made my life black. My Anna-Lisa; she has done terrible thing to me. I have a horrible life. All the time, drink – I spend all my money on drink.'

It transpired that, a dozen years previously or thereabouts, poor Spiro became involved with a tall, beautiful Finnish girl on vacation in Rhodes. They fell in love, or perhaps just lust – Jonathan was not too sure on this point – married, then lived together in Greece, on Tilos. And this is how it continued thereafter for most of each year; whether happily or not Jonathan could not determine. However, each summer the afore-mentioned Anna-Lisa, Finnish whore of this parish, would shoot off to Finland for six weeks, citing family obligations and an existential need to keep contact with her Finnish roots. This was an arrangement that Spiro was, at first, happy to indulge. But as the years passed, he became less and less enamoured of this arrangement as, whiling the summer away in her homeland, she fell increasingly under the influence of her stentorian and disapproving father, a man unlikely to win any popularity awards with his son-in-law. The father eventually persuaded Anna-Lisa not to return to her husband, but to stay in Finland.

For the last few years Spiro had therefore been forced to visit Finland in order to see his wife and children, an arrangement that did not sit easily with the fiery little Greek who thought all Finnish people to be cold, brutal, blood-letting Vikings not worthy to sit at his feet. Unfortunately, he had a nasty habit of letting them know how he felt and on more than one occasion had found himself in hot water with various authorities as a result. And although he was happy to see the children, he always ended up fighting with Anna-Lisa, who, despite his insistence and pleading, had no intention of ever going back to Tilos. Consequently, whenever he visited, they would fight like cat and dog.

Throughout this time, and despite his accusations that she was nothing other than a whore, Spiro insisted that he loved her. Indeed, if it were not for the fact that he still loved her, his life would not be the terrible, black hole that he claimed it had become. Jonathan was greatly moved by the passion with which this last detail was expressed.

The last time Spiro visited Anna-Lisa in Finland they ended up having yet another terrible fight during which he threatened his estranged wife with something that, to Jonathan's ears, sounded like butchery (the Greeks having a tendency to exaggerate). She called the police and he spent a night in the cells. Now, it seemed, she was insisting – quite unreasonably in Spiro's opinion – on a divorce, but Spiro insisted that he would never capitulate.

'Never, never!' said Spiro, determined to convince Jonathan of his seriousness. 'I will kill her first. I will kill myself. I will make a *catastroph*! You hear? A catastroph!' Like a cat-in-hat, or cat-in-hell, thought Jonathan, only no doubt much worse. 'I say, "Anna-Lisa, why you don't send me the children?" but all she say is "I want divorce." She is whore. All Finnish people are shit! I say to her this summer I will take new woman, but not to have children. I have children already. All I want is to see them play on beach here in Tilos but all she say is: "We have nice beach here in Finland"!'

Jonathan nodded seriously. What we have here, he thought to himself, is a failure to communicate. But Spiro, who was now smoking furiously and tapping the table like a demented woodpecker, looked to Jonathan like a man who would not appreciate listening to any opinions that differed substantially from his own. Besides, although only of small stature, Spiro was so wound up that Jonathan did not doubt he was capable of killing someone without a single thought for the consequences. There was something extraordinary about this man's passion, misplaced though it was, and Jonathan found himself fascinated by Spiro and his story, and the way in which he was able to tell it with such candour to a total stranger. Would Jonathan ever have the courage to tell someone else – even a close friend – that he had 'a horrible life'?

Such passion; Jonathan was not sure why it was that Spiro's emotional outburst had affected him so strongly, but he suspected that, despite their cultural differences, there was something in Spiro's behaviour that reminded him of himself. Jonathan had not – at least not as far as he could recall, ever harboured emotions about another person like the ones that Spiro held for his estranged wife. That strange, confusing amalgam of love and hate, of passion and disgust, with its equally ambivalent corollary of pleading and threatening behaviour ... for all its absurdity, there was something intrinsically – *essentially* – human about it, as if Spiro, for all his madness, was only acting the way everyone would act, if only they were not constrained by the dictums of the society in which they lived. Spiro was a man who clearly gave little thought to — and even less forbearance towards — society's mores.

Jonathan had never felt that way about another person, but he did not doubt that he had it within him to behave every bit as extremely as Spiro, given the right circumstances. And seeing that potential, that similarity, suddenly excited him.

'So, you help me?' Spiro was clearly now more impatient than ever before. Roda had failed to materialise with the wine, and Spiro's nerves were in need of a sedative of some kind. If nothing else, Jonathan thought he ought to buy the man a drink.

'Sure,' he said, grabbing his camera and getting to his feet. He was suddenly very excited. He had just had the most wonderful idea, and he had to tell Liz about it before he did anything else. 'I'll just be a moment,' he said to Spiro. He walked into the house and to the back bedroom, where Liz was still sound asleep. He knelt down beside her and rocked her gently until she woke.

'Liz? Liz?'

Liz opened one eye blearily. 'Hmmm?'

'Liz? Are you awake?'

Liz stretched out her arms, yawned, smiled, and then folded her arms around Jonathan's neck. 'Mmmm,' she said, in what Jonathan took to be an affirmative manner.

Jonathan kissed her on the nose. 'I've just had a great idea. Let's get married . . .'

17

'So, where is she then?'
'What?'
'Your wife. Where is she?'
The intruder was still brandishing the gun in his face. Jonathan was surprised by the question. He thought they had finished with Liz, had moved on to other, more important matters, like fear and pain. His mouth was bleeding profusely and his jaw ached from the punishment he had received from the gunman. He was no closer to knowing what was happening, to understanding how this awful thing had happened to him.
'Well?' demanded the gunman.
'I don't know.'
'She didn't leave no forwarding address?'
Jonathan shook his head. Why was he asking all these questions?
'What, she just walked out on you, did she? Have a row or what?'
This time Jonathan had half a mind to tell him to mind his own fucking business, but at that moment, blood still dripping from his mouth on to his white bathrobe, he feared the prospect of pain even more than the prospect of death.

'What you do to her then? Eh?'

'What's this got to do with you?'

'Oi!' The gunman sprang forward and Jonathan lurched back. 'Talk nice, man, or else I'll have to use this. Now answer my question.'

Jonathan closed his eyes tightly. 'What happened between me and my wife has nothing to do with you,' he said slowly, the words clear and distinct. He kept his eyes closed and braced himself for the blow. But the blow did not come. After a moment or two Jonathan opened his eyes. The gunman was still there, staring at him, pointing his gun at Jonathan's head.

'You're going to have to tell me in the end,' said the gunman, leaning back. 'You'll see. You'll have to.' He stood up and stretched, leaving Jonathan cowering on the sofa like a frightened animal.

Jesus, thought Jonathan, still baffled by the turn of events: What on earth can any of this have to do with Liz?

18

In the end, they did visit the other islands and, just as Liz had suspected, whilst Nisiros and Symi both offered greater spectacle — in particular Symi with its glorious harbour — neither provided the stillness and tranquillity that had been so important to her in Tilos. Not that she did not enjoy the other islands. By the time they returned to Rhodes Liz was hooked on Greece, and every bit the enthusiastic proselytiser that Jonathan had been. She could not wait to tell her friends about their trip, and was a little disheartened to discover that no one was terribly interested. Those she singled out had either been to Greece themselves, in which case they found her enthusiasm either quaint or tedious, or they had no intention of ever going, and so found her rather boring on the subject.

Liz was disappointed. She knew that something very special had happened to her and she just wanted to share her new-found knowledge with the people to whom she was closest. She had returned to England relaxed and renewed, as if a great weight had been lifted from her. True, she had had rather more arguments with Jonathan than she had anticipated, but even that had helped her to clarify her thoughts.

For the first time in her life she knew, really knew, what was important to her.

It was not Greece, *per se*, that had been responsible for her change of attitude, but what it had allowed her to do. In those quiet moments on Tilos she had been able to see her own life clearly for the first time since childhood. Other than Jonathan's mostly playful (but sometimes irritating) sexual overtures, there had been no one making demands on her time, no pressures to conform, to think or act in a certain way. She did not have to *be* anyone either. Released from all the usual constraints, Liz's mind had run wild. She had discovered another world – not just the physical, Mediterranean world of sun and sea and siesta, but a metaphysical world too, a world where what was important no longer revolved around what one did, but who one was. It was an extraordinary transformation, and not the sort of thing she expected would happen to her at the age of twenty-five; this sort of revelation, she had always thought, happened much earlier in life. Or perhaps much later. She was not sure. She was, however, sure of one thing: she had returned from Greece with a completely new value system.

Liz had never been especially materialistic, which was why she had, in many ways, suffered previously in a world devoted – or so it seemed – to acquisition. Get a good job, get a big car, get a nice house . . . none of it had ever made much sense to her. Even her enthusiasm for decorating Jonathan's house had been more to do with expressing herself – or a part of her self – than anything to do with owning or possessing a home. Now that Liz had spent time on Tilos, she knew exactly what a good job would be;

one that was leisurely, stress-free, creative. A good job was one that gave you plenty of time to stretch out, to feel free, to do nothing at all if that was what you most wanted. Liz had gone on a two-week holiday and instead of coming back with a suntan and a bottle of duty-free, had returned with a clear mind and a new philosophy on life. Not bad for seventy-nine quid (and spending money).

And she also had Jonathan, of course.

Liz and Jonathan got engaged that summer. They didn't make a big deal of it, celebrating the occasion with a candle-lit dinner and a bottle of champagne, and choosing – for the meantime at least – to keep the information just to themselves. They made private, personal declarations of love to each other and promises which neither of them thought would be especially difficult to keep, even though they did all seem to contain clauses like 'always' and 'for ever'. Still, the event made them both happy and, in its own small way, brought them closer together.

But it was not all plain sailing. As the summer wore on, Jonathan found himself increasingly concerned over Liz's changed attitude to her studies. It had taken all his efforts to persuade her to stay on at college until at least the end of the summer term. On returning from Greece Liz had been all for abandoning her studies, packing a bag and hitchhiking around the Mediterranean. Jonathan had not thought this prudent. And whilst their promises to each other had, in some ways, secured their liaison, it did little to stem the bickering that had, of late, become an integral part of their relationship.

Matters came to a head one evening shortly after

they returned. It was a Saturday and Jonathan's photos had just come back from the developers. Liz had spent most of the day in a dreamy state, poring over the photographs and sighing a great deal. It started to irritate Jonathan in the extreme.

'I do wish you'd stop that.'

'Stop what?'

'All this melodramatic sighing and pining; it's like something out of a cheap Victorian novel.'

'I am not being melodramatic. You just don't understand what a profound effect Greece had on me.'

'So you keep telling me.'

'Well it's true. I'm amazed that you don't understand.'

'Why is it that whenever I make even the most modest of criticisms about your behaviour I get this "you don't understand" crap. What on earth makes you think I don't understand? I've been there, remember? If it wasn't for my telling you about the place . . .'

'In which case you should be more tolerant.'

'Liz, tolerance is one thing, indulgence quite another, and it would be wrong of me to indulge you in the spurious and rather naive belief that college no longer matters now that you've "seen the light".'

'Don't be sarcastic.'

'I'm just trying to make you see sense.'

Liz grew angry. 'If you don't mind, I'd rather you wouldn't keep trying to force me to do things against my will.'

'I'm not forcing you . . .'

'You bloody are. You just said so. You want to make me see sense. Well for your information, I can see perfectly clearly without your interference. You know, you keep doing this: forcing your own opinions and interpretations upon things that have happened to me. You have to let me have my own responses to things. It's worse than when my mother insisted that I mustn't cry. "Don't cry, darling, don't cry." When I was young, I swear, that's all I ever heard. If something went wrong, if I hurt myself or was upset, my natural reaction was to cry. Correct me if I'm wrong, but this sort of behaviour is not unheard of in children. But I wasn't allowed to express myself in the one way that felt natural. "Don't cry darling." Do you know how frustrating that is? It's like being gagged.'

'All right, all right. Go ahead, express yourself!'

'You patronising little shit.'

'Liz!'

'Well you are.'

'All I'm trying to do . . .'

'I know exactly what you're trying to do Jonathan. You're trying to stop me from doing what I want. For the first time in my life I've discovered something that I want to do . . .'

'What, bum around Greece for a year?'

'Maybe. Anyway, how can you talk? What have you done every summer for the past God knows how many years?'

'That's different . . .'

'Of course it is. Because it was you and not me.'

'No, stupid. It's different because I didn't jeopardise my career by doing it.'

'I don't have a career.'

'And you probably never will if you pack in your studies just like that.'

'Oh please . . . you're beginning to sound like my parents.'

'Well, forgive me for showing concern.'

'You know, if you could just remove that taint of sarcasm from everything you say, I might just have some respect for you.'

Jonathan bristled. So, she didn't have any respect for him, for his views and opinions. Well, that was fine; that was just fine. 'All I'm suggesting is that you keep your options open. Finish this academic year and then go travelling in the summer. You've got three months, haven't you?'

'But Jonathan, this isn't about keeping options open by having a long holiday. It's about lifestyles and doing the things I want to do.'

Jonathan took a deep breath. He wanted to tell her to stop being so naive, but he knew this would only rile her. At the same time, he wanted to avoid coming the heavy. That crack about sounding like her parents had wounded him far more than any of the personal insults. Then again, there were moments when what he really wanted to do was slap some sense into her. There were times when it seemed as if she was deliberately goading him. It made him so angry.

'Look, you do what you fucking like. I'm going for a drink.'

'If that isn't typical . . .'

'What now?'

'I'm having a crisis and all you can do is piss off down the pub.'

'Crisis? You're behaving like an adolescent, and I'm buggered if I'm going to pander to your whims for fairy tales. If you want to pack it all in after working so hard to get to college in the first place, you go ahead. But I'll tell you one thing. If you want to have a freer, less stressful life, then you'll have to finance it somehow.

And there's no way I'm going to subsidise your little flirtation with hippiedom . . .'

'No one's asking you to . . .'

'And I can also tell you from personal experience that picking lemons gets pretty tedious after a while. As does picking olives or milking goats or sweeping barns or waiting on tables or washing dishes or any of the other meaningless, back-breaking and soul-destroying jobs that you'll be forced to do to keep yourself alive whilst you're pursuing paradise . . .'

'But . . .'

'No, shut up a minute and let me have my say. There is nothing wrong in changing your life and trying for something different – God knows, I've wanted the same thing for myself a hundred times. But it's senseless going about it when your head is still in the clouds. You've had a holiday romance, Liz, not with some stranger with dark skin and piercing blue eyes but with a way of life that you've never experienced before. But unless you're independently wealthy, you can't live that sort of life all the time.'

'I only want to try it for a year.'

'Okay, and then what?' Jonathan thought about raising the small matter of their engagement but decided that it was not the right time.

'Jesus, I don't know. I'll worry about that next year.'

'You'll be back to square one. Remember why you came to college in the first place? Because you were sick of the sort of dead-end jobs that had become your life. If you pursue your studies, get a degree, then go off and do whatever it is you most want, then at least you'll have a head start when the sight of another goat's tit has you pulling your hair out. Now is that such an unreasonable stance?'

'You're really enjoying this, aren't you.'

'Enjoying what?'

'This little power trip of yours. You know, I really thought you were different . . .'

'Wait a minute, wait a minute . . .'

'What is it, Jonathan? Experimenting with one of your little sociological theories? Well it won't work.'

'What? What's got into you? What is all this?'

'You think you're so fair minded, so liberal . . .'

This was no longer funny. Jonathan could feel his anger rising by the moment. Where did she get these ideas from?

'Why are you being so offensive? All I was saying . . .'

'I know what you were saying. As for being offensive, frankly it seems to be the only way to get through to you. Understand this: I am my own boss, and w hilst I can respect your opinions, it just so happens that I also have my own. Believe it or not, they are a lot more important and a damn sight more relevant.'

And perhaps sensing how angry Jonathan had become, Liz grabbed the photos off the table, stood abruptly and ran upstairs to the bedroom, slamming the door behind her, leaving Jonathan dumbfounded. And still angry. What right did she have to talk to him that way? He had a good mind to follow her up the stairs and . . .

And what?

Jonathan's anger disappeared, but the energy that had powered it had turned into something else altogether, something much less pleasant. He had not followed his thoughts through because he knew where they led, and he did not like it. He had frightened himself, and there was only one safe option open to him: to get out of the house as fast as possible.

In the end it was Liz who capitulated, although her reasoning was always suspect. Partly she stayed on at college because, for all his insensitivities in this matter, she wanted to be with Jonathan, a point further confirmed when they became engaged a few months later. Another part of her suspected that, despite his rather patronising manner, there might be some truth in what he said. Liz no more wished to go back to a series of endless, meaningless jobs than she did to continue studying, but at least her studies, theoretically, could lead her out of the potentially soul-destroying career cul-de-sac in which she had been stuck previously. If she at least completed her first year, it did leave her options open and would give her the whole summer to think about her future. Anyway, what counted in all of this was that she had discovered what was really important to her, and if that discovery was real, then an extra few weeks at college would not harm it. Nirvana, as she saw it, would not be abandoned, merely postponed.

In addition, there was always the chance that as a sort of by-product of all this, Jonathan would stop playing the know-it-all megalomaniac and get back to being a reasonably sensitive and understanding human being. At least that was what she hoped.

With the long summer vacation stretching out before them, Liz and Jonathan started to make plans to travel. Liz's first and – for a while – only thoughts were to return to Greece; somewhere along the line this had become not just a wish but a firm intention. However, Jonathan had to remind her that the height of summer was not the right time for the islands as they would be inundated with package holiday makers and backpackers – remember what the Greek man had said on the ferry to Tilos? Wall to wall Scandinavians. Even Tilos, according to Roda, became crowded during August, although Jonathan had wondered how Roda defined a crowd. When more than three people were waiting to be served at the village taverna she used to say it was 'busy'. Still, there was no doubting that whatever magic Greece had managed to hold on to since it had opened its shores to mass tourism, very little of it would be visible when the place was swamped by twenty million foreign visitors.

This had upset Liz quite considerably. Most particularly, she felt that Jonathan had tricked her. Hadn't he suggested she see her first year through at college and go to Greece in the summer? Wasn't that the carrot he had dangled in front of her to prevent her from just taking off? She tried not to think about this too much, but it was almost impossible for her not to feel a certain resentment.

Liz spent the best part of a week looking for other possibilities. She traipsed around the travel agents collecting brochures which she would scan for ideas. She pored over Jonathan's splendid *Times Atlas of the World* in the hope that the name of a country or city or region would spring off the page and invite her personally to visit. She spent one afternoon in Foyle's thumbing through a hundred or more travel books, looking at the colour plates, wishing herself into the pictures to see if she 'fitted'.

Time and again she came back to Greece, to the islands. It was not that there were no other beautiful places in the world. Who could fail to be seduced by the glorious visions of the islands of the South Pacific or the Indian Ocean, or the magnificent vistas afforded by Alps, Andes and Himalayas? It was not that these places did not appeal to her; she was sure that, having caught the travel bug, at some time in her life she would visit these far-flung corners. It was just that she was not drawn to them now. Besides, Greece was where Jonathan had proposed to her, and although she did not bring this into her conversations with Jonathan, it was something she would never forget.

When, after a week of frustrated research she repeated these findings to Jonathan, she was surprised to find that instead of being sympathetic to her plight, he was actually angry.

'Oh for Godsake Liz! Anyone would think that Tilos was the only place in the world worth visiting. It's just one small, nondescript island stuck out in the Dodecanese whose main attraction is that, lacking main attractions, everyone has left it alone. If you want to experience the delights of the untouched, untouristed wilderness, then there are thousands of places to go! Who do you think goes to Iceland for their holidays? Or Papua New Guinea? Or Belgium? What is this fixation you have with fucking Tilos?'

'Why are you shouting? You have no right to shout at me.'

'Because you're acting like an idiot.'

'Go to hell.'

'Well really . . .'

'How can you be so insensitive about this? You of all people.'

'This is not insensitivity. This is common sense, something which you seem to have left behind somewhere. Probably Tilos.'

'I don't just want to find some un-touristy pisshole so I can have a nice quiet holiday. It's not about that.'

'What exactly is it about, then?'

'Why are you making such an issue out of this? I think you're doing it deliberately to upset me or prove a point or something. Is this what it's going to be like when we're married? With you questioning my motives about everything, time and time again? Is this your power kick operating yet again?'

'Why do you always assume this is about power? It is not about power. I do not derive any pleasure from it. I just want to understand what this is all about. I would have thought you'd be only too happy to have a partner that takes an interest in your emotional and spiritual welfare.'

'You're taking the piss.'

'I'm just trying to get to the heart of the matter.'

'I can't believe I have to explain this to you again.'

'Indulge me. And if you can do it without using words like "lifestyle", "direction" and "meaning", so much the better.'

'Fuck you.'

His hand was in the air before he realised what he was doing, and if it hadn't been for the look of pure, unadulterated horror on Liz's face, he had no doubt that he would have brought it down across her face.

'Go on, try it,' sneered Liz, covering up her fear and shock with a false bravado. 'Just try it.'

Jonathan lowered his arm swiftly. 'I wasn't going to . . .'

'What? What weren't you going to do? Force me to see things your way with a bit of domestic violence.'

Jonathan blushed; he felt awful. It was just a reflex, nothing more. 'Liz, I . . .'

'Don't try explaining, Jonathan. You'll just make it worse.' She picked up her sweater from the sofa and headed for the door.

'Wait a minute, what are you doing?' said Jonathan, realising too late that he had pushed too far this time. 'Where are you going? We haven't finished talking yet.'

'Oh yes we have.'

'Oh come on Liz, I was just . . .'

The door was slammed so roughly that, just as in the most predictable of television sitcoms, something fragile rattled off the nearby mantelpiece and fell crashing to the ground. But Jonathan, who had already opened the door to chase after Liz, did not find out until later that the object in question was the ghastly glass-fronted carriage clock, left to him by his Aunt Harriet in her will.

And when he did return home to discover the breakage, he did not bother to salvage the wreck, but merely swept up the glass shards, brass cogs and tempered steel springs and, wholly oblivious to any metaphorical implications, emptied the broken timepiece into the dustbin.

19

The trip was not quite the total disaster that Jonathan had imagined it might be. Rather than cause any further friction between himself and Liz at a time when she was clearly uptight about such matters, he capitulated to her whims to return to Greece for two months, on the understanding that they head well away from the usual tourist haunts. Returning to Greece was his way of apologising to her for his behaviour, although no mention as such was made of it.

In the end, they set out for the more remote islands in the Cyclades and, with the aid of another of Jonathan's well-researched guide books, managed to have a relatively hassle-free time, albeit without the untainted pleasures of their first trip together.

Whilst the places they visited provided everything that one could hope for by way of unspoilt island life, there was clearly something missing, at least as far as Liz was concerned. It may have been that her expectations were too high or that, in attempting to recapture something of the magic of the previous trip, she was laying herself wide open for disappointment. That the distance between her and Jonathan had widened as a result of her uncompromising stance on college was not something she wanted to dwell on.

Consequently, by the end of two months she was almost pleased to be heading home. Greece was wonderful, but eight weeks spent meandering around its less well-travelled arenas put her previous experiences in perspective; she realised that, for all its wonder, Greece was not the answer to her problem. It soon became clear that, in all likelihood, no place alone would solve the sort of existential difficulties that she found herself up against. Greece would, no doubt, remain special to her, but she would have to do more than just luxuriate in the escapist pleasures of travel if she wanted to capture – and maintain – the essence of freedom that Tilos had instilled in her.

Throughout the trip she had been tempted, more than once, to open up to Jonathan about these matters, but felt that after their steaming rows on the subject, he would be rather less than sympathetic to her plight, and she did not want to give him the satisfaction of saying 'I told you so', at least, not whilst they were still travelling.

It was not that Jonathan had become vengeful or spiteful; she knew that although he often chose to relay his thoughts and impressions in a less than subtle or considerate way, at heart he meant well. It was just that, of late anyway, he had become so intolerant. Sometimes he seemed like a totally different person to the one she knew and loved.

And yet he was no monster. He had a worse temper than she had at first realised, but no doubt there were aspects of her own character with which he was only now coming to terms. If only Jonathan were as thoughtful with her in conversation as he was when they were in bed together, then she would have no reason to be hesitant with him. As it was, she felt sure that, given the opportunity to take the intellectual high ground, he would waste no time in climbing to the top. What made the whole matter all the more infuriating was the fact that, regarding matters intellectual and philosophical, Jonathan was far more erudite and principled than she. It was not that he was always right and she wrong, simply that he had ways of getting his ideas across with such accuracy, precision and clarity that it made her own arguments sound woolly-headed and feeble-minded. He was good with words, there was no taking that away from him; and whilst she could usually hold her own in company, if Jonathan chose to shift into his turbo-charged-nuclear-attack mode, as he often did, he could zero in on her often fragile and tentative opinions and, with ruthless zeal, annihilate them. What's more, he obviously enjoyed it. Liz could understand the pleasures to be had in winning intellectual arguments against one's peers, but she did not understand why he always had to be so merciless when it came to her.

As for Jonathan, the trip had been a perfectly pleasant sojourn in his favourite country, and so he had little to complain about. Besides, the warmth, freedom and easy pace of travel made him perpetually horny, and Liz seemed happy to engage, not just in the more strenuous and active sex that was still, for both of them, immensely exciting, but also in the sort of casual foreplay that was, for Jonathan, as intrinsic and essential a part of life as breathing. If the sun was out and Liz was there beside him, perspiring gently on some forsaken stretch of beach or lounging beneath the branches of some gnarled olive tree, then Jonathan was quite simply incapable of keeping his hands off her. There was something about the way she sat or lay, the manner in which she arranged her limbs, the line of leg, the curve of breast, that he found immensely arousing. And she had such lovely skin; it invited caresses. And as for the wonderful odours that emanated from every pore, Jonathan never found it less than wholly intoxicating. There were times when, especially if they had both been lying in the sun, just being near her aroused him so greatly that if they were in a public place he would have to entice her into a quiet corner; if sex were not possible, he would have her relieve his sexual torments in other ways.

That their conjoining never reached the dizzy heights of that first, too memorable occasion, was, he supposed, to be expected. It was curious, then, that on occasion he found himself getting quite angry about it. Not that he ever said anything to Liz. They never talked about it. Whilst Liz had learnt to accept that some things were truly unique, never-to-be-repeated experiences, when Jonathan was not angry about the whole business, he managed to hold on to the small yet potent belief that, given the right circumstances, the right place and time and joint inclination, then anything was possible. If it did not happen then that was just the way of the world; there was no one to blame. Especially not Liz.

So while Jonathan saw their trip in terms of an extended holiday, for Liz it was a more complex matter, a combination of travel, vacation and retreat. And she wanted to enjoy it fully; although she never said so, Liz was probably as deeply addicted to pleasure as Jonathan.

Realising that he was more or less at the mercy of his hormones, Liz no longer complained about Jonathan's priapic fixation. On the contrary, the sun, the space, the easy relaxation made her feel more physically aware and more conscious of her body, and by and large she was happy to share those feelings with him. She enjoyed his frequent, tactile investigations, loved being the complete focus of his attention, revelled in the sure, certain manner in which he caressed and fondled her; it was guaranteed to turn her on. She was fascinated, too, at how someone as intellectually grounded as Jonathan, for whom words, thoughts, and philosophical constructs represented the highest, most important aspects of humanity, could be reduced to a gibbering idiot by the sight of bare flesh or the promise of sexual favours. She also loved the control she had over him when he was aroused, how careful manipulation of hand, tongue and lips could have him begging for release. And she loved, too, to pleasure him: despite any difficulties that existed between them, and beyond all other considerations, she loved him, and wanted to make him feel loved and wanted in much the same way as he did for her.

However, for all their indulgence in matters of the flesh, by the time they had eaten their last dishes of Greek salad and downed their final glasses of retsina, Jonathan was more than ready to return home. It was not that he had not enjoyed the trip. It was virtually impossible for him to spend time in Greece and not enjoy himself. It was just that, leaving aside the sex, he was beginning to have some small, irritating doubts concerning the state – and implications – of their relationship.

When Jonathan had proposed to Liz it had been strictly on impulse, spurred on by a vision of passion and commitment of which he had not previously realised he was capable. When, following their return, Liz had become restless and difficult, especially concerning her studies, he had thought (at least, he had assumed) that getting engaged would somehow smooth over the sharp edges that existed in the relationship and, more pertinently, would give Liz the sort of emotional stability that he felt sure she needed. Was it not the lack of security that was responsible for her flighty notions of chucking in college and bumming around the world? And wouldn't the promise of marriage provide the necessary ballast to ensure that she no longer drifted, or felt so uncertain of the direction her life was taking?

Clearly, if he had hoped that getting engaged would nip Liz's wayward ideals firmly in the bud, he was sadly mistaken. If anything, whilst travelling around Greece she had become even less certain of what she was doing, even less rooted than previously. On several occasions during the trip he had attempted to broach the subject. But whenever he mentioned, even tentatively, Liz's lack of focus and intention, it only seemed to cause a row, so after a while, he stopped bothering. Whatever it was that was causing her angst, Jonathan decided she would have to sort it out for herself. Yes, he cared about her; and yes, he was her fiancé. But neither of these two irrefutable facts meant that he was responsible for finding her a *raison d'être*. If Liz needed meaning in her life, then she would have to find it for herself. He was willing to assist in whatever capacity was called for, but he was not going to indulge her in the sort of dreamy wish-fulfilment that, he knew, led nowhere. After all, she was not a child.

Once back home, the situation settled for a while. The arguments ceased, the sun continued to shine and, in a spirit of whimsy, in much the same manner as they had become engaged, Jonathan and Liz got married.

The registry office ceremony took eight minutes and thirty-two seconds – Jonathan timed it – and was attended by Dougie from college and Liz's friend Angie, one of her ex-flatmates. The legalities were incidental to both of them, so they made as little fuss about it as possible. However, the fact of the marriage was important, and to celebrate it properly they held a huge party for all their friends and relations. And as they had just had a long holiday, they thought it improper even to discuss a honeymoon. Liz did mention, however, that, all being well, they could celebrate their first wedding anniversary with a holiday in Greece.

There was still a month or so before the academic year started, and Jonathan used the time to catch up on certain menial tasks that he had been putting off all summer, most of which involved correspondence of one kind or another. He also threw himself into a series of household repairs that had been crying out for his attention. Ever since Liz had taken his charming hovel and turned it into House Beautiful, he felt it incumbent upon him to keep the place in reasonable working order. Whereas previously this would have entailed a great deal of moaning and procrastination, now that the house looked so fine, he was less reluctant to apply his neophyte painting and decorating skills to the upkeep of the house. He even relished the prospect, claiming that it was good to involve himself in such down-to-earth practical matters rather than spend all his time inside his head.

That Liz seemed to spend most of her time lounging around in a bit of a daze did not, at first, concern him; in the past he had often been at a bit of a loose end when he returned from a long trip abroad. However, as the weeks passed and the start of term approached, he started to become more worried about Liz's lack of enthusiasm for college. Indeed, her general apathy started to gall him; he could not understand why she was being so weak-willed about everything, so indecisive. He had avoided getting involved for fear of rubbing her up the wrong way, as he had done in the past. But with the start of term approaching, he knew that if he did not say something there would soon be no time to say anything at all: the start of the academic year was so hectic.

And there was something else. Since the wedding, on three separate occasions when he had attempted to initiate some sort of sexual play, Liz had put him off. On the first occasion, muttering something about not being in the mood, she had simply taken hold of his hand and removed it from between her legs where it had been busily amusing itself for several minutes. Whilst this was an unusual response for Liz, it was not unprecedented, and Jonathan had not pursued the matter. The following day she had actually become quite irritated when he had tried to slip her knickers off in the kitchen whilst she was preparing dinner. This was not a common gambit for Jonathan, but neither was it completely new, and on the one or two times when he had played this particular game before, Liz had entered into the spirit of the thing whole-heartedly, whimsically introducing various proximate comestibles into their already highly spiced foreplay, much to Jonathan's amusement and, it must be said, pleasure.

However, on this occasion, she was clearly not interested, and even chastised him for his poor sense of time and place; couldn't he see she was busy? Jonathan's first reaction, like many an unreconstructed male, was to make vague, half-realised assumptions about premenstrual matters.

It was not until she rebuked him for a third time in as many days that Jonathan started to feel aggrieved. His one attempt to question her on the matter was met with a vitriolic bombast. This included a damning indictment of his supposed right to sex-on-demand and some loud and clearly heartfelt assertions of her moral right not to be treated like a whore just because she had, in a moment's weakness, agreed to marry him. If Jonathan had been less than happy about the contents of her barbed response to what had been nothing more than his usual interest in her body, then he could not but be impressed by the vigour with which such a response was made. He let it go for the moment, and spent little time speculating on the possible reasons for Liz's about-turn on matters conjugal, assuming that, whatever they were, they would soon pass and they could return to normal.

That things did not return to normal, or anything like it, certainly played a part in what was to follow.

One evening, just after they had finished eating, Jonathan decided it was time to broach the subject of Liz's lack of interest in all things academic. As expected, Liz responded defiantly, wearily explaining, yet again, that studying did not mean anything to her and that she had decided, after all, not to continue with her degree. This response merely angered Jonathan; the opportunity to study, to pursue knowledge, even for its own sake, was one of the great gifts of a civilised democracy, and he was damned if he was going to let Liz dismiss it with such ease.

'You're a bloody fool, you know that?'

'That's charming. I don't agree with you, so that makes me a bloody fool. For Christsake Jonathan, get off your high horse for a minute and try and see things from my point of view.'

'I've been trying to see things from your point of view all summer, and all I see is a bright, intelligent woman, with great potential, willing to throw away what might just be the greatest opportunity of her life.'

'You're getting to be a bore about this.'

Jonathan sighed. 'You seem to think that this is all very insignificant, that none of it matters, but I can't just stand by and let you squander such a great opportunity . . .'

Now it was Liz who had had enough. If reasoning could not get through to him then she would just have to raise her voice and hope that sheer volume would succeed where diplomacy had failed.

'Opportunity for what?' she yelled. 'To be bored shitless? To be rendered brain-dead because the course work is so stultifyingly tedious? Don't you see, I don't want to be an academic! I don't want to learn facts and theories and other people's ideas about how the world works. I want to discover it for myself . . .'

'You're talking like a bloody idiot . . .'
'I'm talking about how I feel.'
'You know, when I first met you, one of the things that most appealed to me was your apparent maturity. I see now that it was all a bit of a myth.'
'And you're so wise I suppose . . .'
Jonathan felt the anger rising inside him still further. 'There is more to life than bumming around Greece!'
'Oh yeah? Like what?'
The question caught Jonathan off-balance. For the first time that evening — perhaps ever — he was lost for words.
And that was when Liz — sensing that weakness for the first time, seeing the hesitation and the uncertainty — attacked.
'That's it, isn't it. That's what's at the root of all this. Because you're incapable of finding meaning in your life — *true* meaning, not this caring-by-proxy exemplified by your precious sociology — you wish to deny me the opportunity to find it for myself.'
Jonathan sensed something snap inside him, some level of tolerance that had just been stretched to breaking-point, tested to destruction. That crack about caring-by-proxy . . . that was going too far.
'This is not about me, or what you see — quite wrongly, incidentally — as my inability to find meaning in life. I am not the one behaving like an adolescent.'
'No, more like a middle-aged has-been.'
She was really giving it to him now. He had no idea she could be so spiteful. 'That was uncalled for.'
'Yeah, well, the truth hurts sometimes.'
It was as if she had stabbed him in the chest and was now delighting in turning the dagger in the wound. 'Why are you being so cruel?'

'Cruel? Jesus, you can dish it out but you just can't take it, can you.'

Jonathan's mood had darkened considerably. The anger had now been joined by embarrassment. She was trying to shame him, to make him feel small. He wouldn't stand for that. Not from her, not from anyone. 'I was just trying to help,' he said, trying to maintain a sense of dignity that, since this conversation had started, was slowly ebbing away. She had no respect for him, for his opinions. She just didn't care. 'I was just trying to help,' he repeated, a touch of self-pity colouring the words.

If Liz noticed this she did not let on. But neither did she let up her tirade. 'Sure. But what good are your insights, O Voice of Reason, if all you can do is put me down every time I express some heartfelt belief? Now listen to me, just listen to me: I do not want to pursue a degree course in psychology that has become meaningless to me, I do not want to immerse myself in the sort of academic pursuit that you feel is a God-given blessing, and I do not want to spend the next two years in that mediocre college that you think is so damn precious! Got it?'

It was not a heavy blow. His hand was open, his fingers straight but not tense, and the travel was limited; there was no follow-through. But the slap resounded in her ears as if a small explosive device had gone off inside her head. She burst into tears, not from the pain – it had not hurt, just a slight sting – but from the shock.

In the silence that followed, Jonathan looked on in some bemusement, as if watching some incident that did not really concern him from afar. He had never done anything like that before, he had never hit another person. He was not sure what had happened, why he had struck out like that. It confused him. His pulse was racing, his hands sweating, his breathing rapid. He was so wrapped up in his own responses that he was not even thinking about Liz, about whether he had hurt her, about what she might be feeling or thinking. All he knew was that he had done something wrong, something terribly wrong, and that, in amongst all the strange, conflicting responses that were all fighting for position inside him, one thing was certain. He had broken the rules. He had hit Liz deliberately. He had hit her because he wanted to. Because he could. And because it made his heart beat faster.

Part Three

20

'She just walked out on you, is that it?' said the gunman.

'That's it,' mumbled Jonathan. He had had enough now. He wanted it to be over.

'And yet you thought she might come back.'

Jonathan said nothing. He was not just tired, he was mentally drained, and he felt no closer to getting himself out of what was becoming an increasingly intimidating experience. The gunman's sudden interest in Liz had not helped. He did not want to talk about her, not to anyone, and certainly not to a brutal stranger holding him captive in his own home.

That Liz had walked out on him three weeks ago was still something of a bitter pill, and one that Jonathan had to swallow every morning when he woke up to find himself alone. Her departure had come as a shock and surprise to him; he appreciated that they were having a few problems, but he had not thought Liz would just walk away from it all. That's what marriage was all about, wasn't it? Sticking with the relationship even during times of trouble? Not abandoning your responsibilities? Not abandoning your partner? He still felt angry about it. And now this maniac with a loaded gun and an attitude was not content to just threaten his life and have him jump through hoops, he wanted to grub around amongst the details of his marriage. Well he wasn't having it; oh no. There were some things . . .

'You must have done something pretty nasty for her to just leave you like that, eh?' The gunman was shifting around now impatiently, poking him in the chest with the gun as if it were a cattle-prod. 'Come on; what did you do to her?'

Jonathan did not respond, but just closed his eyes and set his jaw firmly. With each poke of the gun barrel Jonathan flinched; the hard metal impacted viciously against his flesh with a violent, localised pain. How much more of this would he have to put up with? Jonathan gazed at the clock; it was not even three o'clock yet.

'Well?'

'Is this what you get off on? Details of other people's relationships?'

'I'm the one asking the questions.'

'Yes, well, now I'm asking you.'

'You're forgetting who's in charge here. Do I have to remind you? Is that it?'

Once again Jonathan was alerted to something not quite true in the gunman's attitude, something not natural. There was the suggestion of something rehearsed, something practised about some of his expressions. And this whole situation. It reminded him of something he had seen once, a play, perhaps Pinter or Beckett, some piece of convoluted theatrical game-playing where the audience was kept deliberately in the dark about the characters' motivations, about their reasons for being there. Jonathan knew it was dangerous to think like this, to think in terms of plays and games and theatre. Such thoughts could just as easily be products of his imagination, his psyche's way of dealing with the unpalatable and barely believable truth of the situation. Pretending things were not real, were not true – that was the fantasist's way out of reality. He knew it was dangerous for many reasons, not least because that was frequently how psychopaths and sociopaths behaved. They manufactured their own realities in order to deal with a present reality that was not to their liking. The irony was not lost on him. Was this what Jonathan was doing now? Was this what this torment had reduced him to? How convenient it would be if it all turned out to be one big sick joke, if the gunman was a hired hand, an actor, turning in the performance of a lifetime. Even as Jonathan considered once again the possibility of this version of events being true, he realised how unlikely it was. But was it any more unlikely than what the gunman claimed to be the truth?

And if it was true, if this was a set-up, then that produced in turn more questions than answers. Who could be responsible for such a masque? Who would want to terrorise him so? Jonathan did not have any enemies, at least, none that he could think of. And who had he harmed so greatly that, rather than confront him with the facts, they had preferred to stage this elaborate scenario in order to extract their revenge? Jonathan was on good terms with all his acquaintances, with his family, with most of the staff at the college, with his students. In fact, there was only one person he had upset lately . . .

'And you've no idea where she is?' said the gunman.

'I've already told you.'

'So tell me again.'

'Jesus . . . I don't know where she is. She left me, okay? She hasn't been in touch since.'

'Must have been bad, eh? Must have been really bad.'

And what if it was? thought Jonathan: it's none of your fucking business.

'She got family, has she? Live nearby perhaps?'

'Look,' said Jonathan, still trying to keep the details of his private life at arm's length from the intruder. 'Why should any of this interest you? You're not interested in me? I'm just a name in a telephone directory, aren't I?'

The gunman nodded.

'So why so many questions?'

'I have my reasons.'

Jonathan looked at him then. 'I have my reasons'? What sort of expression was that? It didn't fit, it didn't fit at all.

'Who *are* you?'

The gunman looked mildly surprised by Jonathan's question. 'Your worst fucking nightmare, in case you hadn't already figured it out. Now, how's about some answers.'

'No, I mean it: who *are* you?'

The gunman shook his head. 'You don't get it, do you? I'm not here to answer your questions.'

'But if you're going to kill me, why should I tell you anything? Are you going to let me go?'

Jonathan's bluff manner, his attempt to make a stand, to assert himself, albeit in a rather small way, backfired badly. He saw the gunman's expression turn especially sour.

'No way,' said the intruder. 'You're a dead man. But in the meantime, having made me curious, I think you should just do as I say. Now, either you answer my questions or I hurt you. I can't make it no simpler than that.'

And as if to ensure that Jonathan was in no doubt about his earnestness, he tossed the gun into his left hand, stretched out the fingers of his empty right hand, like a pianist reaching for the octave, then quickly clenched his fist, tight like a piece of thick knotted rope, and then ploughed it into Jonathan's face.

It was as if his face had exploded. The pain radiated out fiercely from Jonathan's nose like ripples in a pond and in an instant engulfed him in one shrieking, raging howl. He thought for sure that his skin had split wide open, ruptured in a dozen places, so that his flesh now spilled into the air like a piece of ripe fruit that has been hurled against a brick wall. The physical agony ran parallel with an intense and mind-numbing high-pitched whine that seemed to emanate from right inside his ears, and seemed to trigger off a sensation of terrible nausea. The force of the assault had knocked him sideways, so that he found himself lying on one side, his left arm trapped beneath him, his face half-buried in the sofa's cushions where it throbbed in such immense, angry pulses that he thought he might lose consciousness altogether. He had never known such agony before. The pain, blunt and heavy, pulsated through every piece of his skull, reverberating with especial severity at edges and angles; his eye sockets, his jawbones and the top of his spine. He could taste blood in his mouth and the sickly taint of bile edging into his throat. Then, suddenly, the temporary numbness that had accompanied the shock and had shielded him from the worst of the torment vaporised. In the following split second Jonathan experienced the full weight of the pain, like a momentous aftershock, which seemed to detonate inside his head, travel straight through his body, and zero in on his stomach, which duly gave up its contents all over the sofa.

'That's disgusting,' said the gunman, standing up and moving several paces back. 'Really disgusting. Still, I did warn you.'

But Jonathan did not hear the gunman's words of self-justification. His whole body convulsed once, twice, then a third time, as if several thousand volts of electricity had been discharged through him. His senses had either become numbed in a torrent of pain and anguish or were engulfed by the foul smell and taste of his own vomit. He was whimpering, like a beaten dog, unable to maintain any personal dignity. He had never felt more wretched in his entire life, had no idea that the business of being alive, of existing, could be so miserable.

He tried to lever himself into an upright position, but even the smallest move caused him unimaginable distress. 'I need . . . I need some water,' he mumbled from between bruised lips. His mouth and nostrils were filled with the acidic, rotting stench of sick; more than anything else he needed to get rid of that taste, to clear his nostrils and throat of it or else he might suffocate. 'Please . . . I just need . . .'

'What did you do to her.'

Jonathan coughed and then spat on to the sofa; he could not help himself. Surely he was not still questioning him about Liz? It couldn't be.

'Can I have some water? Please, I really . . .'

'Answer my question. Then I'll think about it.'

Jonathan felt the anger and disgust rise in him. How could he do this? Couldn't he see how he was suffering?

Jonathan stared up at his captor, who now stood a few yards away, sneering. 'If you let me clean myself up . . .'

'What did you do to her? Eh? Come on. Answer me. Answer me *now*.' Jonathan saw the gunman raise the gun and point it towards him. He heard the ominous click of the hammer being cocked, and saw in his captor's face a look of such disdain that Jonathan no longer dared to think that he was anything other than what he purported to be: a man at the end of his tether, ready to kill someone.

'I hit her,' said Jonathan, so quietly that, had it not been the middle of the night, the general buzz and sizzle of late twentieth-century life – traffic, radios, televisions, refrigerators, telephones, hi-fis – would have drowned him out.

'Figures. So, now you know what it's like.'

Jonathan managed to pull his face away from the sick-stained sofa and prop himself up on one arm.

'I didn't punch her in the face!' he spluttered. 'I didn't put all my weight behind my fist and smack the living daylights out of her!'

'No?'

'No. What's it to you anyway? What does any of this have to do with you? If you're looking for a reason to shoot me I'm sure you can do better than that.'

'I don't need no reason to shoot you. I've known you were guilty all along.'

'Do I get some water now?'

'When I'm ready.'

The pain and hurt still throbbed through his face relentlessly and blood still dripped from his nose on to his bathrobe where, readily absorbed, it spread out through the fibres in concentric waves, so that the material covering his chest had become pockmarked with irregular, orange-red marks, like a faded floral wallpaper.

'So what was it? A slap? Did you slap her, is that it?'

Jonathan nodded once again. The effort of replying had become too much for him. He did not care what happened now; he just wanted the pain to stop. He would do anything, agree to anything, confess to anything ... just so long as the pain stopped.

'And then what? Kick her a few times? Put your hands around her neck, try a little suffocation?'

'I just slapped her. Nothing more.'

'I'll bet. Women don't walk out on their men just beause of one slap.' There was a long pause. Jonathan managed to get himself sitting upright. The gunman was staring at him unflinchingly. 'Terrible thing, fear,' he said. 'Terrible thing to live your life in fear, innit?'

He had already spoken those same words once that night; Jonathan knew that, knew it was supposed to mean something to him. Once again Jonathan felt that there was nothing random about this intrusion into his life at all, but that it had all been carefully planned. Not a joke, but to hurt him, to teach him a lesson perhaps. And, as ridiculous as it seemed, if this *was* the case, then there could only be one person behind it. The terrible truth had been banging on the door all night, waiting to be let in. It all added up; it even explained the nature of the gunman's questions.

Someone had set him up. And that someone was Liz.

21

Jonathan had a theory. It went like this.

You are sitting at home, minding your own business. There is a knock at the front door. You go to the door, open it, and find two policemen standing there. Despite having been raised on a diet of cheap thrillers and soap operas, your immediate response is not (a) 'There's been an accident, someone's hurt' or (b) 'There is an escaped killer on the loose, lurking around the neighbourhood', but a much more prosaic and revealing (c) How the hell did they find out about *that*?

No matter how honest or law-abiding, everyone was guilty of something. You let your road tax expire, you go an extra two stops on the underground without paying, you say nothing when the check-out girl fails to ring up your packet of chocolate biscuits ... whatever, we are all guilty of some deliberate flaunting of the rules, something we are sure we got away with, something we are certain cannot be traced. But we never feel fully comfortable about it. We may forget about it, push it to the back of our minds, never let it impinge upon everyday life, but then one day there is a knock at the door and the first thing we think is: the game's up.

Five past three. The gunman had not taken his eyes off Jonathan, was still studying him intensely. Jonathan wondered where Liz had found this madman. People like this certainly did not advertise their services in the Yellow Pages. And what was the brief, he wondered. 'Scare him a little'? 'Make him suffer'? 'Kill him'? Surely not; surely Liz was not capable of setting up something like this, issuing instructions . . . was she?

And yet, what other explanation could there be? It may have been unlikely, but it *was* possible: given the right circumstances, ordinary people were capable of committing the most terrible crimes. Clearly the idea was to humiliate him, to hurt him, to settle the score somehow. If so, then the mission had been accomplished. What more could she possibly want? They could just call it a day now; Jonathan could go clean himself up, and the 'assassin' could go back and report to Liz what a great job he had done . . .

'I think you'd better tell me more.'

Jonathan coughed again. The inside of his mouth tasted truly foul; it was all he could do to get the words out without choking.

'There's nothing more to tell.'

'Where is she?'

'You tell me.'

The gunman eyed him quizzically. 'What's that supposed to mean?'

Jonathan sighed. 'I've told you everything there is to tell. I've confessed my crime. I hit her. It was a terrible thing to do, terrible. I should never have laid a hand on her. Don't think I haven't regretted it from the moment I did it. But enough is enough. If I was meant to suffer, to pay for my crime, then I think we can say that the account's settled now.'

'Yeah, but it don't work like that, does it? There ain't no account.'

Jonathan shook his head slowly in despair. 'What is it with you? Do I have to beg? Is that it? Okay, I'm begging you; leave me alone. I accept the punishment that's been meted out to me. I won't call the police, I won't retaliate in any way. I'll leave you alone.'

'If you're still trying to make me laugh, forget it.'

'No, I mean it. There won't be any repercussions; I won't do anything.'

'Of course you won't do anything. You'll be dead.'

'I *won't* be dead. Come on, admit it; I've rumbled you. Whatever your instructions were they did not include putting a bullet in me. That's just way over the top. I should have realised that half an hour ago. Now just let me clean myself up. You can leave the way you came in . . .'

The gunman lurched forward. 'Okay, enough. You've had your fun. Now cut out the smart stuff and start telling me what I want to know. Where's this wife of yours. If you don't tell me, I'll only have to hit you again.'

The sudden threat of yet more punishment made Jonathan's heart sink; he could not take another punch to the face. He could not take another beating. Even the thought made him cower.

'Okay,' mumbled Jonathan. 'Okay. I'll tell you. I'll tell you whatever you want to know . . . but please, let me wash my mouth out; it's almost impossible to talk like this.'

'Get out of it . . .'

'Come on. I'm just talking about a glass of water. What difference could it possibly make to you? Come on, exercise a bit of that power of yours.'

The gunman thought about this for a moment. He looked hard at Jonathan before making his decision.

'Okay. But make it quick. Get up.'

Jonathan was so surprised by the gunman's response that for a moment all he could do was stare at him in astonishment. However, once he saw the gunman twitching the gun at him, he soon made a move. It took an unexpected degree of effort for Jonathan to prise himself off the sofa and on to his feet. He was disturbed to find himself so unsteady, his legs so shaky and unstable; like an old man, he thought. Like a cripple. For a brief moment, just prior to getting up, he had entertained the rather ridiculous notion of rushing the intruder, hurling himself at his legs perhaps to knock him over, but as soon as he was vertical he realised that he did not have a hope of getting away with it: there was only a fifty-fifty chance that he would be able to walk to the kitchen unaided without falling over.

The gunman was right beside him, scrutinising every twitch and shuffle. 'Where is it then,' he said.

'I can use the kitchen sink. It's through there.' Jonathan indicated the doorway behind him.

The gunman strode over to the doorway, reached inside and switched on the light. Jonathan squinted at the brightness. For the first time he was able to get a good look at his captor's face. He was younger than Jonathan had expected, his skin smoother, clearer, and his eyes more alert. Did he look like a murderer? What did they look like? Had Jonathan ever seen a killer in the flesh?

Or did he just look like a man playing a part: an actor, a stand-in, a fraud. And, more pertinently, after all that Jonathan had been through that night, did it matter any more?

'Okay, come on.' The gunman beckoned to Jonathan. Slowly, Jonathan shuffled towards the kitchen. At the doorway the gunman stopped him. 'Be quick about it. And no funny ideas, eh?'

Funny ideas. A curious sensation came over Jonathan in that moment. He found himself, quite unaccountably, smiling, as if there really were something genuinely funny in what was going on, something amusing, worth a laugh or a giggle. The pain of grinning, which stretched and strained his poor, bruised mouth, however, soon wiped the smile from his face.

Funny ideas. Yes, that was what he needed. Not really funny, of course, but clever, smart . . . the sort of idea the gunman was really warning him off.

Did he have it in him? Did he have it within him to come up with something to help himself out of this mess? Surely there was not enough time even to appraise the situation properly, let alone devise a plan . . .

And yet, it did not have to be complicated. It did not have to involve a great deal of effort. It just had to be effective. It just had to work.

Jonathan stepped gingerly into the kitchen, a room he knew as well as any in the house. He remembered how it had looked in its original state, grimy and damp, and how Liz had helped transform it into something quite special. He remembered stripping the walls of the rotting paper, painting the ceiling, fitting the cupboards. He had done a good job. He remembered too their first meal there, together. They had shared cooking duties. It was all rather fun, rather sweet. A room full of memories, both good and bad. And more.

A room full of weapons.

He knew this of course. It was this knowledge that had been playing through his head ever since the gunman had punched him full in the face and made his nose bleed all over his bathrobe. It had been whirling around in the back of his mind because to confront the idea head on, he knew, could give the game away. If he had dared to give the idea any time or space, the gunman might have seen it on his face, and then there would have been no chance to exploit it, to use it. So he had not thought his idea through, he had not allowed it to register on his face, he had not given it its due.

But it was still there, the simple but dangerous notion that, if he could get to the kitchen, he could put his hands on something sharp or serrated or heavy. Something he might wield. Something deadly.

Could he do it? Could he really do it? Not the practicalities: he had no idea whether or not there would be a suitable implement within reach, whether he could grasp it before the gunman knew what was happening. That was not the difficult part. The difficult part concerned whether or not he had the strength and courage to strike a blow. Especially if it meant doing real harm, real damage. Because that was the only sort of blow that would work. If Jonathan was going to do it, going to make an attempt at it, then he had to do it as if he meant it, with the full knowledge that, if he was successful, then the gunman would be fully disabled. And that meant one of only two things: unconscious or, quite possibly, dead.

The stench of vomit still filled his nostrils, threatening to make him retch again at any moment. As he walked up to the sink he could feel the presence of the gunman directly behind him, standing just out of sight. He would be watching him like a hawk.

Was the gun loaded? Was it?

Jonathan did not dare think on this any further. He took the few paces towards the sink with heavy, measured tread, like a man going to the gallows. His face still throbbed with an urgent, unremitting pain that reminded him constantly of the humiliation and terror he had been put through. He could feel his anger rising to the surface.

What was in the sink? Had he washed up from last night's attempt at cooking dinner for himself? Had he? What else was there? Were there knives, skewers, graters, forks, anything within easy reach, anything that could hurt, wound, maim?

Oh God, thought Jonathan, what am I thinking? His hands had become damp in sweaty anticipation, his muscles tense. He was doing it, now; he was thinking of doing damage to another human being, of hurting them. And it did not matter any more whether he was a madman who intended to shoot him dead, or just a hired bully boy, sent to teach him a lesson. It just did not matter. *Mens rea*. Whatever happened now, he was guilty; just like the gunman had said. Guilty.

Could he do it? Could he hurt someone that way, enough to disable them, put them out of action? What sort of person was capable of such a thing? Jonathan knew. A year ago he would not have thought it possible, would not have thought he had it in him to strike out at another person physically, with real anger, with intent to cause harm. But a year ago he had not known Liz. He still had no understanding of why he had done it. Not the slap, of course, that was nothing; just a reflex. But a few minutes later, when she had started screaming at him, that was when those thoughts, those ghastly, potent, powerful thoughts had coalesced in his head, had pumped through his system like adrenalin, urging him to do it, to hit her, to make her shut up, to smack her properly, teach her a lesson. He had dragged her into the bedroom and beaten her to a pulp. It was powerful, overwhelmingly powerful; it had made his heart beat faster.

And here it was again, the same feeling; not forced, not coerced, but perfectly natural. It was there, in everyone, lurking beneath the civilised facade, constrained by the rules imposed by society. You could reel it in, encase it in ritual, smother it with moral arguments, ethical treatise, appeals to higher, more cerebral instincts, but it was always there. Something base, ancient, genetic; to hit, to wound, to kill. Especially when one was threatened.

'Okay, make it quick.' The gunman's voice cut through his reveries like a knife, slicing his thoughts apart. He stepped forward. His whole body had tensed up. Even before he saw it, he had remembered.

In the sink. There it was, the answer to his predicament. Jonathan wanted to laugh ... how he wanted to laugh right out loud at this most absurd of revelations.

Sausages would be his salvation; sausages would set him free.

He had bought them at the local butcher's shop. They were nothing special, just a pound or so of chopped meat and gristle, neatly encapsulated into seven or eight little packages, ready to cook. The sort of food that Liz would never have allowed in the house. And, rather than grill them, which may have been the healthier option but would mean having to wash out a deeply encrusted drip pan and scrub that blasted wire gridiron, he chose the easier option. He fried them. In the fourteen-inch, cast-iron frying-pan that now lay in the sink, unwashed, filled with congealed pork fat.

He knew what he had to do; he played it through at speed in his mind's eye.

'Get on with it; what are you waiting for?'

'I . . . I can't turn the tap on . . . shaking too much . . . you'll have to do it.'

'Do *what*?'

'Please . . . I can't.'

'Fuck this . . .'

Jonathan did not look round. He heard the gunman take one, two, three steps towards him. He grabbed the handle with both hands and in a single, flowing movement, like one of his better two-handed returns on the tennis court, he lifted the dead weight from the sink, swung his body around to the left until he saw his target, then whipped the iron pan around, accelerated it with the coiled energy of his stance so that it followed the movement of his body, and swept the hunk of metal through in a perfect arc. He had just enough time to relish the look of bewilderment on the gunman's face before the solid, flat, weighted base of the pan struck the side of his head with a resounding, satisfying crack. Like much of that evening, time distorted around this event so that it all seemed to happen in slow motion. Jonathan was sure he could see the skull give at the point of impact, was astonished and only slightly sickened by the fountain of blood that spurted from his captor's mouth and, as he went down, began to dribble from his ear.

The gunman crashed to the ground, his limbs flailing in all directions.

You never saw it coming, thought Jonathan, stepping over the fallen body and raising the frying-pan high above his head. You dumb fuck; you never saw it . . .

It was a neighbour at number 19, woken by the commotion in the adjoining house, who telephoned the police at ten past three that morning, claiming to have heard a noise like a gun going off.

22

He pushed himself up onto his hands and knees and tried taking deep breaths. His head was swimming, and his vision was completely blurred, as if he were looking through a steamed-up window. He was in considerable pain; greater pain than he had ever experienced previously. His head felt as if it had been ripped apart by a circular saw, and there was a loud, nauseating ringing sound in his ears.

Cautiously he brought a hand to the side of his head, but he could not bring himself to touch the wound. He knew he was bleeding badly, and even though he felt very groggy, he knew he had to get to his feet.

The effort almost destroyed him; the pain was intense; he feared permanent damage. He coughed, spat out a huge amount of blood; his tongue was bleeding freely from where he had bitten into it. He peered around the kitchen, looking for something to wrap around his head to staunch the blood. He took just a moment or two to find a tea towel hanging on a rack. He did not suppose it was clean, but it would have to do; he could not afford to hang around. Someone would have heard the shots for sure. It was just a matter of time before the police arrived.

He stuffed the gun back into his pocket and, swaying a little, managed to make his way back through the living-room and hallway to the front door. He paused for a moment by the coffee table, snatched up the framed photograph and stuffed it into his pocket.

He wondered whether anyone would be watching, whether it was a sensible moment to make his escape. Not that he had much choice. He would have to risk it. It was still the middle of the night, after all, and the streetlights were not so strong. He would raise one arm, hide his face. The towel, wrapped around his wounded head, would provide partial disguise.

He opened the door a few inches. His vision was a little clearer now, but not clear enough to see if anyone was outside, waiting for him.

What a shame he had had to shoot just then, before he had had a chance to find out where the wife was. If only there had been a bit more time. Not that it would make much difference in the long run; the man was going to get it anyway. He had to. It was fate.

Still, it wasn't all bad news. He had her name now. And a photograph. It shouldn't be too difficult to find her.